THE METHOD TO INFINITE THINGS

MADISON BOYER

The Method to Infinite Things

Future House Publishing
www.futurehousepublishing.com

Cover image copyright: Future House Publishing

Text © 2023 Madison Boyer

All rights reserved. No part of this book may be reproduced in any form or by any means without the written permission of Future House Publishing at rights@futurehousepublishing.com.

This book is a work of fiction. Names, characters, places, and incidents are either the product of the author's imagination or are used fictitiously. Any resemblance to actual persons, living or dead, or to actual events or locales is entirely coincidental.

Paperback ISBN: 978-1-950020-70-6
eBook ISBN: 978-1-950020-71-3

Editing by Kelly A. Taylor

To Colleen Woodward

PART 1

"The whole of science is nothing more than a refinement of everyday thinking." —Albert Einstein

CHAPTER 1

I would be knocked out cold by tonight, but that wasn't how the afternoon started. Everything was normal. And it would have stayed normal if I hadn't received the news of a lifetime just hours before conversing with a dead woman.

You could say it wasn't fair—that the thing which was supposed to be my salvation actually caused me the most trouble in the long run. You could say that. You would be right too. I, however, learned a long time ago not to expect 'fair' from the universe. Especially not one that seemed bent on turning my life into one big irony.

***

Your mind is your greatest asset.

That was the quote engraved on the wall of the chem lab. Its lettering, a matte obsidian color, looked stark among the egg-wash walls and shining platinum equipment. While once the words intrigued me, they had long since blended into the background by this point. Spend two years walking past the same old same old every day, and I guess you start to ignore things like that.

I heard somewhere that the university changed part of it—the quote, I mean. The original used 'weapon' in place of 'asset.' *Hard to imagine the reasoning behind that switch*, I had thought. It wasn't exactly a mantra with which you hoped to motivate the chemical engineering students.

Elbow deep in thick rubber gloves, I pinched a yellow crystal in metal tongs and brought the gem to eye level. Monoclinic facets blinked blonde glimmers around the interior of the vacuum glove box. I rotated the crystal slowly, watching the light scatter, regroup, and scatter again. The sight would always take my breath away. This was the wonder of synthetic science. I may have organized the process—written the equations, pieced together the right molecules—but the laws of physics and chemistry did the rest.

I loved every second of it.

Filling a test tube with acid to the halfway mark, I dropped the gem into the chemical and watched as plumes of gas shot upward. Violent bubbling frothed around the crystal, obscuring it. I waited. The reaction continued for nearly thirty seconds. When the gas finally dispersed and the froth subsided, nothing remained of the yellow crystal but a corroded hunk of rock and a liquid tinged sickly green.

Interesting. Near-instantaneous corruption. I tugged my hands free from the gloves with a squishing suction sound. "Harlow," I said, unrolling my sleeves. "Make a note, please. Sample forty-five corroded upon immersion."

"Done and done," replied a young female voice. It came from the watch at my wrist—practically a permanent addition to my body—and rang out bright and clear despite the device's tiny speaker system. "Any additional comments for this entry?"

Squinting, I leaned in close to the acrylic window that separated me from the greenish vial inside. "Violent effervescence resulted in acid discoloration. Looks gross really." I screwed my lips to one side, grateful I couldn't smell whatever gas now occupied the sealed chamber.

"Noted," said Harlow. "Do you want me putting 'looks gross' in your official records?" There was just a touch of sarcasm in her voice.

"Good point. Maybe leave that part out."

Harlow, a standard artificial intelligence system, had been at my side since I first installed her software six years ago. She'd been a blank slate back then. Fresh from the servers and possessing only a few generic character traits bestowed by the software developers, Harlow's personality had developed over time until becoming what it was now: likable, loyal, wisecracking on occasion. Like most personal AIs, she was designed to match the age of the user in temperament and maturity. I was sixteen.

Therefore, Harlow was also sixteen. At least in a way.

Her constant presence had gotten me through a lot over the years, and I was grateful for our odd friendship. For people like me, friends were often hard to come by.

Hands on my hips, I pressed a button labeled SWEEP and watched as mechanical arms unfolded inside the glove box, rubberized claws extended. They made short work of the cleanup process. With swift, calculated movements, the automated limbs plucked away what remained of my experiments for the day. Any reusable items—like test tubes and vials—would be cleaned and returned to their respective places while spent materials were sent to disposal. I watched the ghastly green fluid disappear in the clutches of one of the claws, knowing the AI system would identify the liquid under 'waste' and discard the stuff.

"There's an incoming message for you," said Harlow. "Should I read it out loud?"

"Message?" I wasn't expecting anything. I shooed wisps of dark hair from my face with the back of a hand. "From who?"

Harlow made a small *oh* sound. "The World's Fair Board of Directors."

I had my white lab coat halfway off my shoulders, but the announcement struck me immobile. Instantly my breath caught in my throat. "*What?*"

Harlow repeated herself. All I could do was stare for a moment or two. Reality felt delayed, sluggish, and oddly surreal. "H-Harlow," I whispered. "Is this what I think it is?" She gave some kind of response, but I forgot it immediately. Maybe I didn't hear it at all. Then, like gradual snowfall, it dawned. An onslaught of nerves kept me frozen, still and unblinking, a glaciated mass too hopeful and too terrified to even move. Had the board finalized the fair schedule at last? After months and months of waiting, did I now have the results? Every possible scenario flashed like lightning through my mind. The good, great, bad, devastating . . . There was heat in my cheeks and a thrumming to my heart, as if my very chest might implode.

"Your vitals have spiked, Cass," Harlow warned. "You really ought to breathe."

"Right." I shook my head vaguely, trying to clear the haze. It helped a bit. My lungs filled with air, and with it, some clarity returned. "Right. Moment of truth, I guess." Faintly, I registered a mechanical hum from some far corner of the chem lab, hovering just at the edge of my awareness as I launched the incoming message with trembling fingers.

An official statement. It appeared via a suspended particle screen in the air in front of me, turning my knees weak like jelly. *World's Fair*, the screen read. A quick scan of the text revealed the long-awaited answer.

Dear Cassiopeia Atwater,

We hope this communication finds you well. Our Admissions Committee, under the direct supervision of the Board of Directors, has reviewed your application.

After much deliberation, we are pleased to extend to you this invitation to the World's Fair.

Attached is a copy of the presentation schedule. Please submit your acceptance letter at least 60 days in advance of your presentation date.

Congratulations,
The World's Fair Board of Directors

I breathed a sigh of amazement.
It was real.
My application had been accepted.
I was going to present my invention at the World's Fair this summer.
"Can you believe it, Harlow?" I collapsed the screen with the press of a button and leaned my weight on a countertop, struggling to comprehend it myself. After two years bent over chemical equations, experimenting with compounds and their applications, and logging countless hours at the Grand Theatre to pay for the university lab fees, my work would finally see the light of scientific endorsement. Even better, landing a spot at the World's Fair all but guaranteed the support of numerous big-

time investors and, if I could pull it off just right, a contract with one of the prominent corporations that were always scouting the fair for fresh innovation.

"Of course I can believe it!" came Harlow's reply. "You are the best scientist there is, Cass. I've never met anyone as smart as you."

"You've never met *anyone* besides me," I said, rolling my eyes.

"That's true. However, I do have access to large informational reserves, and sources tell me that the chances of a sixteen-year-old female attending the World's Fair are 1 in 110,778. Given those statistics, I might reasonably assume you have the highest IQ among your immediate circle of associates."

"Wow, you've gotten really great at compliments."

"Thank you. I try."

I was tempted to linger in the lab indefinitely, mulling over the implications of the news all night long, but I remembered the time with a start and pushed myself up straight. "It's almost 5:30. I can't be late again, or Bautista will have a come-apart. You know how he gets." Even as I spoke, giddiness forced a smile from me. I couldn't help it. I wanted to sing or cry or holler eureka from the rooftops. Every scientist dreams of seeing their work on the world's stage—proof that their idea was worth something, that it might do some good after all. It's a sort of mania really. The fulfillment of everything lived for. And so I let myself pause in front of my personal unit, the one that housed the evidence of all my effort, to let myself take it in for a moment.

There it was.

The best data security device the world had yet seen. Essentially a stop-all against any foreign electrical signal. Its secret ingredient: a synthetic material I'd engineered myself here in the labs. The prototype itself was a flat, carbon-gray wafer no bigger than a teaspoon. Its name, according to official copyright, was CosmiLock. I based the device's simple algorithm on a bit of Harlow's source code. Once demand called for it, the code could easily be replicated on a larger scale. After all, I admitted to myself, demand *would* call for it. Prospects for the inhibitor were practically endless.

The Method To Infinite Things

Impenetrable data protection. A block against the very medium through which all hackers must work: electricity. It would mean the transformation of security worldwide. Militaries, banks, nuclear facilities—all would vie for their own installation agreements.

For all my excitement, I reminded myself not to let daydreams get the better of me. There were plenty of applications for the Lock. Securing my spot in the World's Fair was only the first step. With that out of the way, there was nothing left to do but polish my presentation for the big day. I would worry about contracts and offers later. Sighing, I thought how three months seemed entirely too short a time to prepare; then again, it seemed like the summer couldn't come fast enough.

"Maybe the theatre won't be busy tonight, with the election and all," I said, hanging my lab coat on the hook next to my unit. It was an attempt to take my mind off the fair and reground in reality.

"I find it silly to schedule a performance on an election day," said Harlow, a tone of superiority entering her voice. "Turnout is likely to be significantly lower than usual."

I reached up to tighten my ponytail, draping my charcoal hair over one shoulder, and made for the washing station at the other side of the lab. "That's the hope. If we're lucky, we might get to go home early."

Harlow's haughty tone vanished, replaced by one of childish excitement. "*Ooh*, can we watch one of those new documentaries afterwards? I love adding new information to my system."

I laughed, rinsing my hands at the motion-sensor sink and drying them beneath quieted gusts from the silent industrial dryer. "Remember, it's a school night. Let's see how late it is by the time we get back."

I caught a glimpse of myself in the mirror on the wall and faltered. An unexpected sense of longing—its touch sharp and needlelike—pricked a hole in my enthusiasm. The pain lingered. When I was younger, people used to say I looked like my dad; however, the real similarity lay between me and my mother. Mom used to tell me how jealous she was of my thick eyebrows and tan skin, or "the family indigenous genes." Such attributes came from my father. But all the rest was hers. The curve of my nose, the shape of my jaw, and even the little divot above my upper lip. As a little kid, I'd never understood why someone would be jealous of another person's hair. A nonsensical image of trading my dark strands for her nutmeg waves had occupied space in my brain for years.

The memory took me aback. Where had it come from? I wasn't prone to nostalgia. Too much else demanded my attention. And nostalgia had no place in a science lab.

Yet here it was. For a moment, I dared to wonder what my parents would say about the fair. I imagined, just for a moment, giving my mother the good news. She would hug me. Congratulate me. She would stay long enough to hear all about it. Hope, shallow and endless all at the same time, danced across my reflection in the mirror.

"All right," said Harlow, still occupied with planning our late-night entertainment. "But promise me we will watch the one about deep-sea diving. I've always wanted to know what the ocean feels like."

A glance at my watch told me it was 5:30. Time to go. My backpack in tow, I exited the lab through automatic double doors. Eastern Potomac University was just a short train ride outside Meridian, the capital city of the United North American Republic. Once upon a time, the city used to be named Washington, D.C., but no one had called it that since the world climate crisis caused a planetary overhaul like nothing we had ever seen. Of course, that was eons ago. Anyone around during that time was long since dead. I couldn't imagine a period of earth before widespread nuclear fusion and the national train system, when human beings decimated their own planet in a crazed, self-sabotaging frenzy. A worldwide disaster waiting to happen. It took merging countries into entirely new nations for us to generate enough resources to save ourselves. Only under this new united agenda could we invest in the technology that would start us on the path to restoration.

"Evening." An old man in blue custodial jumpsuit, liver spots speckling a bald head with a few white hairs, greeted me over his janitor's cart. I smiled. He was a regular sight around the lab this time of day. We had a friendship of sorts. A cordial acquaintance nurtured solely within the thirty-second span of our near-daily interactions. He liked jokes. Always the same ones, actually. He seemed to have a rotation.

"What d'ya call a beehive without an exit?"

I paused, feigning thought. "Hmm, I don't know. What *do* you call a beehive without an exit?"

"Un-bee-lievable."

"Now that's a good one."

The man chuckled to himself. He pushed his rattling cart down the hall. I felt somewhat guilty for not knowing his name. Unconsciously, I had always called him *Mop Guy*. I liked the old stranger because he never talked more than this—just told his jokes and moved on. Why couldn't the rest of the world be like Mop Guy?

I waited at the train station outside the university, watching the sleek silver locomotive approach from a distance. Once boarded, I felt the slight pull of acceleration, the smooth power of engineered might, and watched scenery zip past from the leisure of my padded window seat. Stretching green landscapes extended far as the eye could see. There were woods and some small suburban communities, and I even spotted the river once when we crested a hill. Gradually we passed into city limits. The train reduced its speed. Woods made way for high-rise condos, offices, and luxury hotels. I watched buildings of white limestone—Meridian's signature—pop in and out of view.

As a matter of habit, I waited anxiously to spot the Bureau of Nuclear Energy. It was the federal entity in charge of the nation's greatest energy source: extraterrestrial mining and the nuclear facilities that processed raw elements into electricity. They worked closely with the National Space Agency, whose skyhook technology made interplanetary mining efficient and profitable. And there was the bureau now—a magnificent compound—its ethereal white glow coupled with traditional fluted columns, designed to suggest a unity between past and future. The greenest lawn in the city stretched in an elliptic course around the building. And at its entrance stood the flag of the Republic, a blue upper half separated from its red lower half by a thin white stripe and overlaid at the center with twenty-one golden stars—one for each of the twenty-one sectors. Sometimes, when I passed the bureau, I caught glimpses of employees entering or exiting the grounds, and I envied them for whatever scientific advancements were unfolding as a matter of daily routine in their workplace.

***

"Thank you for attending tonight's performance of Chrysanthemums in Blue by Jupiter Pennyworth. Our production will begin shortly."

The announcement rang over the theatre's sound system, fading amongst the plush velvet seats and gilded moldings that trimmed the walls and ceiling. Just as I'd predicted, the Grand Theatre was only filled to half-capacity tonight. Patrons dressed in formal evening attire claimed their seats and chattered to one another while waiting for the play to start. I sat at my usual station: an inconspicuous spot near the front emergency exit where I could direct last-minute arrivals or assist patrons during the production. Dressed in my black crew clothes, I easily blended into the dark tapestries lining the wall. I preferred it this way. Sometimes I could go the entire performance without talking to a single person.

Tension underlaid the crowd, like the buzz of the atmosphere which precluded an approaching storm. The election was at the forefront of everyone's mind. While I usually stayed away from politics, they were hard to escape entirely. Especially when one of my grandmother's favorite pastimes was critiquing the candidates from the comfort of her chaise lounge. Grandam, as I had always called her, was a member of the Illustrious Party. One of two major political ideologies in the nation, it was the party affiliated with Sommer Day. And no, that wasn't a joke. Her name was Sommer Day. She was a vibrant, charismatic woman who liked lighting up screens with her blinding white-toothed smile. This was her first shot at national politics, as the news outlets like to remind the viewers, though she had risen to fame long before now as the president and CEO of a colossal drone and droid production company called Empress Industries. Day kept her hair dyed a strikingly blonde hue, probably to match her name, but if you looked close enough, you could see the dark brown roots peeking out from her hairline.

My attention turned to two old women coming down the aisle, their long sequined evening gowns swishing as they searched for their seats. Their loud attempts at whispering were audible even from where I sat, so

The Method To Infinite Things

I overheard their entire conversation.

"Did you see Sagittarius Seymour's wife when we came in?" said one of the women, whose lipstick shone like polished plums under the fluorescent sconces. "What's she doing at the theatre, of all places, on election night? And alone? Probably left him at home too. If my husband were a senatorial candidate, I would never be so unsupportive."

Amalthea Seymour was here? At the theatre? I'd learned her name somewhere. Where, exactly, I couldn't remember. Sagittarius Seymour was the candidate for the Assiduous Party and the political rival of Sommer Day. The man was not well-known before his candidacy. To be more accurate, he was not as well-known as his *opponent*, whose name seemed to grace headlines at least once a week before she even announced her campaign. Contrary to his party's typical standards, Seymour seemed too reasonable an individual to be running for office. He stood out from the usual crowd of surface-deep gossip hoards that defined this city, almost refreshingly logical in his approach to the most pressing issues. This very quality made me seriously doubt his chances of winning.

"You know," whispered the other woman, in response to the first, "Gisabelle Rosenburg saw them arguing in the garden at Wolf Schneider's birthday celebration."

"Did she?" the first clucked her tongue and shook her head. "If you ask me, they're on the outs. Tragic. Very tragic. And to think how happy they could be if she just focused on his candidacy."

"Precisely. Whether they are on the outs or not, she really shouldn't be so open about it on a night like this."

The first woman released a sigh of exasperation as her downcast gaze searched the numbered rows of seats without success. "Where are these seats?" she flicked a pair of spectacles onto the bridge of her nose. "I cannot see a thing in this lighting. Priscilla, find someone to help. Is there no one in this world to help me?"

I approached, meeting the women in the aisle. "Good evening. May I be of service?"

"Ah, yes, yes," clucked the first woman, not Priscilla. "Where are these seats?" She passed me her ticket. I examined the slip of paper and beckoned the ladies one aisle over, stopping at row D with my arm outstretched.

"Here you are. Seats 15 and 16, ma'am."

The women moved as gracefully as advanced years and high heels allowed. Seating themselves looked like a cumbersome endeavor. I turned to leave, but Not-Priscilla stopped me. "Now wait a moment, young lady." I turned back. "I have seen your face before. Who are you?"

I was sure I didn't recognize these people. Not-Priscilla wore her white hair fluffed into a shape like a cotton ball, and her lowcut sequined gown revealed more wrinkled skin than I cared to see. Most likely she was one of Grandam's friends. "My grandmother is Ophelia Magnusson," I tried.

Nailed it. The woman's face lit up as if she were beholding a newborn baby. "You lovely thing! I know you! You're Mercury's daughter. Why are you working at a place like this, dear? Hasn't your advisor set you up with a good internship? That's their job, darling. If I were you, I would put in a complaint right away."

I swallowed. Not this. I hated this. Being questioned by strangers. Having to recount my own inadequacy. It's not like I put much stock into Meridian's self-important customs anyway, but something deep down inside of me still winced every time this kind of thing happened.

"Unfortunately," I said, pasting on a thin smile, "most internships are unpaid, and I'm trying to save money for college. I don't have time for both."

The woman looked confused. "Your grandmother won't pay your tuition?"

Of course not, I thought. But I didn't say it. Image was everything to Grandam. If she got wind that I'd been tarnishing her good name by spreading the truth, there would be nothing but venom in our house for a month.

"It's not so much that," I began, when in reality it was exactly that. "I want to earn the money on my own. You know—to say that I did it."

"Oh, dear," said the woman, her mouth gaping downward like I'd announced the unexpected death of a loved one. "I hope that's not some outer-sectors notion your father put into your head."

I bristled at the mention of my dad. The inner sectors and outer sectors were not real geographical concepts. They were a cultural phenomenon more than anything. When the United States and Canada merged under one banner to create the Republic, people needed a way to organize the new nation. We couldn't use the terms 'states' or 'provinces' without showing favoritism either way, so we divvied up the land into 'sectors' and called it good. A few years later, scientists had finally engineered and implemented a solution to the climate crisis: self-sustaining nuclear fusion. With it came a wave of societal reforms. Working conditions improved, poverty decreased, and global health was at an all-time high. That lasted for a couple decades. Then came the reemergence of a distinct upper and lower class. Tech giants, corporate CEOs, and other wealthy elite migrated to Meridian and its five surrounding sectors while lower-income earners claimed the other fifteen. No one really meant for the divide to happen. But it happened all the same. We humans need our categories.

Not-Priscilla shook her head as if I were the most wretched of souls. "In this city, you are a Magnusson. Don't let anyone tell you different. Everything your family has, you are entitled to. And don't you forget it." Then she said as an aside to her friend: "You remember Mercury Magnusson's story, don't you? Married a man from the outer sectors. Did it to defy her mother. Absolutely tragic."

Both women gave me a pitying look.

The remark made me want to knock the fluffy white cotton ball off her head. "You're right," I told the women, my face a deadpan. "My father taught me many of his bad habits. Since coming to live with Grandam, I've managed to shake most of them, but some ideas are harder to forget."

"Of course," Not-Priscilla crooned. She placed a reassuring hand on my arm. "That is not your fault. You listen to your grandmother. She is a smart woman, and if you do what she says, she'll clear you of that nonsense in no time." Her hand gave my arm a few pats.

"Yes," Priscilla agreed. "Don't let the past have power over you anymore."

"I won't," I promised. I returned to my dark haven in the corner, glad to be rid of the old crows. For a while I brooded, seething, until the anger wore off and regret took its place. I shouldn't have been so unkind. I was glad my sarcasm hadn't registered with the women. For all their faults, at least they seemed to care. That was a step up from most people in this city. Besides, blaming people here for their selfishness was like criticizing a house cat for shedding on the furniture. They didn't know any better. Ignorance was the stuff of daily living here, and more than likely, neither woman had any inkling what life outside the inner sectors really looked like. They painted my father as a lowlife good-for-nothing for no other reason than where he was born. And me—the daughter of an aristocrat mother and outer-sector father—I would always be a reminder of my family's embarrassment.

Orchestral fanfare blared throughout the theatre. Stage curtains parted, revealing an intricately constructed set and a pair of actors in full costume. I watched the performance with crossed arms, picturing the untold stories of these characters on stage, wondering if their world was much different than mine. Tonight was this play's second showing. I always enjoyed the first week of a new production. The stories were an effective escape. Beautiful and sometimes tragic, they made me feel things I couldn't feel anywhere else. Anywhere except the chem lab, maybe.

"Are you okay, Cass?" Harlow asked. "I'm sorry about that." She was referring to the old women.

I shrugged. "It's nothing. If I let every nosey granny get me down in this place, I'd have lost it a long time ago."

Halfway through the first act, a collective murmur snaked through the crowd. I didn't notice at first; I was so enthralled in the performance. Then the murmurs increased in volume, and my attention was drawn to the flashing notification on my watch. I tapped the screen to bring it to life. A news alert. I read the message: SAGITTARIUS SEYMOUR WINS ELECTION.

I gasped. I had to admit it—the result was surprising. I'd fully expected Sommer Day to claim the majority. Evidently, lots of people in the audience shared my sentiment. The guests hissed whispers among themselves. Their volume rose to a dull throb, the sound of blood pulsing beneath the skin.

A significant upset, for sure. But nothing world altering. Apart from shock factor, Seymour's victory would have no great effect on the affairs of the nation. He'd promised nothing especially radical, and no one anticipated any major policy swings as a result of his office.

So then, why the commotion? I stood. Something felt wrong. The audience grew louder, more emotional.

A man in a tuxedo shot to his feet near the center of the auditorium. He thrust a finger toward someone several rows ahead of him. "No!" he cried. "He cheated! It isn't possible!"

Several hundred pairs of eyes swung to the man. The stage actors froze, then choppily tried to continue the scene like nothing had happened. A woman in a different section stood from her seat to counter with her own proclamation: "Congratulations to Sagittarius and his family," she called in a ringing voice. "Our new senator!"

Like a wave, chaos swelled and erupted in the theatre. The man threw more insults at his nameless target. Who *was* he yelling at anyway? Then I spotted her—the only patron who seemed calm in all this—sitting prone while the rest of the theatre dissolved into anarchy. Even from far away, I recognized her from the news. It was Amalthea Seymour, the wife of Sagittarius Seymour. The one those old ladies had nothing but pitiful words for.

I was on my feet now, both paralyzed and captive. It was like watching dogs tear at each other in a fight; I couldn't look away.

"Rigged!" someone yelled from the audience.

"Get over yourself. You lost!" came the reply from another.

"Day promised. She promised," a man sobbed. "Oh, this will ruin me."

Amid the fray, I saw the senator's wife stand. She made her way to the aisle and walked briskly from the auditorium. The actors on stage had given up by now. The audience was so incensed I thought they might start throwing punches. I should find Bautista. Yes. He'd tell me what to do. I skirted past red-faced men and hissing women, narrowly avoiding the flying spray of one man's saliva. "Seymour has nothing to offer this country. Do you hear me? Nothing at all. Can he keep the working classes in line? Can he protect our private industry? Mark my words. He'll have us groveling right alongside the outer sectors—noses in the dirt—and all we've worked for—*everything* we have—destroyed . . ."

The conversation faded as I left the spitting man behind. I was in the lobby now, searching hopelessly for Bautista, when here came the voice of my manager himself over the auditorium speakers. "Ladies and gentlemen. Please remain respectful of our actors and those trying to enjoy the performance. We request silence during all productions. Please refrain from side conversations and all other disruptions."

He could have been a braying donkey for how much the audience listened to him. Meanwhile, I found where the senator's wife had gone. She was standing in the lobby, facing the front doors. Waiting for her chauffeur, I guessed.

"Appreciated guests, we must request that all private conversations be taken elsewhere or quieted for the sake of continuing the show." Bautista's plea sounded nigh hysterical, his voice a full octave higher than normal as it resonated through the theatre once again.

Outside, a sleek black vehicle pulled into the drive and stopped at the bottom of the theatre steps. At the sight of the car, Amalthea Seymour tightened the shawl around her shoulders, smoothed her hair, and strode gracefully out.

Many of the guests were finally starting to respond to Bautista's desperate announcement, and most were choosing to leave. I knew my boss would be neurotic at their abandoning the show. The guests' conversations, still rather raucous, were transferring to the lobby now. "Please, everybody. Don't crowd," I said. I stared pointedly at a loud disheveled man who appeared to have begun drinking long before tonight's performance. From the corner of my eye, the chandelier lights glinted off something small in the carpet. I looked closer. Was I seeing things? No. There it was again. Near the spot where the senator's wife had just stood. I walked over, stooped down, and gingerly picked up a thin diamond hairpin. I recognized it as part of the same set the woman had been wearing. The pin must have fallen out right before she left.

She couldn't be gone yet. Pushing through the large doors into the cool night air, I shivered at a chill that danced across my arms and neck. She was nearly to the bottom of the steps.

"Excuse me, ma'am!"

The woman looked up. I hurried down to her and presented the pin in my outstretched palm. A confused crease appeared between her eyebrows. Her gaze drifted from the pin to my black crew clothes, then back to the pin.

"You dropped this in the lobby," I explained.

Understanding dawned. Slowly, she accepted the pin with satin-gloved fingertips. "You didn't keep it," she said, voice flat, almost unbelieving. At first, I struggled to grasp her meaning. Then it occurred to me that any sane person in my position would have seen the pin for the opportunity it was. To pawn it for the money at some outer-sector bowery. She probably thought I lived outside the Capital just like the rest of the working class. I couldn't blame her. No teenager born and raised in Meridian would be caught dead sweeping floors at the Grand Theatre for a living.

"No," I said. "It's yours, ma'am."

For one strange flicker of time, like a stall in the movement of the universe, Amalthea Seymour thanked me. It was a moment contained within itself. I felt compelled by the expression on her face to pause, to wait. Wait for what? There was sadness in her eyes. I saw it in the way her eyelids dragged against gravity and the way a furrowed brow could draw friction from forces larger than life. Her hand closed around the diamond pin, and she asked me a question: "What's your name?"

"Cass."

The compulsion remained. *Wait*, the feeling said. I obeyed.

"Cass," the woman repeated, and the sadness tinged her voice. "You have shown me the first kindness of anyone in a very long time. I wish you could know what that means to me."

Returning a hairpin hardly seemed like an act worthy of praise, but I nodded out of politeness. I couldn't be sure whether the woman meant to say more. I folded my arms tight against my chest, hoping to block out the cold. "You're welcome. Congratulations on your husband's victory, ma'am."

Amalthea Seymour drew a deep, tremulous breath of the night air. She gave no thanks for my well wishes. Above us, at the top of the stairs, other guests began filing out the theatre doors. Their piercing stiletto cries reminded me of the seagulls that strutted for crumbs around outdoor cafés in the city. I became restless and wanted to get back to work.

"If there is one thing I have learned from life," said Amalthea—and I turned back to find her blue irises focused on something distant, unseeable—"it is that kindness is the only satisfaction. Do you believe me? No, it doesn't matter. I have never been very kind." She said this to herself, more in a tone befit for personal reflection than anything. I watched the words tumble like powder from her lips. Insubstantial, vanishing.

"Sorry, ma'am?"

Then her eyes were on mine, and she blinked that slow, dragging blink of weighted living. I was uncomfortable. And even more confused. Amalthea reached for my hand, which I hesitantly supplied, and she grasped my fingers in her own. "Forgive me, Cass. Forgive all of us. What's coming will be our doing, but know we tried our best to stop it. You'll understand soon enough. Once you do, I pray that you can forgive us."

A chill—not from the temperature—trickled down my spine. *Forgive us*? Forgive who? For what?

"Goodnight, Cass," Amalthea said.

Her hand released mine. The woman hitched up her gown to descend the remaining stairs. At the bottom, a chauffeur opened the back door to the sleek black vehicle. I saw the partial profile of a man seated within, dressed in suit and tie. Though I couldn't see his face, I instinctively knew it was Sagittarius Seymour, the new Senator of Meridian.

In my palm lay the diamond hairpin, glinting under scattered streetlights.

As other cars began arriving to retrieve their respective owners, guests trickled from the theatre like spilled champagne into the night. Forgotten was the performance inside. Discussion of the election results would occupy each citizen long into the nighttime hours. Their shrill voices, tinny on the air, filled me with renewed exhaustion. I commenced the climb back to the theatre entrance, my mind caught up reliving my interaction with Amalthea Seymour, and tucked the pin into a pocket.

The night was a failure. Bautista—if he weren't struck immobile by hysterics—would be rounding up the crew to launch emergency measures for the recovery of the evening. News outlets might even cover the spectacle: *Outrage in Grand Theatre as Sagittarius Seymour Snatches Election*. I shook my head. I knew how self-absorbed the residents of my sector could be, but did they really need to act so beastly?

That's when the air exploded.

CHAPTER 2

Confusion. I felt this first. Like a fog around my brain, it wrapped me in dizzy static. Lucid dreams accompanied me on the edge of consciousness. I swam through rivers of black oil, fell from soaring heights, and watched faces I didn't recognize race circles around me. The names of Sagittarius Seymour and Sommer Day echoed in my ears with ghostly timbre. I saw visions of angry men and women. They spouted nonsense, their words disjointed, and bashed each other over the head with porcelain teacups and saucers. I dreamt of an impossible staircase that started over every time I reached the top. Woven through it all, there was a sense of something gone horribly wrong.

When I finally awoke, it was to a dim room, starch linens beneath my palms, and the dull thrum of voices far away. Blinking my eyes open, I found myself surrounded by white hospital walls. A heart monitor beeped steadily next to me. I didn't like it. The sound was disorientating.

A layer of gauze wound around my right leg, which was the only part of my body not covered by a taupe-colored blanket. A thin hospital gown rubbed at my collarbone. Oxygen tubes irritated my nose and cheeks. I felt the urge to rip them away but stopped myself.

I looked around the room. As far as I could tell, I was alone. I reached back in my memory, trying to recollect what events had brought me here. I remembered the performance at the theatre. Gossiping women in evening gowns. And a large flash of light. There had been a blast. I struggled to connect the dots beyond that. The blank hospital walls stared back at me, offering no answers. My head felt stuffed full of cotton.

Reaching up a hand, I felt a square of adhesive bandage on my temple. An IV tube trailed from the crease in my elbow. Swallowing, I lowered my arm back down to my side.

How long I laid there, I couldn't say. Sometime later, a nurse walked into the room. She seemed surprised to see me staring back at her. "Ah, you're awake. That's wonderful news."

"What's going on?"

The nurse approached my bed. "Everything is all right. There was an accident at the theatre. Your grandmother is on her way now."

"My head. I feel strange. What time is it?"

"Just past midnight."

"Wh—An accident?"

"Shh," The nurse fluffed the pillows behind my head and adjusted the blankets over my one uninjured leg. "Just relax. I'll alert a doctor to come see you now that you're awake. Everything is all right."

I wanted answers. I didn't understand why this woman wasn't giving them to me. My head felt like a buoy bobbing along the surface of a lake. Every inch of my body was simultaneously heavy and lighter than air, like I could either sink through my bed or float away through the ceiling.

The nurse left the room. I laid back on my pillows, listening to the incessant beep of the heart monitor, racking my brain for any useful recollection at all. "Harlow," I croaked. "Harlow?" My wrist was bare. I searched the room until I spotted my watch sitting on a plastic tray atop a rolling table pushed to the wall. I had to speak above my throaty rasp for the audio sensors to finally pick up my voice. "Harlow, tell me what's going on."

"Cass! I'm so glad you're all right. You've been unconscious for hours."

"I don't understand. What happened?"

"Senator and Amalthea Seymour—"

Just then, a man in a white doctor's coat arrived. Harlow stopped short, a nuance of her programming to go quiet whenever somebody else began talking. "Cassiopeia?" the doctor checked. I nodded. He scrolled along some information on his Loom panel—the nickname for the hovering conglomeration of particles that most high-end watches could launch and collapse upon command. From my position behind the hovering screen, all I saw was his face through the transparent particles. The technology was designed so that only the user could view the information on the screen. "You took quite a fall at the theatre. How are you feeling?"

"Fine, I guess. Can you tell me what's going on?"

The doctor claimed a chair next to my bed. "There was an accident. An explosion to which you were in close proximity. You've sustained a concussion and shrapnel to your leg. The concussion should mend itself through rest and recuperation, and we've already removed the shrapnel. Your leg is healing at an accelerated pace as we speak. The skin should be good as new within a few days."

I dropped my gaze to the bandage wrapped around my lower right leg. I pictured medical AI hovering over my unconscious body, picking out each invasive shard from my flesh. The image unnerved me. "What do you mean, an explosion?"

"A vehicle spontaneously combusted."

My thoughts failed to keep up. Everything felt muddled. Heavy. It took every ounce of willpower I possessed to focus on the doctor's face. "I don't understand. What vehicle?"

The doctor shifted in his seat. He looked impatient. "Please, don't concern yourself about it anymore. You need rest. Your brain needs time to recover from the concussion."

"Don't you have ways to fix this kind of thing? Some . . . drug to make me heal faster?" I was just sentient enough to recognize how weak I felt, like my neurons were only firing at a fraction of their usual speed. How was I supposed to work in a state like this? How could I keep up my research at the lab?

The doctor sighed. "Fixing a leg is easy. We can expedite healing and repair skin cells over the course of, say, 72 hours. It's trickier to heal a brain. You might call it the final frontier of medicine. There are still things we don't understand completely." The man's watch vibrated, and he rose from the chair. "I believe your grandmother is on her way. Don't hesitate to call a nurse if you need anything. For now, get some rest." I listened as the doctor's footsteps receded down the hall.

"Harlow?"

"Yes, Cass?"

"Can you connect to that TV in the corner?"

Harlow paused, and I sensed her hesitation. "Casting capabilities are enabled, yes. Would you like me to play some relaxing music?"

"I want you to show me footage of what happened tonight."

She started to argue, citing the doctor's orders, but I overrode her with a swift command. In response, the mounted screen in the corner of the hospital room came to life. It processed the boot-up briefly before launching into a news report showing footage outside the Grand Theatre, where police sirens cast blue and red glares across the street, and yellow caution tape sectioned off the greater area around a smoldering shell of a vehicle, black with soot. My breath hitched in my throat as I recognized the names scrolling across the bottom of the screen.

A newscaster spoke: "—reporters on the scene of the explosion. We have an updated casualty count—that's four dead and several more injured in a blast outside the Grand Theatre tonight. Among the deceased are Senator Sagittarius Seymour and his wife Amalthea Seymour, both caught in the blast just minutes after Seymour's election victory. Police are asking citizens to stay in their homes. I repeat—stay in your homes. More information regarding the incident should become available soon."

"*Oh my* . . ." I stared, unable to rip my eyes away from the broadcast. "This is live?"

"Yes," said Harlow. "It's horrible."

"Switch reports," I gasped, waving one hand in her general direction, eyes still glued to the screen. Harlow flipped through broadcast after broadcast, each one reporting the same basic details. A few stations replayed footage taken immediately after the blast. Fire still consumed the vehicle in these shots, raging red and black against a stark night sky while first responders doused the blaze with a foaming emulsion. "Dry chemical," I murmured, a matter of habit. I watched the frothy liquid rain over the burning car, slowly quenching the flames, and my lips named off chemical compounds at a whisper. "Sodium bicarbonate . . . monoammonium phosphate . . ." This was a game for me, usually.

To identify ingredients in random solutions. This time, though, it was less a conscious effort and more an attempt to make sense of a senseless situation.

Suddenly I was aware of wetness on my cheeks—tears streaming down my face. If I'd been just a few feet closer to the car, would my name be among the list of dead? An image came to mind of my immobile body flung across the theatre steps, and it was this small detail that broke me. "Who would do this, Harlow?" I wept. The tears flowed, and I had no strength to stop them. My head grew heavier, prompting a strong wave of nausea, and I leaned back on the pillows, searching the ceiling above me for an explanation that wasn't there. Just this very night, Amalthea Seymour had descended the theatre steps, alive and well. She spoke to me—thanked me. Her gloved hand was warm when she gifted me the pin. Had death claimed her so easily?

"I'm confused what you mean by your question. There has been no evidence of foul play. All sources say it was an accident."

I shook my head. "You're good at statistics, Harlow. What are the chances of a freak explosion killing Seymour and his wife the very night he won the election?"

There was silence. "I do not have statistics for such an event. But I imagine the numbers would be quite low."

I sniffed. "Where are my clothes? Do you know where they put them?" My gaze searched the room but came up empty. "Amalthea gave me a pin. It was in my pocket. Is it gone?"

"I don't know, Cass. I'm so sorry."

I squeezed my eyes shut, willing the dizziness to subside. Eventually the heart monitor slowed its frantic pace. It must have peaked while I was watching the reports. Forcing myself to breathe deeply, a voice of reason replaced the one of shock and grief. I remembered my strange conversation with the woman before she died. What had she said? Something about an apology. It was blurry now. Result of the concussion, probably.

Bottom line: The Seymours were dead. Assassinated, most likely, by someone angry enough with the election results to do it. What did it mean? Sommer Day was the obvious next choice for senator. *Grandam will be happy*, I thought.

Oh, no. Grandam. The nurse and doctor said she would be arriving soon. It was the last thing I needed on top of tonight. Even though we lived in the same house, I was usually able to avoid her by deliberately leaving home early and coming back late. Could I fake sleep once she got here? No. More than likely, my nurse would have already told her I was up.

There are numerous chemicals in the scientific world which, when combined, produce such violent reactions as to necessitate protective gear and emergency services at the ready. Take phosphorus and oxygen. The former is known for catching fire upon mere contact with air. That was like my relationship with my grandmother. Our interactions, more often than not, better resembled the tense compromise between resentful roommates than anything akin to familial love.

At this moment, I would rather see *anyone* besides her at my bedside. I considered having Harlow send her a message: *Good news. Doc says I'm fine after all. No need to show up. Seriously. Please don't show up.*

But my thoughts were interrupted by a sound from the hallway. It was the clicking of heels on tile. I knew that sound. Instantly my stomach formed a ball of knots. "Here we go," I whispered to myself.

Grandam appeared in the doorway. She wore a pure-white pantsuit with matching overcoat, pearls, and heels. Her silver-gray hair was fixed to perfection. Now I understood why it had taken her two hours to arrive at the hospital. Far be it from Ophelia Magnusson to go out in public without beautifying herself first.

"Hello," I said.

"Hello," she said back.

I watched her gaze flick over the darkened room, the medical instruments, my injured leg. There was no reading her expression. I waited for her to make the first move—to show me some sympathy if she could muster it. For a while Grandam only stood there, unmoving, as if the idea of stepping foot in the room repulsed her.

"How's a person supposed to see with no lights on?" she said at last. Before I could stop her, she flipped the light switch. Brightness flooded the room. She might as well have taken a hammer to my skull. While the pain meds numbed the worst of it, I still swayed from the sudden rush of vertigo. A groan built in my throat.

"I have a concussion, you know."

Grandam examined the visitor's chair distrustfully, no doubt wondering whether some unseen contaminant might soil the pristine fabric of her pantsuit. When she did sit, she perched on the edge of the chair like a bird. "Have your people turn them off once I leave," she said with a dismissive wave behind her. I could only assume she meant the myriad of nurses passing my hospital room on their routes between patients.

Quiet fell over us, an awkward quiet, the kind that falls upon people who don't talk to each other on a regular basis. Why did she have to be here? I wished she would go and leave me to mourn the dead in peace. The oxygen tubes itched inside my nose, and again I had the urge to yank them out.

"Are you in much pain?" asked Grandam.

"Not really. I'm full of drugs. And they already took the shrapnel out of my leg."

Grandam looked unamused. "That's the extent of it, then?" She nodded. "Good. You have no idea how much this will cost me already. Thank your stars the rest of you went undamaged. I'd have been tempted not to pay the difference."

I lifted my eyes to the ceiling. *Yes. Thank you, stars, for not wrecking my body entirely. We'd hate for Grandam to have to pay the difference.*

She asked me questions about the accident next. I answered them as well as my limited knowledge allowed. I failed to mention my conversation with Amalthea Seymour. Exposing to Grandam the woman's final moments felt like a violation somehow. A desecration, even. I doubted I could vocalize the encounter anyway. Not so soon. Not without fresh tears.

And I refused to cry in front of my grandmother.

Eventually, after exhausting every detail I could recall by memory, Grandam contented herself with watching reports on the television, which repeated the same facts with only an occasional new addition. We waited for a nurse or doctor to return and give an update regarding the length of my stay in the hospital. The halls were busy enough that I figured most medics were occupied with other patients. Half an hour passed before someone arrived. But it wasn't a doctor or a nurse. The man that knocked on the doorframe to my room was clad in a checkered suit the color of peaches and seawater and carried a bouquet of flowers. Immediately, he drew the attention of us both. Grandam sat up straighter and released an audible *oh*!

I had never seen this man before.

"Forgive the intrusion. Ashcroft March. Empress Industries. Director of Public Relations. You must be Cassiopeia?"

The forceful, shotgun style of his remarks took me aback. "E-Empress Industries? *The* Empress Industries?" I stammered out.

The man clutched the flowers, exuding reverence. "I came to offer my sympathies, miss. No one could be more devastated by this accident than those of us at Empress. Our company president, Sommer Day, specifically, sends her deepest regrets to you and the other wounded." He extended the bouquet towards me. "For you."

I accepted the flowers, cellophane crunching in my grasp. A representative from Empress Industries *was* here. In *my* hospital room. Maybe the concussion was skewing my perception of reality. I opened my mouth to reply, but Grandam beat me to the punch.

"Why, how good of you, Mr. March." She leaned forward to clutch my hand. Her fingers felt thin and foreign. "This is a difficult time, but nothing through which we cannot persevere."

You've got to be kidding me. I barely kept myself from rolling my eyes.

"I'm sure you have more than enough on your plate," continued March, "To ease some of the burden I hope you will accept this gift, as a gesture of goodwill from President Day's senatorial campaign." March produced a metallic-looking card from his suit jacket. "You should find enough credits here to cover the costs of your medical care. While no one can turn back time, perhaps this can lessen the blow of an incident out of anyone's control."

While Grandam gushed over his generosity in her demure genteel way, I pursed my lips. Paying the hospital bill in full—now there was an expensive publicity stunt. I didn't question whether Sommer Day could afford it. Empress Industries led the world in drone and droid manufacturing and could likely purchase this entire hospital if Day wanted it. Where were the cameras to capture this charitable moment? Surprising that he brought none with him. Maybe Sommer Day didn't need the media coverage when word of mouth would do just as well in the city.

". . . charming girl," Grandam was saying. "The smartest in her class. I hate to see her suffering like this at her young age." Grandam fixed me with a pained smile. "After all, who knows how her life will be different now?"

So that was Grandam's play. I should have guessed. She planned to milk the situation for all it was worth. Embarrassment warmed my cheeks as each hollow word touched down with that contrived saccharin sweetness she reserved for only the most prestigious of company. I wished she wouldn't. Why couldn't she keep her mouth shut for once?

"Of course," replied March. He glanced at his watch. Sucked in a breath. "Ah, I'm afraid that's my cue. I should be going. Too much work and never enough time." He inclined his head towards me. "What a pleasure to meet you, Cassiopeia. I only wish Empress could do more. My best wishes for your quick recovery."

"—The quickest," Grandam added.

I shot her a look.

"Yes, certainly. The very quickest," said March, one foot out the door.

"—The girl has big things ahead of her. She really cannot afford to be troubled with adverse health."

"I would think not," returned March.

I gritted my teeth in a smile and waggled one hand in the air. "Trust me, everybody, I'm fine."

Now Grandam shot *me* a look.

March tried again to excuse himself.

Please, I thought. *Let the man go*!

Grandam released a melodramatic sigh. "I only hope"—and she

looked March straight in the eye—"that her injuries don't keep her from presenting at the World's Fair."

The room froze. I turned to my grandmother, mouth agape. March, too, had gone still. How did she know about my acceptance to the fair? When I myself had only received the notification this afternoon? I could only assume that, as my guardian, she'd received a letter from the board as well. Grandam gazed at me without remorse. Her eyes gleamed with pride—a rare look that didn't go beyond the surface. I'd seen it before. I knew it was compensation for herself. As long as I was around, she lived life trying to convince others she was still one of them. Still one of the greats. Now she sat beside my hospital bed, triumphant, ticking off the victory that had been too good to pass up. Where was that nurse when you needed her? I'd make her knock me out again just to escape it all.

I definitely had March's attention now. Mortified, I locked my eyes on the hospital blanket and refused to meet his gaze. "You are *the* Cassiopeia?" he asked. "The one whose name appears on this year's fair schedule?"

I was surprised enough to look up. Word sure traveled faster than I thought. "I haven't had the chance to look at the schedule yet." It was as good an answer as any, and it served to confirm my involvement in the fair anyway.

March cocked his head, eyebrows raised. "Yes, well, at Empress we try to keep abreast of any and all developments across the scientific scene. A new name at the World's Fair is something we couldn't overlook. I'll admit—you are younger than I expected. I have never heard of anyone your age being accepted to the fair."

"Well, maybe they're lowering their standards."

March chuckled. I didn't mean to make him laugh. "You've piqued my interest," he admitted, returning his gaze to his watch. "Empress attends regularly, as I'm sure you know. We often acquire our best new innovations at the fair. I will ensure that our representatives stop by your presentation."

I was speechless. Logically, I knew I should thank him. Express my eagerness to talk further. Empress Industries—*the* Empress Industries—was interested in me? The thought sent a thrill down my spine. If the concussion weren't clouding my senses, and if the man weren't in such an obvious hurry, I might have initiated more of a conversation. But March was bidding farewell, and I lay there and watched as the back of his checkered suit vanished around the corner.

Next to me, Grandam nodded with an air of self-satisfaction. I turned to her sharply. "What was that for?" I demanded. "He came to check on the wounded. He gave us money! Did you have to stick your oar in it?"

She sniffed. "It's called networking. It's what successful people do."

"You made me look stupid."

"I made you noteworthy," she countered. She grabbed the flowers from me, smelled them, and settled them on her own lap. "Use your brain for a moment. Thanks to me, you are the only person in this hospital he is going to remember. Thanks to me, you aren't just some girl who fell down and scratched her leg. So zip it. Maybe we can make something good out this mess after all."

Her eyes flitted up and down my body on the word 'mess.' I was then forced to listen as she analyzed every detail of March's visit—what it meant, how it would change things, what kind of reaction she'd get from the rest of Meridian high society once they found out. Through the hum of medical machinery, the quieted chatter of television newscasters, and my grandmother's incessant prattle, I tried to wrap my consciousness around the fact that Empress Industries—*the* Empress Industries—knew my name.

CHAPTER 3

The medical staff tried convincing me to take the rest of the week off school. They even brought in a psychologist: a pale, freckled man who talked about the importance of rest when recovering from traumatic events. His voice grated on me, and I felt bad for wasting the guy's time when none of his platitudes really had much effect. But I listened out of courtesy and soon realized I could make him go away sooner by nodding thoughtfully and saying things like, "That makes sense. I think you're right. Maybe that *is* the reason for all my issues."

They released me two days after the bombing with orders to avoid physical and mental exertion. My doctor sent me with enough pain meds for a week. I used them during my first day back. I didn't like how they caused my brain to lag like a slow network connection, so I ended up dropping the bottle in a disposal inside the police station.

News broadcasts lit up my watch constantly. Ping after ping sent vibrations up my arm, all notifications regarding the "incident." I watched them obsessively. A casualty report included the Seymours' chauffeur and a theatre guest killed through proximity to the blast. Hospitalization numbers registered at nine injured, three of which were currently in critical condition. Was I one of those numbers? Did they count me as a casualty?

At least I found Amalthea's pin safe in the pocket of my work pants. Somehow it hadn't fallen out amidst all the commotion. Looking at it reminded me of her words that night. *Forgive me*, she had said. *Forgive all of us.* I still didn't understand. Her pleadings haunted me. At night

I heard echoes of our conversation like garbled news reports. Sleep was evasive at best.

And then, during fourth period at school, one of the pings confirmed my suspicions—investigative teams found explosive residue within the wreckage, indicating the malicious nature of the attack. I silenced the pings after that. Even without the notifications, I struggled to focus on my assignments. I often caught myself dozing off, but every time exhaustion threatened, memory flashes of flame and smoke jolted me awake again.

One morning, I awoke to pale light streaming through my window. My watch blinked its telltale blue light from the bedside table. I tapped open the broadcast, launching the suspended screen in front of me. The technology had been made possible when scientists discovered how to condense light particles into a panel-shaped area some distance in front of the user's body, according to an individual's preset body calibration. Radio waves carrying visual information attached themselves to the particle surfaces, creating a free-floating screen that moved where you moved. Its inventors called it a lumigraph—Loom, for short. Groggily, I registered that my panel had dropped out of eye level by several inches and made a vague mental note to recalibrate my body orientation sensor.

The broadcast showed a press conference with Sommer Day, her third after the event, explaining once again that she had no part in the death of her fellow candidate and expressing sincere condolences to the families of the victims. When the feed cut back to the studio, a newscaster reminded the audience of the joint Seymour funeral service to be held next week and televised on all major news networks. He then announced a special election to choose Meridian's replacement senator. Out of respect for the dead, the election would not take place until one week following the funeral. The broadcast went dark.

On that note, I would have stayed in bed for the rest of my life. Even my semi-sleepless comatose was better than going outside again. But I couldn't get behind in school. Not when I needed a spotless portfolio for the World's Fair. It was my sole motivation to extricate myself from the blankets and get dressed.

The rising sun peered through my windowpane like a tentative creature testing the day's waters. I dressed in a simple beige shirt, jeans, and jacket. Pulling my hair into its usual plain ponytail, I stared at myself in the mirror. There was no hiding it. I looked terrible.

Resigning myself to the inevitable, I fastened on my watch and made for the front door. I had one hand on the brass doorknob when Letty, Grandam's housekeeper, appeared from the hallway adjacent the kitchen. She carried a bucket of cleaning supplies and gave me a gentle smile. "Hey, you. How's my girl doing this morning?"

I faked nonchalance by smoothing my hair at the place my head had hit the concrete on the theatre steps. The goose egg had receded since that night, along with most of the aching. "Not bad. At least they're tracking down whoever did it. I better get to school. I woke up a little late."

"Cass?" Letty stopped me with concern in her voice. "Are you sure you're okay? Do you want to talk about it?"

When I first came to live with Grandam six years ago, Letty took it upon herself to become a sort of mother figure. She had to be around fifty years old, though I'd never asked her age outright. Over those first few months, she developed a knack for reading into my facial expressions to guess exactly how I was feeling. I was just a timid little kid then, still confused and freshly raw from my parents' divorce, and she was the quiet ghost on the periphery. We rarely spoke to each other in the beginning. Then one night, Grandam locked me out of the house. "Slugs sleep in the garden," she'd said before slamming the patio door. Letty had snuck me back inside, dried my tears, and tucked me into bed.

We became friends after that. Every night she would sit with me, talking and telling stories until I fell asleep. Looking back, I sometimes wondered what time she got home on those nights we stayed up late together. I asked her, once, where she lived. "Right across the sector boundary in Prestiga North," she had explained. "There's a lovely set of apartment complexes. That's where I live."

Every sector—except Meridian—was divided into four cardinal pieces: north, south, east, and west. The distinction was purely organizational. In other words, no class difference existed between the pieces like that separating the inner sectors from the outer sectors. It was the first time

I'd realized how superficial the divide was.

I'd then asked Letty if she had to walk home from Grandam's estate every night.

"No, silly," she had laughed. "I take the train. You can't walk in between sectors."

Normally, I would have been relieved to see her on a morning like this. Even someone less astute than Letty wouldn't have trouble gauging my innermost thoughts today. I should have been eager to unload the pain. She always knew the right thing to say, after all. She knew how to make things better.

Trouble was . . . this time felt different. I wasn't sure even Letty could fix this.

"I'm good. I promise. Besides, I-I didn't even see it happen. I really should get to school."

There was a pause that weighed heavy between us. Still, I kept my gaze locked on a marble vase in the entryway to avoid making eye contact. Putting her off felt unnatural. I hated the feeling. But more than that, I hated the thought of recounting that night—that ugly, ugly night when people's lives evaporated like smoke and somebody, somewhere, laughed because of it. The memory was an acrid thing in my gut.

So though I hated it, I couldn't talk to Letty. Not yet. As my silence stretched on, I heard her give a small sigh. "Okay," she said finally. "That's all right. You be good at school today. I'll see you when you get home."

I slipped out the door.

***

The day passed gradually so that when the final bell released me from class, I had long lost interest in whatever material my teachers were trying to instill in me and my fellow pupils. The other students questioned me incessantly. Word spread how I'd been working my shift at the theater that night. Normally I was invisible at school, but my presence at the bombing changed everything. Everyone wanted details. I, however, had no desire to indulge them. My head started hurting again around midday, so I used the concussion as an excuse to escape the bombardment and generally sequestered myself until school ended and I took my usual route back home.

"I don't get it, Harlow," I muttered, blocking the sun with one hand. Though my sensitivity to light had abated since leaving the hospital, I'd found that direct sunlight was still too much to handle. "Amalthea acted like something horrible was about to happen. Something big. The way she talked—it was all so foreboding. Almost like she knew she was going to die."

"Do you think she had caught wind of the attacker's plan? Perhaps she was warning you?"

"Why would she get in the car though? If she knew what was coming? She might have known someone was after them, but I don't think she had the specifics. Anyway, that doesn't seem to be what she was asking forgiveness for." I shook my head. "It doesn't line up. Something in the future was scaring her, and she said it was all 'their' fault. Who was she talking about? What was it that made her so upset? I just don't get it."

I entered my grandmother's house to the sound of overlapping talking and laughter. *Right*, I thought. It was Thursday. My grandmother hosted her weekly luncheons on Thursday. Being so soon after the bombing at the theatre, she was likely bursting to discuss every detail with this week's friend selection. Everyone would have their own little piece of gossip to convey—whether it was true or not. And those who had been unlucky enough to garner Grandam's displeasure this week through some social misstep or another would have been disinvited from the guest list. Last week it had been some woman named Gladyah Hornbill. I didn't know the details. Excluding people from her luncheons was Grandam's best singular method of revenge. The woman was drunk with power.

I saw the guests milling around the parlor, plates in hand, decked out in their fancy clothes and pristinely placed hairstyles. I counted a husband-and-wife couple, a very tall woman, one lady in extremely high-waisted slacks, another married couple, two women with broad sunhats, and a man who wouldn't stop talking even while chewing his food. All the guests were around my grandmother's age—many retired or close to retiring from their corporate management positions. Either that or reaping the monetary inheritance of a deceased spouse, as in Grandam's case.

During her luncheons, Grandam always had strict rules for my staying out of the way. Normally I avoided most of the thing by being at school. During the summer months, however, when school was out of session, I tended to sit in the garden. I was never interested in the guests' conversations anyway, but especially not today. Since Grandam hadn't seemed to hear me come in, I decided to make myself as scare as possible. I closed the door without a sound and began to skirt around the party to the patio when one of the guests spotted me.

"Hello," she called. It was the tall woman. I turned, suddenly feeling like a trapped animal. She looked like a vision in her gold-trimmed sundress and red lipstick, one hand perched on her hip and the other swirling a glass of some raspberry-colored concoction. "Are you Ophelia's granddaughter?"

I wished she were talking to someone other than me. "Yes," I said, summoning a polite smile. "I'm Cass. And you are?"

"Andora Paybody, love. How nice to meet you." I felt self-conscious of my plain appearance compared to hers. "Don't you live here with your grandmother?"

"Yes."

"Charming. Do you enjoy yourself in Meridian?"

There were many ways I could answer that question, but I didn't have the nerve or the presence of mind to voice any of them. I nodded instead. I hoped she would take that answer and let me go.

"And your parents, do they—well, how should I say it—visit you often?"

She gazed at me curiously. A beat passed between us, in which I wondered how much she had been told about my past. An acidic emotion curdled my stomach, and I responded deliberately, my eyes narrow and unblinking. "No, ma'am, they never visit me."

"Cassiopeia?" Grandam's voice cried out, a mix of surprise and horror. Her eyes flicked from me to Andora Paybody, and I saw her thought process displayed on her face. Her heels came clipping over while her pointed stare bore a hole through my body. "Haven't I told you before not to bother my guests?" She flashed a smile at the tall woman over her shoulder, who responded with raised eyebrows and sipped her drink. "Get out," Grandam spat at me through gritted teeth. "Now."

"Ho there, Ophelia, who's this?" The talkative man stepped forward, seeming delighted to see me standing there. "I've seen you all over the news, young lady! Ophelia, you never told us your granddaughter was the girl from the theatre."

Grandam didn't reply. She glared at me like she might an insect that had invaded her home.

Upon hearing the man's declaration, all other guests gathered around. I was an animal at the zoo. "Tell me, darling," said one of the sunhat women, "were you horribly scared? How traumatic for you. If I were you, I wouldn't be able to sleep for a week after something so dreadful."

"This is providential!" a man with a large polka-dotted cravat cried, coming forward. "My good friend, Alabaster Jennings, was at the theatre last night too, you see." He spoke like a stage performer, one finger raised in the air, eager to capture the attention of everyone present. "While he didn't see the explosion itself take place, he told me about a girl with dark hair running up and down the stairs tending to the wounded. Was that you, my dear?"

Whoever Alabaster Jennings was, I wouldn't trust his word on anything if he thought I was rescuing the wounded while passed out cold.

A collective gasp rose from the guests. Chattering ensued. Grandam looked ready to murder.

Then the sunhat woman covered her mouth with one hand. "*My* friend told me about a dark-haired girl who followed Amalthea Seymour out to her vehicle. Perhaps that was you as well? Oh, do tell us everything! Did you know what was about to happen? Is *that* why you followed Amalthea outside? Oh, my, I'm going to be faint. Tell us, my dear, tell us!" She clasped her other hand to her chest—so dramatic an action I might have thought she was faking if I hadn't lived among these people for the last six years.

Someone loudly hushed the chatter so that everyone fell silent, anticipating my response. I dragged my gaze away from my grandmother's fuming stare. Patrons at the zoo wouldn't leave the animal alone until it performed. How could I relate my account in the shortest amount of time possible, allowing me to escape this group of overly enthusiastic retirees? "I did *not* know what was going to happen," I said. "I followed the senator's wife out because she dropped something in the lobby, and I returned it to her. That was it. I had no more interactions with her besides that."

"What was the belonging?" It was the polka-dot cravat who asked it.

"A hairpin." I shrugged, feeling uncomfortable revealing the late Amalthea Seymour's final moments to these ravenous gossip hounds. "Just a hairpin."

"A cry for help!" gasped a woman who had not yet contributed to the conversation. Her eyes importuned the man next to her. "Perhaps she knew what would happen, so she dropped the pin as a cry for help!"

"Don't be ridiculous, Gloriana. If she knew what would happen, why would she get into the car?" The man who chided Gloriana appeared to be her husband.

"Never mind the pin," said Andora Paybody. When she held one hand in the air, the rest of the guests clammed up instantly. Interesting. Apparently, I wasn't the only one whom this woman made nervous. As silence fell, Andora lowered her raised hand. "*Well, love, you are the last living person to have spoken with Mrs. Seymour before the incident.* Would you mind telling us her last words? Some of us knew Amalthea quite well, and I believe I speak for all of us when I say that knowing the details of her last moments would give us closure."

Others nodded in agreement. My tongue stuck to the roof of my mouth. It was all coming back now. The feel of satin gloves clutching my hand, the hushed surprise in her voice upon receiving the hairpin. Well, love, you are the last living person to have spoken with Mrs. Seymour before the incident. Her last living connection to the world. In this instant, that burden felt entirely too massive to bear. For the first time since the hospital, tears pricked again at my vision. "She . . . she told me thank you. For returning the pin." I shut my eyes, if only for a second, trying to block out my reality. Afraid that if I opened them again, the tears would spill out. "She thanked me."

The room was so quiet I hoped I had imagined it all. But when I opened my eyes again, the group was still there. They seemed contemplative . . . and disappointed.

The polka-dot cravat cleared his throat. "Ah. Suppose we couldn't have been expecting the State of the Union now, could we?" He drank deeply from his glass.

"Still rather anti-climactic though," laughed another.

My ears grew red-hot, an effect that happened when I was either embarrassed or very angry. This time, it was the latter. More than angry. I was furious. I faked another polite smile and beelined out the patio door. Let Grandam and her smug cohort enjoy themselves at the expense of a woman's death. I would have no more part in it. Unfortunately, escaping the thing wasn't that easy.

***

Two days after the luncheon, I was finishing another experiment in my most recent series on hydrophosphates at the chem lab when Mop Guy and his cleaning cart appeared around the corner.

"Yer the one on TV, aren't ya?" he asked.

What could I say? Security cameras had captured the final moments between me and Amalthea before the explosion. News networks played the silent footage on repeat. For the last two days, reporters kept showing up at the house, asking for a statement, but I refused to meet with any of them. Grandam, on the other hand, reveled in the attention. She gave permission to release my school photo to the public. As speculation surrounding the Seymours grew, she even sat for several interviews.

We were more popular than ever. And why? Amalthea hadn't revealed anything of significance to me besides the nostalgic reminisces of a woman bearing an impossible burden. I found the whole thing macabre. Better to leave it all alone.

As far as Mop Guy and his question, I shrugged in response and occupied myself with measuring out calcium oxide for solubility reduction.

"I wou'nt trust Day if I was you."

Surprised by the statement, I looked up. "Sorry?"

Mop Guy shuffled his feet. Unkempt brows twitched over his downcast eyes, and he blinked rapidly as if to build up enough nerve to speak. "I ain't too smart, not like the rest-a-ya," he said, scratching at an arm and not meeting my gaze. "But I knows a bad apple when I sees one. Be careful with a lady like 'er. She's sour all right. Sour and shady too. Ya don' wan' someone like 'er takin' advantage of ya."

Processing this, I considered how to respond. The man seemed to think I was involved with Sommer Day somehow. In reality, nothing could be further from the truth. Ashcroft March may have visited me in the hospital, but our acquaintance stopped there. And yes, Grandam had played up the interaction in her interviews, but it was all just to make herself feel important.

"What do you mean, 'someone like her'? What's she done?" I asked.

Mop Guy cleared his throat. He'd started fidgeting. Probably wanted to get back to work. But he was the one who initiated this exchange, and I intended to follow it through.

"When ya work 'ere long enough," he said, "long as I have, ya hear things. Ya learn what people like 'er do to get where they wanna be. When I saws yer face on them news channels, I thought, 'That's 'er all right. That's the girlie from the lab.' And then I hears how Sommer Day wants ya for 'erself. I thought, 'Now I oughta warn that girlie. A good one like 'er ain't got no business dealin' with a shady lady like that.'"

"I-I'm not with Day," I explained. "I don't even know her."

Mop Guy nodded. "Well, better keep it that way. Ya don' wanna go makin' deals with the devil when there ain't no need. Jus' watch yerself now." Another nod. With a push he got the cart rolling again, and I stared as he shuffled off, looking frail bent over his cleaning supplies.

This was a new development. The tone of the man's voice, the warning it contained, sounded sincere. He really thought Day posed a danger to me. Why? No one from Empress had reached out to me since the hospital. If Mop Guy had heard something, some inkling of collaboration between me and Day, it was definitely nothing but rumors. Speculation. Some wild idea concocted by conspiracy theorists trying to prolong the drama.

I could see them now—gossip columnists watching the footage from the theatre, my private conversation with Amalthea, then learning how Ashcroft March had visited the wounded in the hospital. No matter that he was visiting *everyone* that night. People would take what they wanted from the situation. They'd draw conclusions. And Grandam—I cursed under my breath—Grandam probably contributed to the rumors more than anyone. She'd blasted my involvement in the World's Fair all over the metaverse via her interviews. There was no concealing the fact any longer. And while I should have been grateful for the publicity, I found myself frustrated instead. It wasn't supposed to be this way. The fair was my chance to prove myself, to seal a contract based on nothing more than my own merits and innovative thinking. But how would it be now? Definitely not the objective environment I'd envisioned, where people were considered for their scientific prowess rather than social accolades. Now, anything I presented would be touched by runoff from this media frenzy. If companies showed interest in me, would it be for the quality of my invention? Or just the fleeting popularity of a big news story?

Anyway, I could see where Mop Guy got the notion. But what I couldn't explain was his poor perception of Day. As a custodian, he probably had access to most areas of the university. It's possible he had picked up on a few things—overheard some unflattering information about Day and her company. I should have pressed for more details. As the thought occurred, I hurried off in the direction the man had gone, thinking I could catch him and find out what exactly compelled him to warn me against Empress. I peered down aisles and cracked the main doors to check the exterior hallway, but Mop Guy was nowhere to be found.

Preoccupied, I returned to my lab station. Work felt impossible now, so I packed up for the day and found my way out the winding halls of the university. My watch buzzed with a notification for the Seymours' joint funeral next week. It was to be the largest occasion of the year, complete with day-long television specials on the lives of Sagittarius and Amalthea. The guest list continued to grow as officials from all over the world sent in their RSVPs. According to this newest update, the Secretary of State for the Central-South American Federation and his family were on their way now.

I claimed a quiet section on the train where no one sat within earshot. "Harlow," I said, planting myself in a window seat, "give me all the information you can find on Sommer Day, please."

"Sure, Cass. That's a lot of material. Want me to start with the basics?"

I agreed, and Harlow began reading directly from Day's official bio on Empress Industries' webpage. The information didn't provide much insight beyond superficial details. Day graduated from Hawley University with a graduate degree in business administration at age twenty-three and founded Empress two years later. It sounded like every other Meridian executive's backstory up to this point. Then Harlow landed on an article describing how Day's father went bankrupt when she was just seventeen. The fact surprised me. Here in the Capital, money problems were worse than death, at least in the public eye. Day must have pulled more than a few strings in order to regain her status.

The train wove its way into the city. I watched clumps of people pass on the sidewalks in heavy fashions too illogical for spring. I caught sight of one woman's massive handbag dangling from her arm. It was a crocodile—an actual crocodile. A long scaly tail protruded from the back end and wrapped halfway around the woman's body. The front of the bag featured the head of the creature, its mouth agape as if the woman had dispatched it herself just that morning. "What makes *that* a fashion?" I mumbled. The train quickly left the sight behind, and I watched as the stranger and her lifeless crocodile faded into the distance.

"I'm sorry, what was that?" asked Harlow.

"Never mind. Can you play me some of Day's most popular campaign speeches?"

I fast-forwarded through the audio, gathering frequent uses of 'future,' 'mankind,' and 'freedom.' Fairly standard for a politician. "What about the last three press releases from Empress Industries before the bombing took place?" I asked. Harlow queued the list of videos, and I listened to the voice of someone I recognized—it was Ashcroft March—expound on the virtues of Empress technology overseas, where drones and battle androids fought alongside troops of the Republic to defend the weak and oppressed. Sommer Day herself started speaking, exuberant and likeable, going on about aerospace advancements that would take mankind into the future. There were those trigger words again. The last audio piece was shorter than the others and again featured March: "The technology to heal this nation of its maladies is just within our reach," he proclaimed. "With your support and patience, Empress will soon be protecting not only those abroad, but those at home as well. Watch and wait. We won't disappoint you. Relief is coming. Put your trust in Empress Industries."

I screwed up my face as the speech ended. "What does he mean, 'relief is coming'? What technology is he talking about?"

There was a pause while Harlow scanned audio transcripts for more clues. "They announced a new tech in development several months ago. I'm not finding any specifics."

The train glided to a stop at the station nearest Grandam's estate. Unsurprisingly, the theatre was closed for the time being, which meant I was out of a job until Bautista reopened. I hoped he wouldn't take too long. I needed the money for the university lab fees. Disembarking, I began the walk home. It was only a few blocks.

My thoughts turned to Amalthea Seymour. "Aren't there any more updates on the bombing? Any new evidence?" I asked Harlow.

"Not that I can find. I'm sorry, Cass."

I sighed. None of it made any sense. My hand went to my pocket, where I'd taken to keeping Amalthea's diamond hairpin.

Rounding a corner, I caught a glimpse of Grandam's estate. White stone dormers and dark roofing tiles protruded above the tree line. Glamorous and pristine. That was the standard. Every inch of Meridian declared the wealth of its citizens. You either matched that standard, or you didn't belong. And I was tired of not belonging.

I heard the voices inside before I turned the handle. I stood at the house's front door, hand poised on the brass knob, listening. There it was again. A man's voice. The gardener maybe? Grandam's chauffeur? Neither of them had ever stepped foot inside the house to my knowledge. Grandam must have friends over again, I decided. Fantastic.

Quietly, I opened the door, hoping to avoid attracting attention long enough to make it to my bedroom. But what I saw caused me to stop short of a quick escape.

Seated in the parlor chatting with my grandmother was Ashcroft March.

CHAPTER 4

He wore a strawberry pink suit. Linen. And polished brown Oxfords that likely would have cost me six months' worth of lab fees. Two glasses of water sat untouched on the coffee table.

"Darling," said Grandam, adopting a pleasant smile. "Welcome home. Come greet our guest. He's here to speak with you."

March inclined his head politely.

Explanations shuffled through my subconscious in steady succession. I hardly had time to consider them all. "What a surprise," I managed to say, mimicking Grandam's smile. "I hope you haven't been waiting long. If I'd known, I would have come back sooner."

"Not at all," said March with that distinctive upper-class charm. "I've been quite comfortable. Your grandmother is delightful."

He knew just the way to flatter a person. Grandam flushed with pleasure. She contained it well—she was practiced in these things—but I saw the glint of self-satisfaction dance across her face. Crossing the entryway, I claimed a seat on the sofa next to her. I didn't mistake the glance she cast over my plain clothing, nor did I miss the almost imperceptible curl of her lip that followed.

Ashcroft March leaned back in his chair easily. "We were just discussing the replacement election."

"Oh?" I tried to sound interested.

"Sommer Day has my vote," Grandam assured. "The Magnussons are staunch Illustriots. My husband made numerous donations to the party when he was alive. I've since continued the tradition."

"Your generosity is much appreciated. Though the circumstances sadden us all, President Day remains the best choice for Meridian. Perhaps even more so in light of our recent tragedy."

"How's that?" I asked. Grandam looked annoyed.

"*Darling*," she whispered. "Let's not ask stupid questions."

March either didn't hear her or was pretending as much. "Well, to put it frankly, the bombing indicates the presence of terrorists in our midst." He shifted in his seat, and I caught a waft of expensive cologne from his starched pink lapel. "Forgive my bluntness, Mrs. Magnusson. I don't mean to alarm you. President Day is perfectly suited for Meridian at a time like this because her background has prepared her for it. Empress Industries is the Republic's primary provider of drone and droid technology. National security is a matter of daily study for her."

"Yes, of course," said Grandam. "Perfectly suited. As long as I've known her, I never doubted the fact." On the last word, Grandam seemed to swallow her own tongue. Her eyes widened and she pressed her lips together tightly. Ashcroft March leveled his gaze at her, saying nothing.

The interchange took a few seconds at most, but its oddness was unmistakable. I looked between March and Grandam. What had she said? *As long as I've known her* . . . It *was* a strange way to refer to a woman whose face we only ever saw on TV. Unless Grandam had some personal connection to Day. Really, though, what was the likelihood of that?

I didn't get the chance to dissect it any further. Grandam cleared her throat, effectively signaling a change of subject. "Never mind all of that. I'll let you get on to the reason you've come. What is this you mentioned about salvation for my granddaughter?"

March chuckled half-heartedly. "Of course." He turned to address me. "I'm sure you've heard of our work-study program. The most famous in the world, actually." The man raised his wrist close to his lips and spoke a command into the crystalline watch face. "Ingrid, can you cast to the television in this room?"

I heard no audible reply from March's AI companion. For the first time, I noticed the pea-sized device embedded in one of his ear canals and assumed the short pause which followed his command was 'Ingrid' giving her private reply. Sure enough, here was March nodding his head to thin air. "Thank you," he said, just as the television above the mantle blared to life with an image of smiling students against a campus backdrop.

"Empress Industrial College"—I read the name that appeared across the screen as he spoke—"is a subsidiary of Empress Industries. Currently, EIC fosters more than two hundred student-interns from all six inner sectors. Our students work intimately within Empress itself. In addition to their work in the laboratories, students maintain a rigorous course load provided by our award-winning faculty, the brightest minds on earth." March said this last part with a quirk of an eyebrow and a smirk. A humble brag. "Our corporation has always been interested in providing exceptional opportunities for exceptional students. Opportunities the like of which you will find nowhere else. Children are the future, after all. I'm sure you would agree."

"Yes," crooned Grandam. "I couldn't agree more. Go on."

March prompted Ingrid to switch displays and proceeded to flip through a number of colorful infographics. "What you get is a conglomerate experience—on-site technical work with our top scientists, engineers, and mathematicians, coupled with a premium classroom environment to finish up your high school education." March dipped a nod to me. "Of course, the challenging nature of our program requires all our students to board on location. Our dorms, situated within the rest of our beautiful campus, sit just ten minutes away from Empress Industries' central production facility in Ostentia West."

"And what would this program cost us, Mr. March?" Grandam was the epitome of composure. She waited expectantly for his answer.

"Students fund their own education and living expenses through the time they contribute to the company, ma'am. That's why we only recruit the most talented of students, you see. We've found that members of the work-study program tend to make some of our most valuable technological breakthroughs. Students gain experience in a relevant field, and our corporation benefits in the meantime." March flashed a self-satisfied smile in my direction.

"I see. My goodness. Wouldn't you say this is too good an offer to pass up, Cassiopeia?" Grandam looked at me like she couldn't be prouder. I was used to this behavior in front of guests. So many times, I'd wished she would look at me that way for real.

March's offer *was* tempting. Work study with one of the largest tech companies in the world? It was a dream come true. I knew Grandam would want me to accept. Wouldn't she just love telling all her friends that her own flesh and blood belonged to an exclusive club of big brains working for Empress Industries?

I wanted that kind of future. I wanted it more than anything. I stared at Grandam's luxurious handwoven rug beneath my feet and wanted with all my heart to escape somewhere I wasn't the outcast. Where people valued my talents. Where I could *finally* make something of myself.

I could leave this place behind.

Forever.

"Does this have to do with my invention for the World's Fair? Are you offering me a contract?"

"Wonderful question. This invitation pertains only to enrollment at EIC. That being said, I wouldn't be surprised if an offer to purchase prior intellectual property found its way to you very soon." March smiled. "I have something that may answer the rest of your questions. Ingrid, please present President Day's message for Miss Atwater."

The college infographics disappeared to be replaced by the demure smile of Sommer Day herself. Her appearance looked much the same as always: long blonde hair, a narrow chin coupled with plump, rosy cheeks, and faint rivulets around her eyes signaling middle age. I thought it was a video call at first. I grew conscious of my casual attire, so inappropriate for a meeting of this nature, and wished desperately for a change of clothes.

But no—it wasn't a video call. Just a recording. The woman's jewel-toned voice carried strong into the parlor: "Miss Cassiopeia Atwater, it is a pleasure. Allow me to introduce myself. I am Sommer Day, President of Empress Industries and Dean of Empress Industrial College. Right now, you may be wondering what this is all about. Don't worry. I understand your confusion." The subtle wrinkles at her eyes deepened as her smile grew. "In the wake of the tragedy regarding Mr. and Mrs. Sagittarius

Seymour, I have spent a considerable amount of time interacting with those injured in the attack. You've caught the eye of our corporation. I have never seen academics like yours, nor have I been so impressed by one student's extracurricular achievement. Your name is listed on the schedule for this year's World's Fair!" Day seemed genuinely enthusiastic. Proud, even. "These are high achievements indeed. Given your tremendous record, I would like to personally invite you to join our esteemed institution. EIC is known throughout the world for its rigorous intellectual reputation, and I believe you would be an excellent fit for our academic community."

The significance of this moment wasn't lost on me. There was a sense of gratification, mainly. Like fulfillment of a perfect daydream. None of it felt real.

Sommer Day went on: "I acknowledge the misfortune of this timing. How ironic that tragedy must befall us in order for your talents to come to light. I hope you will allow yourself the proper amount of self-care now, and this that you might make a decision without the burden of recent trauma to cloud your judgment. Your health is of the utmost priority." Day launched smoothly into her closer. "My best wishes for your continued success, and may I have the pleasure of receiving your acceptance letter soon."

There the video ended. When I dared peek at Grandam, she was perched upon the edge of her chaise longue, mouth pressed into such a glossed, taffy smile I wondered how she kept herself from implosion.

I could have accepted on the spot. No doubt Grandam would have liked that. But reason took control and kept me from acting too rashly. "I'll need some time to think about it," I told March, refusing to look at my grandmother. "It all sounds like such a big commitment. Would that be all right? If I thought about it for a few days?"

"Certainly. We wouldn't expect your answer right away. I'll leave you with some digital materials to look over. Ingrid, if you would please."

My watch buzzed, and I assumed it was a notification for the materials March spoke of.

"Take your time," the man continued. "All we ask is that you submit your acceptance letter by the end of next week. If you decide to enroll, that is."

"She won't make you wait long, don't worry!" Grandam laughed. "This is so incredibly generous. Please send my regards to your supervisor. We are enormously grateful for such a tremendous offer."

"I'm the director of my division, ma'am. I have no supervisor. I'll accept the compliment on my own behalf though." March returned her laughter. It sounded hollow.

Grandam sputtered something like 'of course, slip of the tongue, pardon me.' The man smoothed his suit and asked for the maid to see him out. "Why, let me. It would be my pleasure." As Grandam stood and escorted March to the entryway, I remained seated.

Letty emerged from the kitchen with anxiety etched across her face. "Cass," she breathed, quiet enough to avoid being overheard, "are you really thinking of going to that school?"

I met her eye as she lowered herself onto the sofa beside me. Her concern caught me off guard. Matching her volume, I whispered, "It's the chance of a lifetime. I'd be crazy not to accept. Why, is something wrong?"

Letty pursed her lips. "Do you remember my nephew, Jared? I told you about him. He worked for Sommer Day at her vacation home." She glanced past my shoulder, as if worried Grandam or March would return and catch us red-handed. What was this about? I'd never seen Letty this worked up.

"I remember."

"I'm worried about you working for that woman, Cass. Jared told me the things he learned about her. Not good things. Apparently Sommer goes to her vacation home to conduct all the business she doesn't want people in Meridian finding out about."

My mind went back to the university lab and Mop Guy's cryptic warning about Day. It was easy enough to dismiss the ramblings of an old man, but Letty? To hear the same from her gave me goosebumps. "What things?" I asked. From the entryway, I heard Grandam bid March a final goodbye, followed by the sound of the door opening and closing.

Letty leaned closer and spoke quickly. "Meetings. Conversations. Men in military uniform visiting late at night."

"Why's that strange? Day has contracts with the government for her combat drones and droids."

"Yes, but not with *other* governments," Letty said. "These men were foreign. Whatever it was, Jared heard enough to figure it was illegal. Or at least highly suspicious. 'Fringe,' he called it. Nothing anyone with a conscience would want to have their hands in." Grandam's heels came clicking back to the parlor. Letty took hold of my hand, demanding my undivided attention. "I don't trust her, Cass. Please make sure you're thinking this through."

I sat silent, my head swimming, as Grandam returned. "Letty," she said. "You may leave us. I'd like to speak with Cassiopeia alone."

An obedient servant once again, Letty gathered the two untouched ice waters and retreated to the kitchen. I watched her depart. No doubt she'd be lingering just around the corner, listening to every word.

"Sweetheart," Grandam began, the word sounding so unnatural coming from her lips that I cringed. "Can you imagine? This would be perfect for you. All day long you could work on your science and . . . and those *numbers* you like so much. Think of it. What a dream! You are going to accept, aren't you?" Her voice was hopeful.

I was overwhelmed. First the custodian, and now Letty? What was going on? Somehow, Mop Guy had anticipated March's offer even before I did. Maybe he didn't know the specifics. But whatever he'd heard was enough to caution me against Day. Now Letty seemed fixed on the same sentiments. What were the odds?

I trusted Letty. Besides Harlow, maybe, I trusted her more than anyone else in the world. She cared for me, sacrificed sleep for me, and perhaps even risked her job on occasion. And why? She was just that good of a person. She couldn't leave a poor, parentless child to fend for herself.

If Letty thought Day wasn't who she claimed to be, there had to be some truth behind it. I weighed my options. It *was* a priceless opportunity. One I'd be foolish not to take. Besides, what inner-sector corporation didn't dabble in shady business transactions? I'd likely be hard pressed to find one with a spotless legal record.

Yet the worry, the fear, in Letty's eyes made me hesitate. "I don't know," I admitted to Grandam. "I'm going to have to think about it."

Her plastic smile faltered. "What is there to think about?"

"I have some concerns about . . . the logistics. For example, if my obligations to Empress Industries would interfere with the World's Fair. I don't want to go jumping into anything I'd regret."

Grandam waved a dismissive hand. "I'm sure that can be easily sorted."

"And . . . well . . . what about my involvement in the bombing? How do I know this isn't just another publicity stunt?"

The smile disintegrated. In its place, a scowl emerged. "Does it matter? Whatever the reason, Sommer Day has picked you for her program. You can't possibly be stupid enough to turn her down."

I bristled at the insult. "You're right. I'm not stupid. That's why I'm trying to think all this through before diving in headfirst. *It's what successful people do.*"

Anger turned her body rigid as she recognized her own words being used against her. "You ungrateful girl. Don't let your pride get in the way on this. I will not allow you to throw away your future."

"Throw away my future?" The question came out in a single sharp breath. Immediately, I saw the effect of my antagonistic tone on Grandam's face. "I live my whole life for my future. When have you ever cared about my future before today?"

"This is not about me, young lady. Why do you insist on defying me when all I'm trying to do is help you? You heard the man. You will never get an opportunity like this again."

I stood. "You think I buy that? The only time you ever care about me is when you have something at stake. The rest of the time, I'm a nuisance. Is that why you want me in this program? So you can get rid of me a couple years early?"

"Shut up," Grandam snapped. I froze. She came close to me and jabbed her finger toward my face. "I've taken care of you for *six* years. You have no idea what that has cost me. I am the laughingstock of this city. I give everything I have *every single day* to convince people I am not the failure they think I am. That I'm not just the freak whose daughter ran off with some good-for-nothing Outmode and got stuck with her brat of a child."

I reeled. Outmode was a derogatory nickname for people from the outer sectors. It invoked a sense of backwardness, ignorance, lack of civilization. I hated the word. "Trust me, I don't exactly want to be here either."

"Then you will take the offer," Grandam insisted in a matter-of-fact tone. "Go be a scientist. Isn't that what you always wanted?" Her eyebrows shot to the sky. "What's that look now? You're surprised, aren't you? You're surprised I know about your dreams. See, I have paid attention to you. And I know that if you give up this program, you'll never get anything half as good ever again. So swallow your self-righteousness, or whatever you want to call it, and take the offer."

My eyes went in the direction of the kitchen, where I could see Letty's uniform just visible around the corner. "And what if I don't?"

Grandam was fuming. I watched her jaw work back and forth. Then she lifted one palm and slapped me across the face. The force made me stumble. I was stunned. I brought my hand to my cheek, touching my fingers to the stinging skin. Grandam had never hit me before. Suddenly, I flashed back to my family's house in Exulta East. The outer sectors. I was ten years old, standing in our kitchen with my mother. I couldn't remember what I had done to anger her. All I recalled was the pain of her slap, my shock, and the look on her face after she did it. At first, she stayed angry. Then slowly, her expression had fallen. She pulled me into her arms and apologized over and over. "I'm sorry, baby. I'm sorry, I'm sorry, I'm sorry . . ."

Grandam's face, unlike my mother's, remained hard as stone. She leaned in so her nose was mere inches from mine. "You will accept a place in this program, or you will no longer be welcome in this house. Do you understand me?"

I ground my teeth together to keep my lower lip from trembling. My whole body had become coiled like a spring—an instinctive fight-or-flight response. I was no longer concerned with Day's offer. I could easily make a decision later. For now, there was only hate. Anger, tremulous inside me, had risen to the point of no return. I'd known it was coming. How, I couldn't say. But the moment was here, and my choice was obvious. I made it in seconds. "I understand you," I whispered, then retreated down the hall to my bedroom.

"Where are you going?" Grandam snapped at my back.

"To pack!" I returned, slamming my door.

As I paced the room, shoving articles of clothing into a duffel bag, I felt nothing but rage. My cheek throbbed, but the pain was minimal compared to the fury inside me. I should have left eons ago. Grandam never wanted me anyway. I was tired of living under her thumb. Maybe Day's offer was the final incentive I needed.

Stomping back and forth like I was, I barely heard the quiet knock from the hallway. "Cass?" Letty's soft voice was muffled by the door. "Can we talk about this? Will you let me in?"

I dug through my closet, throwing sweaters, jeans, and underwear onto my bed. My world was spinning so fast I could barely speak. "No, I-I'm busy. Don't worry about me." What else was there to take? A second pair of shoes. My hairbrush. Toothpaste and toothbrush. I'd have to get those from the bathroom last of all. A strange feeling came over me as I turned around and around the room, checking off items. Was this all I had? For the first time, I realized how empty the space really was. Wasn't I more than this? A duffel bag's worth of belongings and the clothes on my back? How had I lasted here so long?

Letty was waiting for me in the hallway when I opened my door. Her face creased with worry when she saw my duffel sitting on the bed. "You can't be running away? Where will you go? Have you even thought this through?"

"Yes," I said. It wasn't necessarily a lie. I had entertained the idea before, after some of my worst fights with Grandam, but I'd never had the courage to leave until now. The upcoming fair was something tangible, something guaranteed, and it calmed my nerves about the future. Besides, I'd felt different since the bombing. I knew now that life wasn't permanent, that anything could snatch it away. Why, then, should I waste mine in a place

THE METHOD TO INFINITE THINGS

I was so hated?

I retrieved my toiletries and paced back to the bedroom to pack them along with the rest. "Where? Where will you go?" Letty's tone was anxious. "Can't you come stay with me until this blows over? People say rash things when they are angry. Your grandmother was flustered. That doesn't make it right, but it doesn't mean you have to go. Please. Please, come stay with me instead. I can't let you go out there on your own."

I swung my backpack onto my shoulders, then hoisted the duffel in one hand. The thought of leaving Letty was the worst. I hugged her tightly. She clung to me in return. Finally, I pulled away. "I have to go. I promise, I'll be okay."

Letty's hand grasped mine. "*Please*, Cass."

"It's okay. I'll talk to you soon. Promise. I have to go." I let my fingers slide from her grip and turned down the hall. In the parlor, Grandam was seated on the sofa, arms folded, long nails tapping against one elbow. She responded to the sound of my approach, her eyes flitting to the duffel bag. We shared a brief, tense look before I made for the front door.

"Are you happy, then?" Grandam asked dryly from behind me. I paused. Grandam removed her pink heeled shoes, stood, and padded across the rug to snatch a candy from the dish on the mantle. "Happy to be leaving me?"

I gave no answer. The truth was—I was, for once in the last six years, hopeful for my future. Hopeful, despite the lingering anger inside and a budding fear of the unknown.

"Be good to Letty," I said.

She snorted and popped the candy into her mouth. Was that it, then? Was that all the goodbye my grandmother would give me? When she crossed to the window and stared out instead of begging me not to go, I took that as my cue for dismissal.

I walked marched from the house and down the front walk, turning south at the street in the direction of the metro. It was a straight shot from our nearest metro platform to the train station. There, I could take a train out of Meridian and down to Loyala.

Loyala South, to be exact. It was a rural area, the polar opposite of the Capital. The thought of living there had always appealed to me somehow. Not only did the rolling fields and farms spark some pleasant, unidentifiable emotion in me reminiscent of bedtime stories my father used to tell, but I also had connections there. Connections I hadn't seen for a long time.

If there were a voice of reason that should have been kicking in right about now, it was nowhere to be found. Nothing short of an apocalyptic event could make me return to that house. My pounding heart kept time with my footsteps on the concrete, and I felt surer of this than anything I'd ever done.

Breathing deeply, I started planning. What to say, how to say it, and what to do if none of it worked after all. The idea involved some risk, yes. But I wouldn't think about that. Not when every step I took felt like leaving behind an eternal winter in exchange for a long-awaited spring. Not when I was just starting to wonder what possibilities lay ahead.

With every step, I came closer and closer to seeing my sister.

CHAPTER 5

The train slowed as we approached Loyala's capital. My fingernails dug nervously into the fabric of my backpack. Through the window, I watched scenery pass in a rush, the station growing larger in the distance. My stomach was a ball of knots. I'd questioned my decision for the length of the two-and-a-half-hour train ride. What if my sister didn't want me? Suppose she didn't live here anymore? I tried to ignore the anxiety. Getting out of Meridian was the best decision I ever made; I was sure of it. I still fumed over Grandam's words to me. I felt the memory of her stinging slap across my cheek.

It was enough to silence the doubts.

With a gentle lurch, the train came to a gliding stop in front of the station platform. I stood, burying my nerves deep down. Passengers shuffled forward, a mass of unassuming-looking people not prestigious enough to travel in the reserved coaches, and I fell in line behind an oil-stained ball cap. Probably a mechanic on his way back from the Capital.

The evening air carried some strange smell like decaying earth and wet pavement. I located the outdoor screen display showing arrival and departure times, a convoluted spiderweb of numbers scoured across a color-coded map. I spotted my destination—a tiny dot near the bottom of the map—accessed only by another train said to arrive in thirty minutes. Claiming a bench to wait, I watched the locomotives stop, start, and speed away on their levitating tracks. The train that brought me here from Meridian closed its sliding doors around a fresh load of passengers. I watched the long gray canister disappear out of view.

There was no going back.

***

At last, the second train deposited me in a small township of stretching green fields and unassuming buildings. I checked the address my sister had sent me over a year ago. She'd written it on the corner of a package delivered for my birthday, and I had digitized the address for safekeeping. Now I was glad I did. Inside the train, a screen indicated the stop: Sam Fellow, Loyala South. Everything matched. I descended the steps into humid afternoon air. I was one of only three passengers to do so.

Adjacent to the train station, a town square appeared to be the focal point of this place. A monument drew the eye first of all. It was a woman. She clutched something in one arm. A book, maybe. That detail alone dated the statue at least fifty years. Paper books had dropped out of favor ages ago when governmental policies declared them a waste of natural resources. The statue looked like bronze, but its surface had developed the dull green tint of oxidation from years exposed to the elements without proper cleanings. Meridian landscapers would have a fit at the sight.

The train's other passengers weaved around me. I let them pass. Large brick buildings formed an angular horseshoe along the square's edges, and rough cobbled walkways converged like the spokes of a wagon wheel at the center monument. Weeds grew between stones and infiltrated any grassy segments of the square. I thought again of the immaculate grounds in Meridian, knowing none of this would ever make it past the inspections of city officials.

With the other passengers far enough ahead, I spoke into my watch: "Harlow, directions, please?"

"You are closest to Town Hall at the moment. Follow this street north for two blocks, and you will arrive at your destination."

"That's it? She's that close?"

"This appears to be a very small town."

Harlow's directions led me past storefronts and modest homes. I'd spent most of my childhood living in the outer sectors, but our neighborhood was always suburban in feel. Neighbors lived side by side in Exulta, their houses ordinary but comfortable, with upkept yards and smooth concrete sidewalks. This place—Sam Fellow—was unlike anything I'd ever seen. The streets were empty, the pavement cracked and faded. I found no sidewalks. Instead, the road blended seamlessly into the wild grass at its edges. Most houses looked weathered by time and elements. Few were built with brick or stone, and most featured chipped siding, slanted roofs, and quaint front steps. What did people do for entertainment here? There were no theatres, botanical gardens, or recreation facilities. No visible concert halls or museums. And strangest of all, it was *quiet*.

So quiet.

Two streets north of the town square, I arrived at a home with the number I was looking for next to the front door. A colorful patch of spring flowers grew in a swath of earth beneath one of the windows. "Harlow?" I whispered.

"Yes?"

"I'm nervous. I haven't seen her in so long. What if she doesn't want to talk to me?"

"I guess you won't know until you knock."

Taking a deep breath to steel myself, I opened the front gate, strode up the walkway, and rapped four times. The moments that followed felt like an eternity.

I waited. And waited. No one came to the door.

I frowned. Had I miscalculated? Was this not the correct address? I checked the number on the house again. Everything matched up. I braved another knock and waited, waited . . . but the house remained silent.

"She's not here," I said finally. The reality sunk in, making my chest ten times heavier than usual. What was I thinking? I should have known it was a stupid idea. You can't show up to someone's house a year after last speaking to them and expect a hearty welcome.

"Maybe she stepped out of the house for a minute?" asked Harlow.

The prospect gave me a little hope. I walked back towards the gate. "Let's try again later." Though I projected a tone of confidence in my voice, the truth was that my enthusiasm had started crumbling by the second, and every optimistic notion that drove me here over the last hour and a half began looking more like the delusional hopes of a child than my usual careful calculations.

"Would you like me to message her?"

"No. I mean—um—don't bother her. I say we try again later and see if—"

A lock clicked, and the door squeaked open on its hinges.

I spun around, nerves firing in every direction and heart leaping out of my chest. But it was not my sister that stood in the doorway of the house. It was an old woman, her eyes and cheeks deeply wrinkled. She gazed at me curiously. My first thought was how awfully petite she looked. A hunch made her appear even shorter than she was. Short and frail, like a strong gust of wind might tip her over.

"Hello," I stammered. "I'm so sorry. I'm looking for my sister, Andromeda Atwater. I thought this was her address." I was painfully aware of my duffel and backpack—how they made me look, how impertinent I must seem to this woman appearing unannounced on her doorstep.

"Andie," said the woman in a crackling voice. "Andie. You're home early."

"Um . . . what?"

The woman motioned me closer and cupped a hand around one ear.

Stepping forward, I said loudly, "I'm not Andie. My name is Cass. Andie is my sister."

A degree of clarity shone in the woman's face. She looked me up and down, as if confirming what I claimed was true, then tapped a finger to her temple. "Bad eyes. You get that in old age." She smiled.

"Right." Feeling awkward, I pointed within the house. "Does Andie live with you?"

The woman nodded.

This was news. Andie never mentioned a roommate. Actually, she hadn't said much at all about her life during these last six years. I suppose I'd never thought to ask. Not knowing how to respond, I shifted my weight from one foot to another. How ridiculous I must look, not even knowing such a simple fact about my sister. Apart from her occasional visit to Meridian or a package in the mail for my birthday, interactions between us were few and far between. I blamed it on our parents' divorce. Andie had been eighteen when they separated. In a way, I thought she took it harder than me. At ten years old, I had little idea what was truly going on, but she witnessed it all. The frequent arguments between her and my mother proved how tense their relationship had become. By the time Dad left and Mom made the decision to place me with Grandam, Andie had moved out. It was a blurry memory of which I had little recollection. The older I got, the more my memories from that time got fuzzier.

"When will she be home?" I asked the woman.

Her glossy eyes focused off to the side. She hummed in thought. "Come back at six o'clock."

"Six o'clock," I repeated. I glanced at my watch. That was still an hour away. What in the world was I going to do until six o'clock?

The woman nodded again in confirmation.

I adjusted the backpack on my shoulders. "Okay, great. Thank you so much. I'll come back then." Unsure where to go from here, I retraced my steps back to the town square. A few people exited a storefront off to my right. One member of the group smiled at me as they passed. In response, I increased my pace to give off an air of decided purpose. Great. I looked like a lost tourist with my duffel and backpack, and I was stuck here until my sister returned. Maybe this wasn't such a good idea after all.

I was headed for the train station, where I figured I could wait until sunset, when a building in the square caught my eye. A faded inscription on its face read 'library' in carved stone. *Library*. I paused. Could it be? Cracked concrete steps led to the front doors of the two-story edifice. Its brick was faded—in places, crumbling. I'd never seen a real library. I climbed the several stairs and creaked open one of the doors. Expecting to be met with the musty staleness of antique paper, I was instead hit by a strong waft of antiseptic cleaner. I stood in the entryway of a large room covered in not bookshelves but hospital beds. Confused, I wondered if I had misread the inscription outside.

Most of the beds looked unoccupied. Some had curtains drawn

around them. Besides a ticking clock on the wall, the place was painfully quiet. I decided to leave. Clearly, this wasn't what I thought it would be. Before I could go, there was the sound of footsteps on the floor overhead. Someone descended a wooden staircase in the corner. Dressed in navy blue medical scrubs and carrying a clipboard under one arm, the new arrival met my gaze. "Hello," she said, pacing to a desk that sat at the end of a long row of beds. "I thought I heard the door open. How can I help you?" The woman looked about thirty, with thin glasses and hair pulled into a bun.

"I'm sorry. I thought this was a library. Y-your sign out front, and all."

The woman in scrubs cocked her head just a little—a look suggesting I might be in need of the hospital's professional psychiatric services. I turned to go. The train station benches sounded more appealing than ever. As I pivoted, I nearly smacked directly into a girl entering the library—hospital, whatever it was—from the outside. She was spewing words at a mile a minute and didn't look up as she crossed the threshold. "Okay, Citrine. I just got back from the jail. They won't let us take—Oh!" she jumped in surprise when our noses nearly collided. The girl stepped back, shoving voluminous black curls out of a darkly tan face. "You scared me!"

"Sorry." I waited for her to move, but the girl remained in the doorway, looking at me oddly. The attention made me uncomfortable. "Well," I mumbled, "I'm going, so if I could just . . . ?" I gestured behind her.

"Oh! Excuse me." The girl hopped to the side. She squinted closer at me. "You look familiar. Are you from around here?"

I shrugged off the girl's question with some uncommitted response. Being in Loyala felt strange enough already, and I couldn't help feeling like a lost puppy wandering the streets in this strange interim before my sister came home to take me in. Admitting my situation felt embarrassing. Thankfully, the girl didn't seem to notice how I danced around her question so vaguely.

"Wow. Doesn't she look like someone, Citrine?" The girl with the dark curls fisted her hands on her hips, looking to the woman in the scrubs for input. Citrine, or so I assumed, raised her eyebrows in response.

"Yes, she looks like someone. Everyone looks like someone, Tahlia.

Themselves, primarily."

For a second, Tahlia seemed to process this. Then she scoffed, a sound coupled with a wide-open smile that spread across her face. "Oh my gosh, that's not what I was talking about." She addressed me again: "What's your name?"

"Cass."

"Do you have a last name?"

"Cass Atwater."

"Atwater," Citrine repeated. She was shuffling papers into a file cabinet with her back to me, but she glanced over her shoulder to take in my appearance. Her eyes looked me up and down. "You must be related to Andie."

A fleeting feeling pricked at my heart. My surprise must have been obvious. "You know Andie?"

"Sure. We're friends. I think she works today, doesn't she?"

"Does she? The lady at her house told me she wouldn't be home until six."

"That would be Zinnie," replied Citrine. "Her children are all gone, and she refuses to check herself into a rest home, so Andie keeps her company, does the grocery shopping, that kind of thing. Zinnie discounts the rent in exchange." She smiled. "How are you two connected?"

"She's my sister."

"So that's it!" said Tahlia. "I knew you looked familiar. You two could be twins! I love Andie. She comes to the clinic sometimes."

"I . . . I didn't realize she wouldn't be home today," I admitted. "I'm here to visit her."

Tahlia's face lit up even more than before, and Citrine walked out from behind the desk. "Well, you're more than welcome to wait here until she arrives if you want. In case you didn't catch it, I'm Citrine." She placed one hand against her chest. "And that's Tahlia. She helps me run the clinic here. Anyway, feel free to make yourself comfortable."

I started to protest. "No, please, I couldn't bother you—" But Citrine shook her head.

"It's no problem at all. If a library is what you want, Tahlia can show you what's left of our collection upstairs. Tahlia?"

The girl nodded enthusiastically. "Yes! Follow me." She started toward the stairs but halted and spun on her heel. "Oh, I almost forgot. About the jail—"

"That's all right," Citrine interrupted. "I gathered as much."

Following Tahlia, I took one more glance around the clinic. This wasn't like the hospitals in Meridian, all sterile uniforms and tile floors and high-tech equipment. Tall arched windows along the back wall drenched the room in light. The floor was wooden planks, swept clean of dust. Most of the nightstands held vases filled with tiny wildflowers. A modest place, maybe, but evidently managed with great care.

"We serve all patients from here to the next town, fifty miles away," Tahlia said. We were climbing the stairs now. Each step creaked with the sound of ancient wood. "Whatever the medical need, we cover it. Citrine is training me to be a nurse." She sounded proud. "My family doesn't live here actually. I come here for the school year and go home in the summers. We live in Loyala West. It's nice there, but I like it better here. The boys are cuter, and the school dances are funner," she whispered, twisting around to wink at me.

Not knowing how to respond, I was grateful to emerge onto the second level of the building. I noticed what must have been half a dozen bookshelves pushed together in a corner, stripped of any volumes, leaving an open area in the middle of the room with a circular rug and a few armchairs. The windows up here were smaller than those downstairs. And under the windows sat an antique chair and desk, its top bare.

I looked all around. ". . . Where are the books?"

"Over here." Tahlia beckoned. I followed her to a small cabinet with glass doors. Inside were three carefully arranged rows of books. "Most of them were sold or donated years ago. I don't know any more than that, really. You like to read?"

"Not much more than the next person." I removed a book from the cabinet entitled *Every Bird Knows Sarah*. The glossy cover felt smooth in my hands. Because of their rarity nowadays, I'd only held a physical book once before—back in Exulta. My father brought one home from work after finding two dozen old copies in a utility closet. He called it an antique. I still remembered the texture of the paper flitting across my thumb like the kisses of a hundred butterfly wings.

"So what's your story?" Tahlia asked, curling into one of the armchairs.

"Sorry?"

"Your story. Where did you say you were from?"

I placed the book back in the cabinet and settled onto a chair across from Tahlia. She blinked at me, expectant. "Meridian," I replied, measuring my words carefully. "Actually, I was born in Exulta. I've lived in Meridian for the last six years or so."

"I've never met anyone from the inner sectors. What's it like?"

"Nothing very special, trust me." I averted my gaze to the window, which looked out on the town square below. I could just see the tallest tip of the monument from here. How would I describe my life in the inner sectors? Frankly, I wasn't sure. There had been highlights. For example, it wasn't until I moved in with my grandmother that I installed Harlow. And she'd become the closest friend I ever had. Then there was Letty. Kind, generous Letty. I wouldn't trade a single day of the last six years if it meant I'd never have met her.

I couldn't forget my research either. The sweat-filled pursuit of my every waking hour. It was my whole life. The ground-breaking CosmiLock that bore my trademark had been my daily outlet; it was going to be my salvation. Where would I be without the opportunities afforded by Eastern Potomac's top-tier facilities? The inner sectors had given me chances I would get nowhere else. "How long are you visiting your sister for?" Tahlia asked, tucking her feet farther beneath her body in the armchair.

"I don't know exactly," I answered. "I planned to talk to Andie once I got here. Kind of a spontaneous trip."

"*Ooooh.*" Tahlia leaned forward. "She didn't know you were coming?"

The question struck me as a strange thing for her to clarify. "Uh, no. I guess not. Is that important?"

Tahlia sucked in her lips, her eyes going wide. "Did she already tell you?"

"Tell me what?"

Tahlia covered her mouth with her hands and released a squeal. "I thought Andie would have told you. Don't get freaked out. The police finally arrested the guy. They have him in jail now."

"What guy? What are you talking about?" I could have shaken her.

"I can't believe I'm the one to tell you," Tahlia breathed. "It's only the biggest thing that's happened here since Georgie Folsgren dumped her fiancé for that bucktoothed boy down the street."

"For crying out loud, Tahlia. What is it?"

"Someone named Jeremy Polluck. He grew up here. A year or so ago, he went into the army. Got shipped out overseas somewhere. But guess what? Just last week, he came back. Army people called it 'mental duress' or something. Listen, I'd call it more than mental duress. I'd never seen a crazy person before, but now I'm sure I have."

The air between us had gone very still. Whatever this was about Jeremy Polluck, it gave me chills down to my bones. "What do you mean, crazy?"

"He started walking around the streets at night, trying to break into houses, and *screaming*. Gibberish, really. I've never heard anything like it. Citrine wants to bring him here, to the clinic. That's where I was just now, the police station, before you came in. She wouldn't want me saying anything, but oh well. I went to talk with the chief. He wouldn't budge. Says the guy's unstable and has to stay locked up."

I was barely conscious of a door swinging open downstairs and heavy footsteps—then voices—resonating through the floorboards. Sure, the inner sectors were a breed all their own, but nothing this bizarre had ever crossed the table during my grandmother's weekly luncheons. Perhaps these things were better covered up in the city. Certainly no one connected to such heinous gossip would want their friends knowing about it. Grandam was humiliated enough just to have an Outmode for a granddaughter. Neither she nor anyone else in her social group would survive something as scandalous as a deranged relative.

The memory of Letty's earnest warning against Sommer Day came to mind. Why? Maybe because *that* conversation had left me unsettled as well. But then I realized: Tahlia said Jeremy Polluck was a soldier. An army vet, albeit a young one. And what had Letty said about men in uniform visiting Sommer's vacation home? Her nephew had overheard enough to suspect a conspiracy of some kind, possibly involving foreign military officials. If Jeremy Polluck had spent time overseas, I wondered if he might know something about it.

"Isn't it fascinating?" Tahlia continued. "Think about it—your first day in the outer sectors, and you're landing right in the middle of all this. I can't wait to hear what Andie has to say about it all."

"Tahlia!"

The call came from downstairs, making me jump. Citrine, probably? Her voice was muffled by the floorboards. "Tahlia, I need you down here *now*."

CHAPTER 6

Tahlia leapt to her feet. "Hurry," she said. "Follow me. We might need your help."

"What is it?" I asked, scrambling after her. I heard heavy footfalls from the ground floor. Someone was here, and by the tone of the voices, it seemed urgent. "Sounds like a patient emergency," said Tahlia.

My eyes widened, and I hesitated. I'd only arrived in this town half an hour ago. I already felt like an intruder. "Wh—I'm not trained for that," I protested.

But Tahlia was already halfway down the stairs. She looked up, cocking her head to one side. "And? You're not in Meridian anymore, you know. We do things differently here. Hurry."

And just like that, she was gone. Steeling myself, I followed a step behind her. Already my imagination was conjuring up images of broken bones and gaping wounds. Whatever the emergency waiting below, I reminded myself it was just biology. Another branch of science. Nothing I couldn't handle.

But then I saw the boy. How old was he? Not older than seven or eight, I guessed. A man—his father, probably—clutched the shaking child in his arms. Even from here I heard the wheezes. The labored scratching of each breath he dragged into his lungs. I saw the look of panicked helplessness on the father's face as he watched his son struggling for air. Citrine voiced the diagnosis: "It's an asthma attack. Tahlia, prep an IV. And Jason,"—she pointed to the father—"set him down on the bed. He has to remain upright. Laying down will only make it worse."

Though I hadn't studied much of the body's chemistry, I knew enough to identify the symptoms of an asthma attack. My mind went back to elementary school. It was second grade, and one of my classmates had returned from recess in a state of half-choked desperation. Her face, twisted in pain and fear, still lingered in some far-off corner of my memory. It was my first encounter with the condition.

"Where's his inhaler?" I asked Jason, accompanying Tahlia to the boy's side.

"We ran out. The new shipment hasn't come in yet."

"It's true," Tahlia said. "We've been short on supplies for weeks. The shipment's been delayed."

Citrine arrived holding a small gray box wrapped with a rubber tube. She placed it on the bedside table. "This is a nebulizer. It'll open up his airway," she explained, uncoiling the tube. There was a face mask attached to one end. "Micah, can I put this mask around your head? Good. My machine is going to start making noise now. It's nothing to be scared about. Just means the medicine is working." She broke the cap off a plastic cartridge filled with clear liquid and poured the contents into the machine. "Okay, three, two, one—"

She flipped a switch. There was a buzzing, whirring sound as medicated steam traveled the length of the tube and into Micah's face mask.

"Breathe it in," said Citrine. "That's it. Let the medicine do its work."

Micah rolled over in the bed. "Dad?" What with the mask and the whir of the machine, his voice was barely audible.

"I'm here," Jason told him. He enveloped the boy's small hand in both of his own. "Deep breaths now. You're going to feel better in no time."

The next sixty seconds weighed heavy with unspoken tension. Micah's ragged gasps slowed to a steady rhythm. Tahlia had an IV ready, waiting for Citrine's signal. I watched relief spread across the young boy's face as the medicine took effect.

"What is that?" I asked Citrine, indicating the discarded cartridge.

"Sodium chloride solution. Clears the mucus from the trachea." She took out a stethoscope and listened to Micah's lungs. To the father, she asked, "What caused this attack? Has he been sick?"

Jason shook his head. "He went into the neighbor's hay field with a friend. We've told him not to since the hay always triggers his asthma. Usually he has an inhaler for this kind of thing."

Citrine nodded. "It happens. Thankfully, it sounds like he's reacting well to the aerosol." She put away the stethoscope. "I don't think we'll need that IV after all."

Micah continued with the nebulizer for ten more minutes until all the solution ran out. He looked better by the time Citrine took off the mask. Weak, but better. "Ow," he complained, rubbing the front of his shirt. "My chest hurts."

"Your lungs were working extra hard trying to get you oxygen. They're tired. Give it a couple days and the soreness will go away," said Citrine.

It was a welcome sight for Micah to be breathing easy again, but something about the situation bothered me. I tried identifying the source of the feeling with no luck. When I heard that the boy would need to stay at the clinic through the night for monitoring, I searched the cabinet upstairs for children's books and brought Micah an assortment of the stories. His family arrived before long. There was a mother, one daughter, and two other sons. When they rushed to Micah's bedside, Tahlia and I backed off to give them space.

"Do shipments get delayed a lot?" I asked her.

"More often than you'd think. And sometimes the boxes are missing half of the supplies we ordered. It's so irritating."

Irritating? I thought. It was criminal. "Can't you do anything about it?" I asked.

"Like what? All the suppliers are based out of the inner sectors." Tahlia shrugged. "If they decide to send us half our order, there's not much we can do to change their minds."

How could it be that a clinic didn't even receive enough supplies for the surrounding town? Micah was safe only because his father got him to the clinic in time for emergency treatment. But without an inhaler at home, the boy might not have been so lucky. I realized now what was bothering me. In the inner sectors, I'd received medicine that regrew the tissue in my leg within a matter of days. But out here, even a *child* couldn't receive the basic care he needed. I was angry. Did people in Meridian know about this? Did corporate suppliers realize the effects of their carelessness on communities like this one?

I banished my frustration to the background, however, when Micah's siblings grew restless and started playing with the hospital equipment. I entertained them with games on my Loom long enough for the parents to speak with Citrine undistracted. Then Tahlia and I prepped overnight accommodations for Jason and Micah while the mother said goodnight and took the rest of the family home. Fading daylight cast the clinic in a creamy orange hue. How long had I been here? My watch put the time at 7:00. "Woah. I'm late. I was supposed to leave an hour ago."

Tahlia glanced at a clock on the wall. "Would you look at that. I completely forgot. Will you stop by again before you go back to the Capital?"

Though I wasn't planning on ever going back to the Capital—at least not to live with Grandam again—I nodded and smiled. "I'll drop in. I promise."

Next, I thanked Citrine for her hospitality. She was organizing files at her desk. I approached with my duffel bag and backpack in tow. "Thank you," I said, and she looked up from her work. "I'm off to my sister's place. It was really nice meeting you and Tahlia. You saved that little boy's life today, and I think the town's lucky to have someone who cares so much."

Citrine fixed me with searching eyes. "You were a big help too, Cass. If you don't mind me asking, does Andie know you're here?"

I gulped. "Well . . . no. Not exactly. It's a surprise."

Those searching eyes seemed to see right through me. Could she somehow read the truth on my face? I never was a good actor, but I tried my best to appear sure of myself under the woman's measured gaze. Secretly, I dreaded what might come next. Would she reprimand me? Put me on the earliest train out of town? Or lecture me on the dangers of inserting myself where I didn't belong?

But I reminded myself that this place wasn't Meridian. Citrine wasn't Grandam. And out here, I wasn't the outcast I was in the city.

Still, it was a relief when Citrine cut the prolonged scrutiny and resumed filing her papers. "You know, I've been through a rough patch or two myself. There were times I felt no one in the world could understand me." She scribbled a note at the bottom of one page and tucked the sheet into a stack of a hundred others. "I just hope you know you're always welcome here. If you need anything, anything at all, don't hesitate to reach out."

Her words gave me pause. What angle was this? I was doing my best to decode the real message behind her offer when the thought hit me: she was being kind.

"Oh. Well, thank you. I appreciate that."

The evening sun cast a warm glow across the town as I walked back to my sister's house. I remembered the way well enough. As I walked, I thought of Micah and tried to focus on his smile rather than the pinched tightness of his face as he struggled for air. The image refused to fade, and my heart threatened to burst. I reached the house with the spring flowers under the window and the single step leading up to the door. My sister's house. I tried not to overthink as I made my way up the front path and knocked. Waited. There were footsteps inside. The knob turned, and there was my sister. Her straight black hair, identical to mine, lay across her shoulders as a frame for her tan face. She was beautiful. I had always thought so. Now, her perfect eyebrows rose in twin arches when she saw me.

"Cass? What are you doing here?"

I eked out a tentative smile. "Surprise."

Her response read on her face like the pages of a book. First, shock—eyes full of consternation, and her mouth turned down, gaping. She saw my backpack and my duffel. There was a flash of concern. She went to speak, then stopped herself. Confusion. Suspicion. "What are you doing here?" she repeated.

We stood there like that for half a beat—me on the porch, her just inside—trying to make sense of each other, I guess. Something felt off. I sensed it the moment Andie opened the door. She didn't look happy. Why wasn't she happy? "I—uh, I was wondering if I could stay with you.

For a bit. Grandam isn't exactly thrilled with me right now." I forced a chuckle. "I mean, when is she ever, right?"

Andie didn't laugh. She actually looked close to sending me away. In a moment of panic, I thought she might. But then—and relief let me breathe again—my sister stepped back, opened the door wider, and ushered me inside. "Well, you better come in. I'm just making dinner."

My feet felt glued in place. I broke them loose with some effort, following Andie into the house. The entryway, a pale peach color trimmed with floral wallpaper, gave way to a living space on the righthand and a staircase on the left. It was small. A fraction of the size of our childhood house in Exulta. Then there was the smell. How to describe it?

In the kitchen, cracks riddled the tiled floor like light waves breaking from a prism. I sat at the small breakfast table. Andie worked at the stove, her back to me, tossing ingredients into a pot for dinner. How I wished I could read her thoughts. The air hung heavy with tension as neither of us spoke. I imagined she was struggling to find something to say, just as I was.

"So," I tried. "It's been a while. How have you been?"

She shrugged. "Not bad."

"What are you up to these days?"

"I'm a concierge at a resort in Augusta."

"That must be a long ride." Augusta was the outer sector just west of Loyala. Since it bordered El Golfo—previously known as the Gulf of Mexico—on its southern edge, I knew the area was popular with inner-sector tourists looking for a vacation spot.

Andie shrugged again. "Train gets me there in less than an hour. It's not bad."

I ran out of questions quickly, and Andie wasn't much help at all. She sliced carrots and potatoes at a rapid pace. It made me nervous watching her chop away, blowing the vegetables all to bits, and with enough force to rattle your teeth in your head. I was grateful when she finally put the knife down.

"How long will you be staying again?"

I hesitated at the question. I'd been so preoccupied with getting here that I hadn't thought through the remaining logistics. How long *would* I be staying? "Well—I'm not exactly sure. Long enough?" I said it like a question. Andie seemed appeased by that answer on the surface, seeing as she went silent again, but it was hard to tell with her back to me.

"And your plans after this?" she asked.

I fidgeted with the strap of my watch. The connotation was clear enough. I sensed it in her voice. If there was one thing I learned from Capital society, it was how to read subliminal messaging—the unsaid social cues lingering just below spoken conversation like a hidden bedrock beneath the sand. "I have some prospects," I said in answer to her question. "The timeline isn't exact. If you let me stay with you for now, I won't have to go back to Grandam's ever again."

Andie's movements were agitated. Suddenly, she spun to face me.

"I just don't get it. You had it so good in Meridian. I've always known I didn't have to worry about you because you would always have everything you need. Didn't you think this through? Why would you give it all up?"

I gaped at her. I guess I'd been expecting more. A hug, maybe? A smile? Instead, my sister couldn't seem to grasp my presence. Or maybe she didn't want to. It was hard to tell.

"Why would I give it all up?" I repeated. "You've met Grandam. You know she made my life a living hell. And you're criticizing me for wanting out?"

My sister rolled her eyes. "I'm not criticizing you. It's just . . . you don't know what it's like having to fight for everything you own. When you move out for yourself, you'll understand."

"I understand now. I know what I had. But that didn't make anything easy."

"Well, at least you were safe." Andie snatched up a wooden spoon and plunged it into the bubbling pot, working the thick brew around and around. "I don't know if I can take care of you out here. I barely make enough to cover my own rent. And what about your future? Universities, internships? We don't have the same opportunities out here. Not like the inner sectors. You'd be better off going home and making up with Grandam. I'm sorry, Cass. I just can't give you the same things she can."

I stared down the steam rising off the pot. My anger, my hurt, felt like that. Like hot gas evaporating off my soul and condensing on my tongue. I might have released it all on my sister now: the uncertainty of six years, of wondering what she was doing, where she was, why she didn't come visit me more often. "You don't—" I bit my cheek to stop myself, clenching my teeth against the words. Tears beat against the back of my eyes, and my chest rose and fell with shaky breaths. "You don't have to take care of me," I began again, more evenly this time. "I just need somewhere to stay until . . ." Until what? The fair? That was still months away. Until I enrolled at EIC, then? Yes. Except—maybe not. I hadn't decided. I still needed more time to process Letty's strange reaction to the offer. "I-I don't know exactly how long. No longer than two or three months. You won't even know I'm here."

"That's a long time."

"Yeah, well, I'll be able to reimburse you by the end of the year."

Andie set down the spoon and crossed her arms. "Oh? You got a ship coming in?

I returned her sarcasm with a glare. "Actually, I'm going to the World's Fair. Give me time to sign a contract, and I'll pay you back for everything."

There was creaking overhead. Zinnie moving around upstairs, probably. Andie just looked at me for a while. I scowled at the kitchen wall.

"Seriously?" she asked.

"Yeah. Seriously."

Andie closed her eyes and shook her head. "You're being ridiculous."

"No, I'm not. I want to stay here."

My sister laughed once. Wryly. "You don't know what you want."

"Stop that! Stop treating me like a little kid!"

"You *are* a kid. You're only sixteen. Try to understand my perspective here." She spun to face the stove again, but not before I glimpsed her eyes blazing with the same anger I felt rising in myself. There would be no stopping it now.

"You're not trying to understand *my* perspective!"

Andie slammed the saltshaker onto the counter so violently I thought it might shatter. "When did you become so impossible?"

"I don't know. Maybe around the time my family left me to fend for myself." There. I'd said it. Let her try to talk herself out of that one.

A scoff. Andie fixed her gaze somewhere beyond the kitchen window, her eyes roaming, erratic in her exasperation. "Maybe instead of complaining, you could appreciate having a house to live in and food handed to you every day. Some might call you lucky."

"No one forced you to move away, Andie."

"Oh really? Where was I supposed to go? You think Grandam would take me in? You can't remember, but Mom and I never got along. Grandam still hates me for it to this day." Andie chewed on a thumbnail, her eyes unfocused. I recognized the nervous tick. Seeing that she hadn't kicked the age-old habit since we'd been apart was somehow reassuring, like maybe there were other parts of our life together that had been preserved as well.

"Look. All I'm saying is you could have visited me a little more. I just wanted to see my sister."

"That's what this is about? You want more visits? Fine. I promise I'll visit you more. Happy? Now can you go back to Meridian?"

Her words stung, but I raised my chin and set my jaw. I hadn't come this far to back down now. I'd never return to that house, no matter how my sister argued. How was it that my presence could be so unwelcome wherever I went? Andie was the last blood relative I had left. If she didn't want me, who would? It was like being abandoned all over again. The nervous hope I had felt on the train ride here—it dissolved like sand against a rolling tide.

"I'm not going back," I whispered. Andie's eyes showed a mixture of anger and something less certain. A beat passed between us. I felt my heart pumping, pumping inside my chest. How would she react? Would there be more attempts to convince me? I wished I could read the ambiguous expression of her face, the way she set her jaw in a mirror image to mine. I waited. I was determined not to give in.

Then, unexpectedly, Andie relaxed like the headstrong will had gone out of her body. She came forward, pulled out a chair, and joined me at the table. For a second, we said nothing. Her thumb rubbed at some nonexistent smudge on the tabletop. "Listen . . ." She dragged her gaze up to meet mine. "I'm sorry I haven't been in your life more. I guess I've just been scared, is all. My whole life I've felt a responsibility to be . . . I don't know . . . someone *bigger* than myself. For you. To make up for the times when things weren't so perfect. When Mom and Dad weren't the perfect parents. And once you went to live with Grandam . . . well, we were the smallest people in the world. You needed someone so much bigger than me. I'm just sorry. I'm sorry I haven't been a better sister for you."

All my budding retorts, the righteous justice brewing at my lips . . . it all came to a standstill. I'd been prepared to argue my case. She *owed* this to me, after all. She was the one who rarely came around after Mom and Dad left. She was the one who made herself scarce in my life. The least she could do was take me in for a few weeks until I found a place of my own. Now, my anger faltered, and I shook my head automatically. "You have been a good sister."

"No," she insisted. "Not all the time. I ran away. And I left you to grow up with only that witch for company."

A laugh burst from my mouth. It surprised me as much as her. "You can't call her that!"

"I can and I will," Andie returned, sitting up straighter. But a smile crept across her face. I was reminded, briefly, of our childhood together in Exulta. Andie used to play tricks on our father when he got home from work. I always watched from a hiding place. Her face as she ran past me, impish and aflame with delight, had never left my memory.

"So," my sister continued, "to answer your question, of course you can stay with me. I haven't always been there for you, but I can be now. You'll stay here. It will be like old times."

Old times. How would that be? The thought made me smile.

"Now, just so you're clear, this isn't a free ride." Andie shoved her chair away from the table. "You live here, you help out. Which means helping me with dinner. I want these dishes cleaned before we sit down to eat." She indicated a sink full of odd cooking implements and day-old plates. "Water *and* soap. None of those tricks you tried to pull when you were a kid."

"Already bossing me around? Maybe I won't live here after all. You're mean."

That got a laugh from her. I rolled up the sleeves of my jacket as she handed me a sponge. "If you think that's mean, get ready for spring cleaning. I'll make you wish you were never born."

I plunged my hands into the basin of soapy water. Old times. Maybe she was right. Maybe we could pretend everything was back to the way things used to be.

Just me and her.

I dared to believe it.

CHAPTER 7

Tahlia promised to meet me Monday morning for my first day of school in Sam Fellow.

I registered on-meta the evening before. Something about submitting my forms with the district's education system made the move feel infinitely more official. *No going back*, I thought. The hardest part—at least, the part I expected to be the hardest—was acquiring Grandam's signature on the registration papers. I sent her the electronic document, along with a brief-as-possible message politely asking her permission to enroll at Sam Fellow High School. The blank space requiring my legal guardian's signature glared like a taunt from the screen. It was torture, waiting for her response.

When I received her version of the edited document, filled out to its entirety, I was both relieved and strangely pained. She hadn't even bothered to write a message back.

I tapped *submit* and watched the loading spiral morph into a glowing green check mark. The strange pain disappeared. The relief of new horizons filled me up. And something else—nerves, I realized. It didn't last long though. No anxiety was enough to make me regret my decision.

Come Monday morning, the town awakened with sounds of chatter and distant dogs barking. I met Tahlia near the clinic. Apparently, the old library also served as her living quarters away from home. We walked down a gravel road that led out of town. This was the way to school, she clarified. Few people drove vehicles in Sam Fellow since cars had become so expensive after the federal train system negated the need for individual transportation. At least in Meridian, we had the metro to carry citizens within the city limits itself. Here, everyone walked. Tahlia claimed it was a short trip to the school, only twenty minutes on foot.

She chatted while we went. "I am *so* glad you are coming to school with us. When you told me you were here to visit Andie, I didn't realize you meant long-term! Now you'll *really* get to know the town. I'm so excited to introduce you to my friends."

Buildings receded farther down the road. They were replaced by grassy stretches and willowy trees. We reached a vast field fenced off from the road and speckled with grazing sheep like marshmallows thrown over a cake. Then someone called out to us from behind. Tahlia turned. "Oh! That's my friends," she exclaimed, waving one arm in greeting. "Stop here. We'll wait for them. I promise, you'll love them."

"Hey, Tahlia," said a boy as he approached. I got a look at his face. He had curly blonde hair, close-set eyes, and a facial structure chiseled by the gods. White teeth glistened as he smiled. He was the quintessential pretty-boy poster child. "How's it going? Who's this?" The boy aimed his gleaming smile in my direction. Behind him, others arrived—an athletic-looking girl who looked me up and down; a boy and girl pair I assumed were siblings, given the similarity of their faces; and a boy whose brown hair fell across his forehead and flipped out over his ears.

"This is Cass," Tahlia said. "She's from Meridian. You know Andie Atwater, the girl who lives with Zinnie? This is her sister." Tahlia cocked one elbow, palm upward, like a game show host introducing its newest contestant. If only I possessed even a fraction of her enthusiasm. I could have used the confidence right now. With everyone's eyes on me, I stood stiff like a statue and offered a mirthless 'hello.'

"Who's Andie Atwater?" the blonde kid asked. His mouth rarely closed, I noticed. Not even while he was breathing through his nose.

"Of course you wouldn't know, Nash," Tahlia replied with artificial sweetness. "It would take caring about something other than yourself."

Ouch, I thought. But Nash didn't seem to mind the jab. In fact, his grin widened even more.

"Cass, this is Nash, Venetia, Dangelo, Evie, and Rollie. Don't worry, you don't have to remember all their names today. I know it's so much to take in!" Tahlia tossed her head back and laughed. The girl named Evie gave me a shy, welcoming wave. How old was she? It was hard to tell. She was smaller than all the rest, with big round eyes and dark eyelashes. Her skin and hair were a warm brown color. Dangelo, who I assumed was Evie's older brother, shared all of his sister's features except for the shy smile. His mouth seemed locked in a permanent frown. I couldn't decide if that was his natural look or if I'd already done something to offend him.

"You're from the Capital?" asked the athletic girl. She was the one Tahlia had called Venetia. In what seemed to me an unnecessary show of affection, the girl pressed up to Nash, entwining her fingers with his. She left no question—the two were clearly together. "What are you doing all the way out here?"

I opened my mouth, but Tahlia responded for me. "She's visiting her sister. Why else would she be out here?" I thought I heard a touch of acidity in her voice. "People visit people, Venetia."

The response hardly seemed to faze Venetia. She rolled her eyes but remained focused on me. "Are you staying long?" she asked with a forced smile. "I mean, does that matter?" Tahlia laughed pointedly. "C'mon! What's the problem?"

Venetia glared. "I thought you *Splurges* were too good for people like us. That you think we're all dirty and stupid. Do you think *I'm* dirty and stupid?"

The use of the disparaging term for inner-sector elite, coupled with the snide question, caught me off guard. She had to be joking. Yet the look on her face suggested otherwise. My consternation lasted what seemed like an eternity, long enough that I could only stare at her while my brain *click, click, clicked* to process her statement. She'd called me a Splurge. And for what? The mere mention of my being from Meridian? I knew people in the Capital could be hostile toward outsiders, but I had no idea the same sentiment existed out here. I couldn't decide what shocked me more—Venetia's outright animosity or the fact that she'd taken me as part of the socialite crowd. She thought *I* was one of *them*?

"I never said you were." I went to turn away, already feeling my cheeks going hot.

"Well, I don't want you functioning under any false assumptions," the girl said to my back. "If you thought you were going to come out here and walk all over us, then get that idea out of your head right now. I'm not stupid. And I don't think you're better than me."

A general silence dropped out of the sky and settled among the group like fallout. Nash threw a glance in Venetia's direction, but she ignored him. The whole thing felt incomprehensibly odd. In Meridian, I'd trained myself against those frequent encounters with nosy old ladies and mercenary classmates patronizing the "poor little girl" from the outer sectors. The stinging barbs of their calculated remarks had pained me in the beginning, until I learned how to use the elaborate pity as fuel for my work. Instincts built over half a lifetime don't fade easily: I knew how to deal with people who wanted to pass their judgments on my history, my life, my character. I looked the girl in the eyes, as if daring her to say more. I didn't dignify her accusations by clarifying the fact that I wasn't actually from the inner sectors at all. Not technically, anyway.

At first, she returned my stare defiantly. Then, if by only a fraction, the hardness in her face wilted. She looked away. I counted it as a small victory.

Someone out of my view started clapping—*clapping*—slowly, like at the end of a performance. It was the boy with shaggy hair. His name was Rollie. "Great, Venetia," he said, straight face and all. "Really great. I think she fell for it." With a quick glance around the group, I saw I wasn't the only one looking confused. The boy continued, addressing me like he didn't notice my bewilderment: "Sorry about that. See, it's a tradition we've got. Anytime someone new comes into town, we try to make them feel as bad as possible. If you pass, it means you get to stay. Nice job."

Venetia opened her mouth to protest, but Rollie cut her off. "What did you say your name was again?"

"Cass."

"Great. Nice to meet you, Cass. Don't worry about Venetia. She struggles socially. It's tough on all of us." He was now leading me forward, beckoning the rest of the group to follow. "Come on, guys. We're gonna be late."

When the last of the boys—Dangelo—ran up and started whispering fiercely to Rollie in stifled laughter-speech, I was able to slip away to walk beside Tahlia. "What was that all about?" I murmured, quiet enough so Venetia wouldn't hear me, though it was probably unnecessary. She had dragged Nash at least ten yards ahead of the group and likely couldn't hear anything over the *crunch* her stomps made on the gravel road.

Tahlia seemed embarrassed to answer. She tried to shake off my question with some noncommittal response and change the subject. I insisted. Finally, she sighed. "It's not your fault. Rollie was right; Venetia is just mean sometimes. And . . . not many people around here have good feelings toward the inner sectors. They think you're self-important and everything. I don't mean *you*, obviously. Just in general. It's not your fault. I can already tell you're not like that at all."

"I'm not mad, Tahlia. Really. I'm fine." I gave her a smile to ease her anxious conscience.

"Oh, good. I'm super sorry about that. Thank goodness Rollie said something. I didn't know *what* to do. Oh, I hate it. Venetia is the worst."

"Are Venetia and Nash . . . ?"

"Yeah. They're a couple. Long as I've been here, they've only had eyes for each other." Tahlia's mouth turned down in a scowl as she peered ahead at their backs. "Not that I care. Anyone crazy enough to date Venetia is a few planets too removed for my taste."

I laughed. "A few planets too removed?"

Tahlia pursed her lips. "It's something my mom always says. It means Nash is just as nuts as his girlfriend if he's keeping her around."

"Hmm. Sounds more like out of the galaxy if you ask me."

She slapped one hand to her mouth to stifle a snort. "Too much inhaled space air."

"That'll do it. Probably stuck too long in orbit." I waved one finger in a circle next to my head.

Tahlia was clutching her shaking abdomen. "Wait, wait! I can't take it."

"I bet their heads are so hollow, all the other atmospheres were too dense for them but this one."

She let out a guffaw that caused Evie to stare at us. "What are you guys laughing about?"

"Nothing important," I replied, while Tahlia's curls waved back and forth as she gasped for air. "Just extraterrestrials among us."

When Evie gave me a peculiar smile in return, I counted her as an ally. I made up a mental list and placed faces of my newfound acquaintances in three different columns. Tahlia, Rollie, and Evie—friends. Dangelo and Nash—to be determined. Venetia—basically the worst.

We arrived at the school building about half a mile outside the town. It was small. The red brick exterior looked old, with weedy vegetation and overgrown shrubs along the walls. Inside, there were three classrooms in total. Unlike my school experience in Meridian, we didn't move from class to class throughout the day. All the instruction for my age group happened in one classroom under the supervision of a single teacher.

The curriculum wasn't difficult. I found myself distracted often. Mostly, I thought about Venetia's comments from this morning. It was a revelation of sorts—the negative opinion people here held towards the inner sectors. And for good reason too, in the case of Citrine's clinic.

I wondered if the same feeling existed across all fifteen of the outer sectors.

CHAPTER 8

"I want to see the soldier in the jail."

"Excuse me?" Andie sat at the kitchen table eating a bagel smothered in cream cheese. It was morning. My second day of school. Zinnie sat with us, picking at a bowl of fruit. She rarely spoke. I'd familiarized myself with her quiet presence early on in my stay.

"Tahlia told me about the soldier that went crazy and got sent home. She said he's in the jail. I want to go see him."

Andie looked at me like I'd suggested something laughable. Since I wanted to secure a place in her good graces, I didn't say anything about the piece of cream cheese stuck to the corner of her mouth that was making her look pretty laughable herself right now. "Why on earth would you want to do that?" she asked.

I couldn't tell her my real reason—that I suspected the man might know something about Sommer Day's foreign military involvement—so I went the safe route instead. "I want to talk to him. Sounds like what he needs right now is company, not isolation in a jail cell."

"Look, you can't ogle at people just for the fun of it. Do you realize what you're asking? Jeremy is highly unstable. He's not in any state for visitors."

The way she said his name cause me to pause. "You know him?"

Andie shrugged. "A little. I met him before he went off and joined the forces."

"Then you've got to understand. Don't you want to help him? Talk to him, at least? Please. I'm not asking you to help me break him out or anything. I just want to see him."

Andie considered for a moment, then relented. "Fine. When do you want to go?"

"After I get back from school?

"I have work."

"After you get back from work then."

"It'll be late," she reminded me.

"I know. It's fine."

Andie stood, taking her bagel with her, and made a face at me as she passed. "You're a weird kid, you know that?"

"You have cream cheese on your mouth."

The jail was everything I expected a small-town police station to look like. I couldn't remember where I'd acquired the stereotypical mental image, but somehow this place fit the bill perfectly. The exterior was red brick—much like the school building, suggesting the two were built during the same time frame—with a bronze plaque that read Sam Fellow Police Station in squarely chiseled lettering.

Inside, an officer near the door acknowledged us from behind a desk that was effectively drowning under piles of haphazard papers. "How can I help you?" he asked, looking disinterested.

"We're here to visit Jeremy Polluck," Andie said.

"You family?"

"Friends."

The officer responded with a grunt. He stood with a degree of creaking—both from the office chair and possibly his knees—and motioned for us to follow around a dividing wall that led into the back half of the building. There, a sequence of three cells lined one side of the room.

"I heard you say my name," said a male voice. "Who are you?"

Within the corner cell, a slim young man stared at us from under hooded eyelids. He sat on a cot with his elbows on his knees. Stubble covered his chin. And his hair, plastered to his forehead, looked soaked through with either grease or sweat.

The officer shoved his hands in his pockets to wait. Andie approached the cell.

"Hello, Jeremy. Do you remember me?" She asked.

Jeremy fixed her with a dull, watery gaze. "No. Who are you?"

"I'm Andie. We knew each other before you enlisted."

I watched his Adam's apple bob up and down. There was no recognition in his face. Jeremy ducked his head, his shoulders shaking. "I don't remember anybody."

"Jeremy . . ." Andie paused just outside arm's reach of the cell. She motioned me forward. "Jeremy, this is my sister. I thought you'd like to meet her. I heard you've been in here for a while. We came to talk if you want. Do you want to talk?"

Small sobs came from the man. I realized with a start that beads of sweat covered all his exposed skin. His clothes were saturated with the stuff, and his hair—his hair dripped with it.

"Does he have a fever?" I asked the officer. The room was warm but not any warmer than could be expected for a humid day in spring. It certainly wasn't hot enough to drench a man in sweat. An electric fan hummed in one corner, rotating waves of cool air throughout the room. Jeremy's appearance didn't make any sense.

The officer shrugged in response to my question. "The doctor came by. Said there weren't no fever. She had me turn that fan on though."

"Why is he not in the clinic?" I demanded.

"Not this again. I'll tell you the same thing I told that other girl who came by. He's in a dangerous state, all right. I let him out, no telling what terror he'll work up next."

I turned away from the officer. Jeremy remained on the cot, his sobs coming quieter now, his shoulders still shuddering. He began to mutter something under his breath. The words were imperceptible. "What was that, Jeremy?" asked Andie. "What did you say?"

More muttering. I stepped as close to the bars as I dared. Jeremy whined a high-pitched sound, similar to the noise of a dog in pain. Was he in pain? Straining, I finally picked out a few of the garbled words: "Head . . . *aaaah*, wrong . . . not right . . . my head . . ."

"He says something's wrong with his head." I looked at the officer. "Is he injured?"

"Look, all I know is after getting sent back from wherever they had him, he wudn't acting right. That's my job, to take in guys like him. You need anything more, you better talk to someone else."

Jeremy grasped his head between both hands. I heard him more clearly now. "Why . . . why in my . . . my head . . ."

Andie spoke loudly to be heard over the fan and the man's own muttering. "Jeremy, can you tell me what's wrong? Do you need help? Do I need to get the doctor?"

In a flash, Jeremy leapt from the cot and slammed his body against the cell bars. "You want to help me? *Get it out of my head*!" he screamed. Drops of sweat flew from his soaking wet hair. Andie lunged backwards from the cell, and suddenly the officer appeared, a barricade between us and a wild-eyed Jeremy clutching at the bars like a madman. The thing startled me so badly I scampered half the length of the room in my haste to get away.

"Back on your cot, Polluck. Now!" The officer threw a fierce scowl our way. "Visiting time is up. It's time for you to go."

I didn't need to be told a second time. I fled the station, only realizing after I'd stumbled out the front door that I hadn't bothered to check whether Andie was behind me. She was. She looked as shell-shocked as I felt inside. My mind was spinning a thousand miles an hour. It didn't help that I could hear my heartbeat loud as gunshots in my ears.

"What was that?" I stammered.

Andie covered her mouth with a hand, eyes wide in alarm. "I had no idea it was that bad. That's not the Jeremy I used to know."

"What happened to him in the field?"

"I don't know. I just don't know. He needs psychiatric services. I need to talk to Citrine."

"Tahlia told me they already tried transferring Jeremy to the clinic. The police wouldn't release him."

"Yeah, for good reason," Andie scoffed, glancing back at the station. "He needs help, but a doctor will have to come to him. Not the other way around."

"What did he mean, 'get it out of my head'? He might have picked up an invasive substance. A parasite or poison. Maybe micro-shrapnel if he was involved in combat. Something a medic could have missed." My thoughts turned to my leg, and the AI surgeons operating to pick out the scattered bits of wreckage from the bombing. My leg was healed now. The skin barely showed a scar. But if Jeremy had suffered a blow in combat, maybe he sensed some lingering disturbance that was affecting brain function. The theory was a reach. I supposed there was always the possibility of simple stress-induced insanity.

"I'm going to talk to Citrine," said Andie, chewing on a fingernail "She's a friend. I bet I can find out more. Are you coming with me or going home? It doesn't matter to me."

"Sure, I'll come. Actually—no. You go ahead."

Andie left, and I lingered outside the police station, thinking of Jeremy. Something about his behavior struck a chord that resonated far away, like a distant memory or faint inclination. "Harlow?" I said out loud.

"Yes, Cass?"

"I need you to collect all the information you can find on traumatic brain injuries."

***

Once every few days I used my free hours after school to take the train into Meridian. I learned to time the train schedule so I didn't have to wait half an hour for the Sam Fellow line like that first day. Returning to the city made me feel nervous, like bugs—in the form of prying eyes—were exploring my skin at every turn. But I needed to be here. I needed access to the lab at Eastern Potomac. It was an irrational thing, to feel so on edge. Grandam was the only one I dreaded meeting, and the chances of running into her were slim. Still, I watched my surroundings warily. The city felt more foreign than ever before.

Per usual, I began my work in the lab with a routine hand washing and donned the white lab coat that draped over my hips like a muumuu, too wide to look flattering. For the last two days, I had scoured every source available having to do with the human brain. I spent over an hour inside the metaverse examining each of the organ's parts, from the cerebellum to the brain stem to the various lobes. I tested virtual scenarios to get a sense of what symptoms might follow trauma to one part of the brain or the other. Ultimately, I'd determined that Polluck's altered behavior—even his body's disrupted temperature regulation, evidenced by an excess of sweat—could be originating from any number of locations inside his head.

The lack of conclusions frustrated me. I needed more information. Today, exhausted from the informational goose chase, I decided to set Polluck's case aside and work on the CosmiLock presentation instead. What with the events of the past two weeks, I'd neglected to compose much of anything. It wouldn't be smart to put it off any longer.

Someone entered the lab. I raised my head from the presentation interface spread across my workstation. Enough cabinets separated me from the doorway that at first, I couldn't see who it was. A university student, probably. While I always scheduled my lab hours during the lulls between university classes, sometimes a chem major or two came by to work on projects outside of hours.

I'd resumed work on my presentation when a young man walked around the corner. "I'm sorry," he said, stopping short. "I didn't know anyone was back here."

"No problem. Am I in your way?" I started to clean up my things.

"Not at all. Actually, I wonder if you can help me. I'm looking for the mineral samples."

He must have been new here. Most likely a university freshman. He didn't look more than a couple years older than me. I pointed at a storage unit embedded in the wall, a panel on its front for selecting which sample the algorithm should deliver out the distribution tube. "Swipe your ID card for whatever you need. It'll make you enter an access code for anything stronger than aluminum though."

"Thank you." He went to use the machine, and I couldn't help noticing his appearance as he passed. He was dressed in a blue checkered button-down with kakis and a skinny necktie. His hair, thick and golden brown, was styled so it swept up at all the best angles. It was great hair. Not that I paid much attention. What did I care how his hair looked, all soft and thick and perfect?

I focused on my work instead. But after the muted thrum of the unit's distribution system stopped, the college freshman hadn't left. I snuck a glance up. He was setting up shop at the table *right next to me.*

"Do you mind if I work here?" he asked.

"Be my guest," I said, even while asking myself what kind of social Neanderthal sets up shop in the only occupied corner of an otherwise empty lab. Common sense, much, buddy? I tried to ignore him as I resumed work on my information slides.

"What's your major?"

I looked up again. He unloaded notes and a textbook onto his table. Part of me wondered if he was talking to me. *Duh.* Of course he was talking to me. We were the only ones here.

"Actually, I'm still in high school."

How could a person look interested and disinterested at the same time? He managed it. "No kidding. What are you doing here?"

I swallowed, but my throat was dry, and I felt an urge to cough. "They, uh"—cough—"they let me rent a space."

"For, like, school projects?"

"More like personal use." *Oh, no.* Personal use? I could imagine what he was thinking about me now. I had no life. I had absolutely no life to speak of.

"Hm. Impressive," said the guy.

I swiped at random components of my presentation, trying my best to look too busy for conversation.

"I'm Leo. It's my first year here."

I nodded politely.

"If it's not already obvious, I'm new to chemistry. I just switched my major. My adviser says I should come here on the off-hours for extra 'applied learning.'" Leo framed the words with air quotes. "Honestly, I don't even know what that means."

I chuckled. "Then maybe it's a good idea you're here after all."

"Maybe so." He went quiet for a bit, long enough that I suspected that was the end of things. It was not. "What did you say your name was?"

"Cass." I gave a tight-lipped smile. "Nice to meet you, Leo."

"Mutual. What's that you're working on now?"

I nearly replied with something vague and dismissive. Then I stopped myself. This could be my chance at redemption from the awkwardness of earlier. "I'm putting together my presentation for the World's Fair."

"No way. You're presenting at the World's Fair?"

"Yes." No matter how I tried to contain it, I felt the tips of my ears burning red.

Leo looked like he didn't believe me. "You. The World's Fair. I thought you said you were still in high school."

"I am." Now I was getting peeved. Who did this guy think he was? "I've worked hard. I don't pay the university just to play around with their lab equipment."

Leo lifted his hands defensively. "All I meant was that I'm impressed. I've never met anyone smart enough for the World's Fair. You must be a genius to get in." He peered at me under quirked eyebrows.

I glanced at the time and decided we were done here. "It's late. I need to head out. Thanks for keeping me company." I managed another of my tight-lipped smiles. My chair made a sound like screaming chipmunks as it grated across the floor.

Leo stood as well. "Hey. I'm sorry if I said something wrong. I didn't mean to offend you."

"You didn't offend me. It was nice to meet you. I really do have to go. Good luck with your 'applied learning.'" I mimicked his air quotes from before.

He laughed just a bit. "Maybe I'll see you around?"

"Maybe." I used it as my cue to walk off, logging out of the presentation interface with the tap of a button. I didn't breathe easy until the lab doors had swooshed closed behind me and I was alone again, walking down the hallway.

Harlow piped up. It had been so long since we'd talked, I'd almost forgotten about her. "You know, you could try relaxing around people. You come off a little unapproachable sometimes."

"I didn't ask him to invade my workspace and ask a million questions."

Harlow hummed, a sound tinged with the automated whir of her synthesized voice. "That is exactly the attitude I'm talking about."

I scoffed, ignoring the twinge that told me she was right. "Look, I don't have time to flirt with boys right now. I have bigger things to worry about. I have to focus on the fair."

"I understand. I'm sorry to press."

My sharp tongue softened, and I felt guilty. "No, Harlow. I'm sorry. I think I'm stressed over this Jeremy Polluck deal. I can't figure out what's wrong with him, and it's driving me crazy."

The cool evening air was a godsend as I emerged out the building's main doors. Dusk had fallen. I walked the few streets to the train station, thinking about boys, and Polluck, and the fair that would determine my whole future. I rode back to Sam Fellow in an obstructed reverie, watching the landscape flicker past like answers too far from my grasp.

CHAPTER 9

Andie and I were playing on the sidewalk outside our home in Exulta East. Andie, of course, was far into her teenage years and pulled me, at eight years old, inside our small wagon. Our parents were inside the house. Dad had just come home from work, but Mom had been working remotely these days. Laughing, Andie and I had watched our father as he walked into the house and closed the front door behind him. Even from outside, we heard the argument start. We saw our parents through the front parlor window, facing each other and waving their hands wildly.

My sister pulled my wagon farther down the sidewalk, out of view of the window. "Don't worry, Cass. Let's pretend to be an airplane." She started pulling me faster. "You ready?" she broke into a run, launching me and the wagon as fast as I imagined an airplane might go. When I opened my mouth and laughed, wind puffed out my cheeks from the inside. I had to hold on tight to the sides of the wagon to keep from falling out.

Then I was somewhere else.

I was inside my grandmother's house in Meridian, but it was empty. I looked through every room and still found no one. Eventually I wandered out front, stepping down the long walkway that led away from my grandmother's front door. When I reached the street, I saw my mother and father. Dad was walking away from me in one direction, and Mom in the other. I suffered a moment of indecision. Somehow, I knew I could only follow one of them. Whoever I didn't choose would walk away forever. I started to cry, confused and torn. Uncertainly, I began running after my mother. When I finally caught up to her, she turned, and her face scared me. Her expression looked foreign, angry, and empty.

I backed away from her and ran toward my father instead. But he was already gone. I ran as far as I could, looking for him. People gave me strange looks as I passed. From the sky, I suddenly heard the sound of gunfire. I glanced up and saw a drone flying toward me, releasing an endless stream of bullets that exploded against the ground, rapidly advancing to the place where I stood. Once again, I began running with all my might. My legs weren't fast enough though. Panic filled my chest. I felt like I was tripping on thin air. My panic continued as I heard the bullets getting closer and closer, always on the verge of overtaking me, yet cruelly drawing out the moment so I was forced to keep running for hours and hours. Overwhelming dread filled me, never subsiding, and I wondered every second whether I'd feel the biting impact of bullets against my body.

My eyes snapped open to shapes in the darkness.

I lay in my bed surrounded by the blackish gray of pre-dawn, and I knew I was not alone. I saw their forms outlined against the walls of my bedroom. Enough moonlight filtered through the blinds that I could distinguish their shifting shadows, occupying space that should have been empty. The dream had left me unsettled and anxious. Was I still dreaming? Whispers came from the dark.

"Don't stand there."

"Move over."

"Shut up."

"*You* shut up."

I kept my body still as possible. How had they gotten inside? Sleep still clouded my brain. I could still be dreaming. Should I run?

There was mumbling I couldn't make out. Shuffling along the carpet. If they approached, I would swing. I would run for the door. What if they blocked the door? The window led only to a one-story drop outside. It might be better than facing them. I wished I could roll over to get a better look, to count the numbers.

The shuffling stopped. My heart froze, suspended, waiting. Listening.

"Ready . . . now."

The lights flipped on. I shot to my feet—a bad idea. My eyesight blurred, stung by the light, and dizziness slammed into my head. But I saw the intruders, looking not at all like I'd feared in the darkness.

"Woah!" Nash extended a hand toward me, palm open. "Calm down. It's just us."

"Why are you in my room?" I gasped.

Tahlia clapped her hands giddily. The others were there too: Rollie, Venetia, Dangelo, and Evie. They squinted at me under the florescent bulbs.

"What, you've got a problem with friends dropping by unannounced?" said Rollie, hands in his pockets.

My eyes were beginning to adjust. I shook my head. "Excuse me?"

"We're kidnapping you!" Tahlia burst out, practically bouncing with glee.

I realized now why my bedroom was crammed full of uninvited guests. And here I'd been ready to throw the first punches and jump out a window. Seeing that all of them were fully dressed, embarrassment washed over me. How ridiculous I must look in my rumpled pajamas. "Are you kidding me?" I whispered, conscious of Zinnie and Andie whose bedrooms sat directly below mine downstairs. "I thought the house was being robbed. You scared me to death."

"I've got to admit," said Dangelo. "Your reaction was golden."

"How did you get in here?"

"Your sister let us in."

"In the middle of the night?"

"It's almost morning," Tahlia clarified. "Besides, she knew we were coming. You can't do what we're going to do any other time of the day."

I gaped at her. "Who breaks into someone's room while they're sleeping?"

"I don't see the problem," said Rollie, turning to Dangelo. "Is there a problem?" The other boy shook his head innocently.

"Hurry, put on something warm. It's chilly out there!" Tahlia led the way down the stairs, leaving me behind to change. I was almost too dazed to notice Venetia's loaded glance around my room as she left. Almost.

Muttering curses under my breath, I used the bathroom, brushed my hair, and dragged on a hoodie and a pair of jeans. I grumbled down each step of the staircase until reaching the living room, where everyone waited for me. Andie was there too. She still wore pajamas, and no doubt she'd be returning to bed after releasing me to my captors. I flashed an expression of mock gratitude. "Thanks for nothing."

"Anytime. Enjoy yourself now." Her grin reveled in my displeasure.

We filed out the front door. I shivered against the cold. Rollie and Tahlia whispered in tones I couldn't hear, pointing different ways and making conspiratorial gestures. Finally, Rollie approached. "Cass, you're going to come with me and Dangelo. The rest of you, go with Tahlia."

"What if we want to see her reaction?" Evie asked. It might have been the first time I'd heard her speak. She was a slight sweet-mannered girl. Usually, her brother dominated the conversations to the point where I almost forgot she existed. Now, her hazelnut eyes looked eager as she importuned Tahlia and Rollie.

"I need three people with me," said Tahlia. "Dangelo?"

"Are you sure you can handle it, Evie?" asked Dangelo.

The girl nodded. Her brother shrugged and moved over to Tahlia's group. Evie took his place, giving me an enthusiastic look that both warmed and unnerved me. What exactly did Rollie have in mind?

"Let's go," he said, taking me and Evie in an opposite direction from the others. He flipped on a flashlight, the beam cutting a trail along the dim street. "The sun will come up before too long. Better be safe for now. It gets a little rocky where we're going."

"Where *are* we going?"

"It's a surprise," came his reply. I should have known it was pointless to ask. Rollie led us from the cracked pavement of residential streets onto a dirt road dividing two fields and disappearing over a hill not far in the distance.

"You do realize this is a little concerning. I'm supposed to follow you down a dirt road to the middle of nowhere?"

"Evie, tell her I know where I'm going."

"He knows where he's going," she confirmed. "It's fun. I can't wait to see your face."

Her words didn't make me feel much better. We started climbing the hill's gentle slope, Rollie's flashlight bobbing along the ground ahead. Grasses, I didn't know what kind, lined the sides of the road. I wondered if at any minute some nocturnal rodent might come scurrying out of the weeds into our path. How much farther did we have to walk?

Rollie was right—the sky was brightening a bit. Dark gray turned to deep, muted blue. I saw the horizon take on a faint glow. The light was enough for me to see more fields ahead, as well as some buildings next to the road. A farm, I realized. There was a large, steel pavilion coupled with an elongated structure reminiscent of a barn. Except, unlike a barn, the top curved like half a cylinder and was covered in stretching white material. A greenhouse? Maybe. We weren't close enough to be sure.

Rollie clicked off his flashlight. As the farm got closer, I got a whiff of the smell. Instinctively, my hand went to my nose. "Wow. Is that where we're going?"

"Yep. Welcome to a little slice of heaven."

"I don't like the smell of heaven."

"You get used to it. Come on. Follow me."

We deviated from the road to reach the white-covered structure, which was settled back among fenced wooden stalls and old farm equipment. The smell reached its full potency here. I braced myself. Rollie unlatched a rolling metal door and sent it curling upward with the sound of steel grating on steel.

Inside, a hundred sheep and lambs, startled by our arrival, skipped across a straw-strewn floor. Bleats rang out from all corners. And the smell—like musty grain and nature's routines—hit hard as a train.

"Sheep." It wasn't a question or really even a statement. The word just slipped out, an expression of my mind's consternation.

Evie giggled. "I knew this would be fun to watch."

"Let's see . . ." Rollie retrieved a few quart jugs from hooks on the side of the barn, unfazed by the sheep that milled about his legs. "There are six of us total. Three quarts . . ." His lips moved silently as he tallied numbers on his fingers. "Three quarts should be enough." He handed me one of the jugs.

I gathered his intention. "We're milking sheep, are we?"

"Yeah." He said it like the fact was self-explanatory.

I pursed my lips. "We're not milking all of them?"

"Not us. One of the other farmhands will come by later for that. Milking them all by hand would take forever. That's what the milking parlor is for."

I'd done a lot of things other people might consider uncomfortable. How could this be any different? I followed one ewe with my eyes as she waddled to a hay-filled trough stretching the length of the barn. Other ewes fed alongside her. The lambs, on the other hand, ran together in a separate enclosure, leaping into the air one after another, copying each other's movements. They were a sea of dusty charcoal wool and boundless energy. I watched them rush from one edge of the barn to the other, their tiny bodies never tiring.

It took me exactly three seconds to fall in love with them.

"Why are the lambs separated from the ewes?"

"We separate them at night," explained Rollie. "That way, when we come in the morning, the ewes can get milked before going back to their lambs. Over here." He walked us to a platform connected to an enclosed chute. "Time to choose your sheep."

"What?"

He indicated the double lines of ewes feeding along the trough. "Pick one. Anyone."

The smell still assaulted the senses, but I lowered my hand to scan the swath of animals. I watched their pudgy, wool-covered bodies jostle into one another, their bleats ringing out like an asynchronous medley. I pointed at a sheep close by who looked relatively cleaner than the others. "How about her?"

Rollie herded my selection up the chute onto the platform, where she bleated until he directed her nose into a bucket of grain and closed the neck brace that kept her from running off. Rollie showed me how the milking was done, then made me finish the rest of the quart. It wasn't all that difficult once you got the hang of it. "Now I can brag to all my friends about how I know how to milk a sheep," I said. Evie laughed.

"I bet you have a lot of friends back in Meridian, huh?" asked Rollie, trading the full quart out for an empty one.

My enthusiasm waned just a bit as I contemplated my answer. ". . . Not exactly. It was more a figure of speech, I guess."

"That's hard to believe. You seem like the kind of person everyone would want to be friends with."

I turned to Evie and asked if she wanted a turn. She took my place at the ewe's side. Wiping my hands on my jeans, I stepped back from the platform and found a stool to sit down.

Rollie scratched his head, shoving the other hand into a pocket. "That was supposed to be a compliment, but if I said something wrong—"

"No, you didn't say anything wrong. I just never made a lot of friends in Meridian. Everyone there thinks you're only as good as your connections." I shrugged. "It's a lousy way to live."

"You talk like you're not from there."

"I'm not, technically. I've lived there with my grandmother the last six years or so, but I was born in Exulta."

"Exulta," echoed Rollie. "Outer sectors?"

"Are you surprised?" I gave a smile.

"Not surprised. It doesn't change how I think about you."

That took me aback, and I stiffened. "How's that?"

"*I think you're a good person.*" Rollie reached up a hand to pat the ewe's neck. Content with the grain, she gave him no acknowledgment in return.

I think you're a good person. The statement, made so casually, may as well have been an observation regarding the number of sheep in the barn. We hadn't even known each other a full week. How could he possibly know whether I was a good person or not?

"People in Meridian might disagree with you."

"What, 'cause you were born in Exulta?" There was just a touch of irony in his voice.

That's one reason, I thought, but I said nothing.

"If that's the case," Rollie said finally, "then they're wrong. Tahlia told us how you helped that kid having an asthma attack at the clinic."

"I didn't do anything. Tahlia and Citrine did all the work."

"That's not what she said."

I pulled my knees up to my chest. "She's too nice. She'd compliment a tree for existing."

Rollie smirked. Evie announced that the ewe was out of milk and released the brace from around her neck. The animal clipped down the chute, replaced by a second sheep Rollie led onto the platform. He offered to take a turn at the milking. Evie shook her head and helped this new sheep find the bucket of grain. "I don't mind."

"Suit yourself." Rollie handed her the last empty quart.

I decided to change the subject. "What's the plan for all this milk?"

"That part's a surprise," said Evie. She gave me a secretive grin.

"Oh, good. The morning surprises aren't over."

"Did you think they were?" said Rollie. "You underestimate us."

Evie rubbed stray hairs from her face with the back of a hand. She sneezed loudly. When Rollie tried to take over again, she sniffed and shook her head. "I have allergies," she explained as an aside to me. "That's why Danny didn't want me to come with you. It's the straw. He worries too much."

I gestured to the barn door. "If you needed to go outside, I could—"

She shook her head again. "Not you too," she said with a look of comic reproach. "I might be small, but I'm stronger than I look."

Rollie herded another ewe to the platform while Evie released the neck brace and patted the last animal on the head as it scampered away.

"Come on," Rollie said to me as Evie started the next milking. "You can hold the lambs."

Surprised, I looked at the bounding balls of wool, still chasing each other in restless circles. Something childish leapt inside me at the prospect. "Can I?"

He chuckled. "I'll take you over there." We walked to the lamb pen. Rollie unlatched the gate and pulled it open just enough to squeeze through. The lambs skittered off at our approach, long ears flapping.

Some of them jumped in the air repeatedly with wild kicking legs. Some tripped over one another only to roll upright again.

"They're funny," I said. "Like little kids. How do we get a hold of one?"

"Like this." Rollie walked a few paces into the flock, waited, and scooped a lamb into his arms as it ran past. The animal bleated in alarm at first, but Rollie rubbed its ears and neck, and that seemed to soothe it. "Here. Sit down."

I lowered myself cross-legged into the straw. Rollie placed the lamb into my lap. When it jerked away, I copied Rollie's example of rubbing its ears and whispering softly. "Hey, little guy. It's okay. See? There we go." I stroked its soft wool, feeling the lamb's warmth on my legs.

Rollie was laughing. I turned to him. "What?"

"You've got the biggest grin on your face I've ever seen."

"I could sit here for hours." I ran two fingers along the lamb's soft muzzle and cradled its body carefully. Neither Grandam nor my mother had ever allowed pets in the house, so I had little experience with animals. For the first time, I could imagine why some people took to the lifestyle so completely.

"For the record . . ." Rollie started, and I met his eyes. ". . . I do think you're a good person. That's my own judgment, not Tahlia's. And I would much rather judge someone on their character than where they come from."

The lamb lay still in my arms. Maybe it was the proximity of the animal that produced a flicker of warmth inside me, or maybe something in the tone of Rollie's voice convinced me he was sincere. Either way, I chose to enjoy it for just this moment.

"What is it like in the Capital?" Rollie asked.

I decided to answer honestly. "On the outside, it's beautiful. It's got the most amazing buildings and gardens you'll ever see. There's a theatre on 16th Street where I worked. They put on these plays that took your breath away." For a moment the memories overlapped, taking me to a place where the Capital existed only in its beauty. In such an imaginary place, I almost regretted leaving. Soon, though, the darkness crept back in. I remembered the loneliness, the heartbreak, and I sighed.

"You're not going back, are you?" Rollie asked.

"What? How did you know that?"

"You talk about Meridian like it's in the past. If you were going back, you would keep everything in present tense." He sat beside me in the straw, calming the lamb when it wriggled and bleated again. "So, what's the problem?"

"It is beautiful," I admitted, "but it never felt like home. I wasn't welcome there. Not like I've been here."

"Why were you not welcome?"

If only I could explain the answer to that question. *Why wasn't I welcome? Let me tell you, Rollie. My mom humiliated our entire family when she ran off to the outer sectors with some working-class good-for-nothing, and my grandmother never forgave me for being born.*

I settled with something more palatable. "The people in Meridian, they have rules. Rules for how to look, how to act. And unless you follow the rules, they don't want you there. Does that make sense?"

Rollie nodded. "I think so."

The lamb finally escaped my grasp, and I let it run away to rejoin the others. In its absence, my legs felt chilled and empty. I contemplated whether to go on. Rollie couldn't really want the whole story. Besides, I had no intention of giving it to him. My life in Meridian was a shadowed lockbox in time. I feared that opening it up, even just an inch, might bring everything flooding back faster than I could stand. As if to confirm my fears, the image of a burning vehicle flashed in my vision. A diamond hairpin. "Never mind." I smiled. "It's not important anymore. I'm living with Andie now, and we're happy."

Rollie didn't push the subject. "Good. I hope you like it here. We don't have fancy things, and we don't live like royalty, but you'll find that most people here are good. If you ever need anything, you can always count on someone to help."

It was then that Evie called us back to the milking chute. We gathered up the quarts and started back to town. The sun had risen fully, sending delicate whisps of steam up from the cold earth. Fading colors decorated the horizon like tissue paper after a late-night party. We walked mostly in silence—my companions were not exactly talkative—but I didn't mind. Every so often, when he wasn't looking, I stole glances at Rollie. The boy with hazel eyes and no judgements. A term from the science and mathematics realm came to mind, and I realized it described Rollie perfectly. He was an *outlier*. Something that deviates from the norm.

And while I didn't know much about Loyala or its people or their ways of life, I knew now that I wanted to find out.

CHAPTER 10

We met the others at Dangelo and Evie's house back in town. Tahlia, Nash, Venetia, and Dangelo came back from their own excursion with a bucket full of fresh strawberries. Tahlia pulled me aside and whispered in my ear. "There's a wild patch about two miles away from here. It's our secret. Don't tell the Arroyo kids. They always want to know, but they'll spoil it for everyone if they do." She shooed away a snickering child who crept close and tried to eavesdrop. "Stop that, Carlos, or you won't get any at all."

A plump woman welcomed us inside—Mama Celeste, she had me call her. She took the quarts of sheep milk from Rollie and poured the creamy stuff into one large pot over the stove. While the milk heated, she demonstrated how to boil and mash the strawberries to a sugary pulp.

"Jam," I realized. "And cheese?"

"It's to *die* for," Evie crooned, leaning over the stove to inhale the sweet, fruity scent rising off the mash.

"Evangeline, *mi niña*, you will burn your nose."

"I will not, Mama. You worry too much."

Mama Celeste said something in Spanish, too fast for me to catch, and Evie laughed loudly. "No, Mama! You are the mean one!"

Mama Celeste noticed me lingering nearby. I felt embarrassed to have been caught staring, but she only beckoned me closer. I joined the woman at the stove, where steam rose steadily from the pot of milk. Mama Celeste smiled. "You are a curious one. I see it in your eyes. You like cooking?"

"Not cooking, exactly," I admitted. "I like science. Making things into something new."

Mama Celeste nodded in understanding. She passed me a double handful of lemons, showing me how to roll the fruit on the countertop to break up the membranes before squeezing out the juice. One by one, I removed the seeds as we waited for the milk to reach a simmer, at which point Mama Celeste added the juice and bid me wait a while. "Ten minutes. Then come and see," she instructed. The allotted time passed, and together we hovered over the simmering pot. Curdles had formed a lumpy layer on the surface of the milk, a chemical reaction to the acidic lemons. "Science, yes?" said Mama Celeste. "*Haciendo algo nuevo.*"

I smiled. "Yes. Exactly."

She drained the whey from the clumps using a cheesecloth. It was a time-consuming process, one which required her to string the cheese up for half-hour increments until all the liquid had dripped away. We gathered around the table white we waited, snapping sugar peas to curb our appetites and listening as Nash told some joke involving a king and a pelican. He botched the punch line, and Venetia pursed her lips when only a few halfhearted chuckles sounded in response.

"What? That was a good one!" Nash protested.

"In what world?" mumbled Dangelo.

Tahlia laughed one of her vibrant, ringing laughs. "Work on that delivery next time."

Mama Celeste served breakfast, a spread of thickly sliced bread, warm cheese, and strawberry jam. I'd never tasted anything quite like it, not even in sampling the leftovers of Grandam's opulent luncheons in Meridian.

Tahlia made everyone laugh with impressions of the curmudgeonly man who yelled at them when they shortcut across his property to the berry patch. I don't know how long we sat around the kitchen, eating and laughing and swapping stories. Before I knew it, Dangelo and Evie were washing plates. Tahlia and the others were standing, slowly shifting towards the exit like elastic stretched out, only to return for one last comment, one last joke followed by laughter. It was over too fast.

Outside, the morning was bright and humid. The sun hung like a lazy dog cocking its head at us from above. I waved goodbye to Mama Celeste from the doorway. The others bid farewell. I started toward home and wondered if the sheep cheese had done something to my digestive system. But no, that wasn't it. Whatever this feeling was, it wasn't so simple as an upset stomach.

I got to the square, with its central monument standing tall, the whole space deserted except for some birds picking their way along cracks in the sidewalks. I found shade in the shadow of the woman statue and sat. The sunshine felt good on my face, so I closed my eyes and let the sounds of Sam Fellow wash over me.

Science. It was the one thing, the only thing, proven to be irrevocably, undeviatingly trustworthy. Up until now, I'd navigated existence by way of a theoretical lens: each piece of life predictable. Manipulatable, if you had the grit for it. It was logic, not feelings, that bound the best minds. At least, that was my philosophy.

Sometimes in science, variables arose that undermined everything you thought you knew. Externalities. Contradictions, even. Those were the pieces that just didn't fit. In that case, a good scientist knew how to rework the hypothesis. She could abandon preconceived notions in favor of better information, no matter how rooted the original paradigm, no matter how hard she'd worked to create the first. Change was good, after all. Change meant progress. Change meant answers.

Life outside the chem lab wasn't nearly as simple, but at least in Meridian I'd learned the patterns. There, society was built on patterns, and I'd learned them quickly after my parents left. That understanding had kept me afloat. Without it, I wouldn't be here. I wouldn't be preparing for the World's Fair in less than three months. I would be nothing.

I could deal with externalities in science, but what was I supposed to do when people got involved? People weren't supposed to deviate from their patterns. Their selfish, selfish patterns.

Suddenly, the world wasn't making much sense anymore. Maybe the majority of people were not selfish, as I'd thought. Maybe there were places, like this one, where rivalry and greed weren't the norm at all. It was a difficult thing to accept—the thought that your whole perception of the world might be wrong. I breathed in the scent of spring blossoms blooming and distant sheep farms carried on the wind, and I felt more torn about my future than ever.

"Are you Cassiopeia Atwater?"

The voice startled me. I raised my chin, squinting at the source of the question. I didn't recognize the man who stood looking down at me. His shaved head, coupled with the thick, burly beard covering the bottom half of his face, called to mind images of wandering mountain men and gnarled sailors.

"Can I help you?" I asked.

The man's mouth settled into a scowl. "John Brown. Pleased to meet you." He didn't sound pleased at all. "I know what you're thinking, and trust me, I don't want to be having this conversation either. I'm here because we've got a problem."

"Excuse me? I don't think you have the right person."

"Are you Cassiopeia Atwater or not?"

I stood. When I did, I was happy to see that the man was at least an inch shorter than me at his full height. It made me feel superior. At least a little. "No, I'm not."

"Liar. I know who you are."

I bristled. "Then why did you ask?"

John Brown, as he called himself, retained his unfriendly glower. "You've been looking into the case of Jeremy Polluck."

I imagined the statement was meant to intimidate me, or at least throw me off. It wasn't going to work. "Is it a crime to visit people in jail? What are you, a cop?" I hoped my disdain came through in my voice. Who was this man, to approach me out of the blue and act like *I* was in the wrong? My irritation increased every second I stood talking to him. Did he realize his rude behavior only made me want to turn and walk away more with each passing second?

Brown pulled a device out of his pocket. I looked at the thing, confused. The device was small. The size of his palm, maybe. Its rectangular face reflected sunlight into my eyes. He punched at the screen, then turned the thing around and shoved it towards my face. "See this? This is a record of every digital search you've performed within the last week. It should concern you. You know who else has access to this information? Empress Industries."

I got a glimpse at the screen, including several entries having to do with brain anatomy and traumatic injuries. I made a swipe for the device instinctively, but Brown yanked it out of my reach. "How did you get my search history?" I demanded.

"Please. Don't make me be obvious." He pocketed the device again.

"What do you want? Who are you?"

"I'm your neighbor, *genius*. I live here. I know about everything that goes on in this town, including everyone that comes and goes. For example, I know your parents divorced six years ago. I know you've been living with your grandmother ever since. I even know you've been accepted to the World's Fair." Brown huffed. "I thought that meant you were smart."

"Is that supposed to make me trust you more?"

"I never asked you to trust me. Never listen to anyone who asks you to trust them." Brown stepped closer, shoving one finger into my face. The height difference was clearer now. I stood my ground, getting more incensed by the minute. Brown continued, "I've investigated Empress Industries for years now, and I know they can't be trusted. Something tells me you know that as well."

I considered this short rude man. I couldn't explain how he knew the things he did. He might have no regard for social etiquette, but he'd gotten my attention. I was interested; I couldn't help it. "What about Empress?" I asked.

"We can't talk here."

"I'm not going with you anywhere."

Brown huffed. "Fine. Meet me inside the bakery. Ten minutes. *Not now*," he hissed as I moved in that direction. He glanced around us, looking paranoid. "You do know where the bakery is, don't you?"

I responded with an icy glare.

The man took a step back. "Bakery. Ten minutes." He slunk off, his shoulders hunched as he walked. I made a face at his retreating back.

What could he possibly have to say to me? I sat once again on the bench beneath the monument, crossing my arms with a huff. Would I be stupid to do as Brown asked? Common sense told me not to meet the stranger at the bakery like he wanted me to. But curiosity gnawed at me. *You know who else has this information? Empress Industries. They can't be trusted. I have a feeling you know that as well.* Brown knew something. If he knew about my past, then what was the possibility of him knowing more?

I hadn't given much thought to my interaction with Ashcroft March in my grandmother's house right before I left to come to Loyala. Too much had happened, I suppose, for me to really consider it. March showed interest in my project for the fair, and he wanted me to enroll in Empress Industries' special academy. So what did Brown mean when he said I should be concerned about Empress having access to my search history? Sommer Day was not my enemy. She might still be my future boss. The week wasn't over yet, and I still had time to submit my letter of acceptance to Empress Industrial College. Why, then, should I be concerned about anything this stranger said?

By the time I'd worked every number of possibilities over in my head, I had more questions than I'd started with. Burning for answers, I ignored Brown's injunction to meet him at the bakery in ten minutes and marched to the building early. A bell chimed above the door as I entered. Brown was settling down at a table, steaming drink in his hand, when I spotted him, and he spotted me.

He let out a sound of exasperation. "Are you kidding me? I told you to wait ten minutes."

I sat across from him at the table. "Tell me what's going on."

Brown glanced at the shop's counter, where a worker organized pastries behind a glass case for display. "Fine. But keep your voice low. Sommer Day is trying to get you to work for her, is she not?"

"How do you know that?"

"Again, don't make me be obvious. I hate being obvious. You were there when Day killed those people outside the theatre." When I widened my eyes, Brown waved one hand in the air dismissively. "Yes, I know about that too. Don't look so surprised." He leaned forward and clasped his hands on the table. He probably didn't think I noticed, but his fingers fidgeted nervously. "Look, you don't strike me as a dumb person. You know Day blew up that car so she could be senator. You know what she's capable of doing to get what she wants."

It was a bold claim—to suggest Sommer Day herself was the one who set off the bomb. I may have considered the thought before, but never with any degree of seriousness. What did she have to gain by being senator that she'd go through such extreme means to secure the position for herself? The woman already had everything. She was wealthy, powerful, and influential. What more could a person want? A shiver ran down my spine, and I got the sense that something bad was going to happen. "What *does* she want?"

Brown took a sip from the steaming mug before him. "How much do you know about neurochips?"

CHAPTER 11

The bakery door opened, and in walked a customer. I didn't recognize her. Instantly, Brown went silent.

"Come on," I hissed at a whisper. "What about neurochips?"

Brown ignored me, sipping at his drink like nothing in the world mattered. When the bell chimed again, and the woman was gone, Brown set down his mug. "I told you to keep your voice down. If anyone hears about this, there's a very real danger that you will not make it back home tonight."

"Are you threatening me?"

Brown rolled his eyes with what seemed like more melodramatic flair than was needed for the situation. "I'm *protecting* you, smart one. Along with this whole town. I think Empress is responsible for Jeremy Polluck's condition. I've been tracking Day's agenda for a long time. She's trying to create a neurochip able to give android capabilities to a person."

"What? Why?"

"Why not? I imagine she became dissatisfied with her roaring monopoly and wanted more." Brown took a drink.

"How does that connect to Jeremy Polluck?"

"Good question. I think Polluck has found himself a victim of Day's philanthropy. An unknowing recipient, if you will. You visited him at the jail, yes?"

I barely registered his question, as caught up in my thoughts as I was. I remembered Polluck's wild, tortured appearance. What had he screamed at Andie? *Get it out of my head.*

"Yes. You're saying Day implanted him with a neurochip?"

"Speculation. Obviously, I haven't been able to confirm. It was several months ago when I first started picking up hints about the chips. I can only assume Polluck's condition is a result of her research."

The horror of the concept unnerved me. One hand fluttered to the back of my head. A chip implanted in the brain? "You think Polluck is one of her test subjects."

"I think Day could hardly secure willing volunteers for testing the chips without going through a laborious legal process. It would take years, maybe decades. A little background for you—the Day family has always considered themselves a rung above the rest. Couple that with the customary inner-sector disdain for us outer-sector scum, and I doubt Sommer Day has much objection to experimenting on the lower class."

Brown had to be lying. It was unthinkable. "Where did you learn all this?"

The man blinked and looked away. "I hardly think that matters."

"If you don't tell me, I'm walking out of here right now."

"You are genuinely the most unbearable person I've ever met." Brown sat back, his scowl in place once again. "Once upon a time, I was a Senior Lieutenant in the army, 43rd Infantry. Don't ask why I left. I had my reasons. I made a promise to uphold freedom. I do it in my own way now."

"So you're a mercenary?"

Brown's scowl deepened. "Did you listen to a word I just said?"

I held up my hands. I was talking to a lunatic. A retired veteran with a complex and too much time on his hands. I decided to humor him. "Fine. How do you plan to stop Day from implanting neurochips in people?"

"To begin with, I need you to stop researching via unencrypted browsers. Empress Industries is the largest drone and android manufacturer on the planet. It's safe to assume they've figured out how to send a notification to headquarters when someone's search history gets a little too close to the truth."

The idea wasn't completely off the rails. Empress likely knew everything about me *and* my search history, just like Brown had known that information himself. Sure, it was an invasion of privacy, but I wasn't naive enough to dismiss the strong possibility. "Look, I'm getting ready for the World's Fair. I need to do research."

"You are fine to continue your research. Simply avoid topics that might make you the target of a murder attempt."

I screwed up my lips. "If Polluck is really as sick as you say, I can help you fix him."

Brown scoffed, finishing off the mug and thudding it down on the table. "Who said I wanted to fix him?"

"You're going to leave him to suffer, knowing what you know? That doesn't make you any better than Day."

For the first time, Brown looked at me without derision or irony. He seemed to be considering. "How exactly do you plan to help, huh?"

I looked at my hands in my lap. "Well, first you have to tell Citrine at the clinic about the neurochips."

"No." He said it so adamantly I looked up in surprise.

"You have to tell her," I exclaimed. "If you suspect information that could improve his treatment, you have to tell her."

"Negative. It was never a part of my plan." It was clear that he wouldn't budge on this. "And you, for one, must swear that you won't diverge anything about the chips to anybody."

I felt no obligation to keep any promises I made to a lunatic. Still, if any of what he claimed was true and Empress learned that I knew about the chips, there would be repercussions. Day was capable of anything to preserve herself. Anything at all to keep her schemes from being jeopardized.

"You have to swear," Brown repeated, seeming to read my thoughts.

"Okay, okay," I said, and Brown relaxed, if only just a bit. "Why are you telling me all this?"

The man across the table paused. "Day is interested in you. She's shown as much. Whatever you've done to attract that interest . . . well, I had to get to you before she did."

"You think she's going to reach out to me again?"

THE METHOD TO INFINITE THINGS

"I am sure of it," said Brown.

I sucked in a slow breath. "I don't trust you, you know."

Brown didn't miss a beat. "Good. Don't."

PART 2

CHAPTER 12

It was after school on Monday, and I was ready to catch the train to the university labs. Tahlia had asked me to stop by the clinic to help pick out her dress for the upcoming school dance. Spring Fling or something or other. It was boy's choice. She was giddy over Dangelo asking her. Part of me wondered why it was necessary for another person to help pick out something as simple as clothes, but I kept my mouth shut. Far be it from me to bring her down from the clouds.

"I like this one, but what's with the bow around the waist? I'm not a child." Tahlia swiped through a digital dress catalog on the medical screen inside the clinic. "Look at this one," she paused on an image colored a variety of pastels, like frosting on a cupcake. "It's bright, happy. I like that. Cass, you've got to pay attention if you're going to help me pick."

"Sorry." I pulled the stethoscope out of my ears, returning the instrument to where I'd found it. "That one's great. Dangelo won't lose you in a crowd."

Tahlia huffed, hands on her hips. "Well, that's not the effect I'm going for." She swiped left for the next image. "Definitely not that one either. Am I *trying* to seduce all the men? Ha, not this time, at least."

Citrine came down the stairs, greeting me as she descended. "Good seeing you again, Cass. How are you?"

"I'm fine, thanks. How are things with the clinic?"

"Not bad. Slow today. In this line of work, slow is a good sign."

"Cass is helping me pick out my dress," Tahlia explained, still glued to the screen. She examined a teal number with lace across the top half and along the hem. "At least, that's what she's supposed to be doing."

"I'm sorry, I'm not very good with this kind of stuff. You should have asked Evie or Venetia."

"As if I would ask Venetia for anything." Tahlia rotated the model figure on the screen, viewing a bright pink tea dress from all different angles. "I wish I knew my measurements. Shopping on meta is impossible. I never know which size is going to fit me."

I got an idea. "Wait." I removed the watch from my wrist, speaking into the microphone. "Harlow, this is my friend Tahlia. She needs you to do a body scan for her measurements." I extended the watch towards Tahlia, instructing her to put it on. She looked perplexed. "Go on," I said. "Put it on. You'll give it back to me in a minute."

Hesitantly, Tahlia accepted the watch and fastened the strap. Harlow's voice emanated from the speaker. "Hi, Tahlia. I'm Harlow. I'm going to perform a quick body scan and configure your digital image."

"Who? What?" Tahlia looked at me for answers.

I laughed. "She's an artificial intelligence operating system. Everyone has them in Meridian. Not Harlow, specifically, but variations."

"Scan complete," Harlow announced.

"That was fast," Tahlia said. "What now?"

A knowing smile threatened at the edges of my mouth. "Harlow, connect to this screen. Transfer Tahlia's image, please."

"Sure thing, Cass." A 3D rendering of Tahlia appeared overtop the web page, from her buoyant curls down to the very shoes on her feet. The real-life version of Tahlia gasped in wonder. She rotated her image in circles, the same way she'd done with the pink dress.

"It's amazing. That's actually me. Did you have more tech like this in the inner sectors?"

I shrugged. "Nothing hugely different from the stuff you're familiar with. The university where I do my research—they've got some impressive tech. You should see it."

Tahlia was looking at me with a curious expression. "You never talked about your life in Meridian. Will you tell me more about it?"

What was there to tell? My daily routine was nothing to get excited over. I contemplated whether to tell Tahlia about the bombing outside the Grand Theatre but decided against it. Some things were better forgotten. So what *did* I want to talk about? Grandam's petty luncheons? My high school where I never felt accepted? It wouldn't be prudent to reveal the details of my invention until the World's Fair, so that was off the table as well. "None of it's very interesting," I said, rubbing my arm. "You probably don't want to hear it."

"No, I do." Tahlia sat on the edge of an empty hospital bed. The old springs squealed and squeaked in protest. "I remember now. Andie told us about you one time. She came to the clinic with the flu . . . or maybe a sprain . . . I honestly can't remember. She told us her sister had been on the news for winning the school science fair."

It had been me. That was more than two years ago. I won the fair for my project on nanowelding. Drawing conclusions without access to advanced equipment had been difficult, to say the least; it was then that I started reserving the university labs and begun work on the CosmiLock. "I didn't know Andie knew about that," I admitted.

"Oh, you should have heard her. She was so proud. She told us you were a genius."

"*Oof.* No, thanks," I replied, executing a few functions on the screen to bring up Tahlia's personalized dress measurements. "Here you go. This is what you wanted, right?"

She glanced at the measurements, her gaze only mildly interested. "Looks good. So did you have a boyfriend in Meridian?"

I jerked, startled. "A boyfriend?"

Tahlia laughed. "Yes. A boyfriend. What? Is that a foreign concept to you?"

"Of course not," I said defensively. But Tahlia saw through me like a glass window. I turned away, searching for something with which to busy myself. Anything. I came up short. "Thing is—I've never had time for stuff like that. What with work and school . . . it's never been important to me."

"Fair enough." She swung her legs back and forth in the air, looking completely innocent, yet something sparked in her eye. "Rollie seems to like you."

I scoffed out loud, not meaning to. "*Rollie?*" I contemplated the possibility. It was ridiculous. Rollie had been kind to me, but only because he was a good person. His demeanor, always cool and perpetually aloof, made me assume he lived on some higher invisible plane of thought than the rest of us. He showed no interest in the gossip everyone else so often exchanged on our walks to and from school every day. He joked with Dangelo and Nash but rarely interacted with the girls. I figured it impossible for him to possess romantic inclinations toward anyone. "You're seeing things. There's no way."

"He's different since you showed up, Cass." Thalia's eyes were wide with sincerity. She planted her hands on the bedspread, leaning her shoulders forward like she was about to tell a secret. "Before you got here, he'd been so serious for weeks. This is the first time I've seen him happy again."

What did she mean? Whether Rollie was happy or not had nothing to do with my arrival. Tahlia must realize that. But now I had to ask: "What was wrong with him before?"

Tahlia shook her head. "Well, I can't say. Patient confidentiality and all that."

"He's sick?"

"No. But I can't say, really. You'll have to talk to someone else. All I know is he wasn't himself before you got here, but now he's back again. You must have worked some kind of magic on him. Even if you don't realize it."

The thought felt absurd, yet I enjoyed a small prick of pleasure—and something harder to identify. It wasn't infatuation. Why would I have a crush on a boy who clearly didn't have feelings for me?

"I like him as a friend," I admitted. "He's sweet. But that's it."

"All I'm saying is I wouldn't be surprised if he asks you to the dance."

I became conscious of Harlow, who was definitely listening to this entire conversation and would have a thing or two to say about it later. Embarrassment washed over me. "He barely knows me. Besides, it's too late. Isn't the dance coming up soon?"

"The last day of the month," said Tahlia. She pinned me with a look under fluttering eyelashes. "Just under three weeks away. Plenty of time for him to ask you, I'd think."

The look on my face must have given away my fears because Tahlia started laughing. Sighing, I manipulated a few controls on the screen until the pink dress from the web page appeared over top Tahlia's scanned avatar, creating a virtual try-on session. The distraction served its purpose. Tahlia gasped in delight, hopping up from the bed to see for herself. For a while, I watched her flip through dozens of dresses, trying each one on in turn. Ultimately, we settled on the same pink gown from before.

I'd lost part of the afternoon by the time I boarded the train to the university. I was preoccupied by Tahlia's comments. Logically, it would have been best to forget and move on with my life. But of course, it wasn't that easy.

At the lab, I quickly learned that restricting my own search history required more Herculean willpower than I possessed. I forced myself to let twenty-four hours pass between any searches traceable back to Polluck and ambiguous ones at that. It was torture. If I were to learn anything more about Day's newest technological endeavor, I'd need to encrypt my device. The only problem was figuring out how.

Just as Brown had predicted, I received a message from Ashcroft March. Coincidentally, Leo was here again too. He worked in silence at his own table, present only in body. I braced myself and launched my Loom panel to read March's message.

Dear Miss Atwater,

We at Empress Industrial College are pleased to announce a one-week extension of our application deadline. Your success is very important to us. While we do not offer this benefit to all our applicants, your academic record exceeds our high standards of excellence. We would be honored to receive your application. Please complete and submit the attached form via the link below.

Best,
Ashcroft March

Madison Boyer

Head Public Relations Manager
Empress Industries

Leo stood, crossing behind my table on his way toward the restrooms. I sensed him peering over my shoulder as he passed. What was the guy's deal? Was a little privacy too much to ask?

I relaxed once Leo disappeared from view. Obviously, I couldn't accept March's invitation. I would never work for Empress Industries. Even the thought turned my stomach. If Brown was right about this, what else was he right about? Could all of his words be trusted? The man had told me himself not to trust him. Where did that leave things?

I pressed a thumb to my temple, and, sighing, swiped the message away. It had already been a long day. My presentation for the fair was half-finished. I decided to throw myself into the work for twenty more minutes before going home. It meant condensing my notes into comprehensive reports for the board of directors and designing animations both professional and interesting enough to catch the eye of whatever companies were present at the thing itself. There was still a lot to do, and the date was only drawing closer.

Leo returned. Not for the first time, I noticed that distinctive inner-sector swagger in his step. You could tell he had money just by looking at him. His family probably lived in Meridian. Business moguls, maybe. Or tech entrepreneurs. The latter seemed likely given Leo's presence here, in the chem lab, and not the business building across campus. I'd bet on the fact that no one had ever forced him to work a day in his life.

I tried ignoring him, but he stopped at my table, gazing down at me. I looked up slowly. "Do you need something?"

"I'm sorry. I admire the way you work."

The way I work? I had to stop myself from scoffing. Who did he think he was? What was he trying to get at, anyway? I dismissed the comment and returned my attention to my work, but when I still sensed him over me, I stopped and looked up again. "Really, what is it? I know I'm not that interesting."

"Would you be so surprised if I said you were?" he asked. He moved to the adjacent table and claimed a seat, leaning forward, his eyes locked on mine.

This time, I did scoff. Not on purpose. More than anything, I was shocked. And nervous. Something about Leo's tone was approaching unfamiliar territory for me, and I didn't like it. Or maybe I did. That was the problem. I couldn't decide.

"Why do you come in here all the time?" I blurted, trying to take the subject off myself as heat trickled to my cheeks. "I've noticed you don't use the compressor, the centrifuge, none of it. You just sit there with your notes. What is it you're doing, anyway?"

His answer took me aback. "I'm designing tech for interplanetary space travel."

"Sorry?"

A smirk crossed his face, and he looked away. "Yeah, space travel."

"Sounds ambitious for a freshman."

"I think you've got to be to make anything of yourself."

For once, I agreed with him. I paused to regard him more seriously, concentrating on the expression of his mouth, the shape of his eyebrows—trying to get a reading on this boy. Was he legitimate?

"I thought you were here to get extra applied learning."

"Still am. I needed some kind of project to channel all this application and all this learning."

I laughed just a little. "I'm sorry to break it to you, but we already have interplanetary travel. Or do you intend to reach beyond the solar system?" I was referring, of course, to the skyhooks patented by the National Space Agency. Overly simplified, the skyhooks functioned as enormous rotating slingshots to grab payloads from Earth's upper atmosphere and 'fling' them into space at the desired trajectory. Constructing the hooks cost much more than any one country could afford, but it became feasible once the climate crisis forced most nations to combine with others and pool their resources towards the technological overhaul. Skyhooks made asteroid mining possible, which in turn provided resources for sustainable nuclear fission. The world had benefited ever since.

Leo had not lost that look of self-assurance, but I thought I saw a glint of annoyance in his eye. He covered it up immediately. "Skyhook technology is only the start," he responded. "There's infinite space our species has yet to discover. I want to create the means to explore that space."

This told me that at least he knew what he was talking about. The way he spoke sounded like a reprimand, but because I didn't much care for Leo, I didn't find it hard to disregard him.

"You must be a fan of Sommer Day," I said. "You sound just like her, going on about deep space and the future of our species."

"Day is smart, and she knows how to get what she wants, but she wastes too much time making sure the public likes her. Getting things done takes grit, sometimes negotiation, but not everyone's good favor."

That's certainly not something you worry yourself about, is it? That's what I wanted to say but held my tongue.

Leo continued: "If I were Day, I would spend less time persuading the people that what I'm doing is right and more time just doing it. She sets herself up as some savior taking the human race into the future, but all I see is a whole lot of waiting and not enough acting."

The narrative gave me an odd feeling. Leo talked like revolution was just over the horizon. Did he know something about Sommer Day that I didn't? What was she planning, exactly? Leo might have information. His family probably ran in important circles and associated with any number of top executives. I wondered if I could get anything out of him.

"Have you heard about the new technology from Empress?" I asked casually.

Leo raised one eyebrow just a bit and began busying himself with data on the embedded tabletop screen. "I thought it was common knowledge."

"Only as much as Day's reported to the press."

"You think I have insider information." Leo shook his head. "I know nothing more than you. Empress doesn't go around disclosing their secrets at dinner parties."

"No kidding. You don't mince words, do you," I muttered.

"I only say things like they are. Does that offend you?"

I manufactured a thin smile. "On the contrary. I'm more used to pretense and charade. Your tactlessness is refreshing."

Leo bristled, then relaxed. He regarded me for a moment. "Pretense and charade," he echoed. "Care to explain?"

I wasn't going to yield, though I was unsure where this conversation might lead. "It's Meridian. It's the culture here. You wouldn't understand."

"Enlighten me."

I released a breath. Leo was a product of this place. Fine manners and social strategy were bred into his blood. Clearly, though, he cared less about the game than others. "No one here is genuine," I said. "You can never be sure the version of them you're getting is the real one or just a front to make themselves look better for the situation."

"And?" he prompted.

Now it was my turn to raise an eyebrow. "You don't agree?"

"No, I agree." He said it without pause. "But you place so much value on being genuine. To me, it's not that important of a trait."

"You're telling me that people could lie right to your face, and you wouldn't begrudge them for it?"

Leo had started fidgeting. Not a nervous kind. But agitated, like I had struck a chord. "I value honesty. Just not *that* much. If someone lies to me, they must have their reasons. They're probably trying to advance, just like me. It's my fault if I let the lying get in the way of whatever I'm trying to accomplish."

I was dumbfounded. "Is that all life is for you? Getting ahead as much as you can?"

"Isn't that what life's about *for you*?"

Now that got me. I found myself looking away from him, at my work, shuffling things here and there as I tried to think of an answer. "No, that's not what my life is all about. I value happiness and the happiness of others, I think."

"I do too. I just prioritize my own happiness."

"Is success happiness?"

"What else could it be?"

Leo was simultaneously a cookie cutter mold of all the people from here and, at the same time, not at all. Once I thought I understood his angle, something changed my mind and confused me all over again. We were not friends. I couldn't call him that, really. We interacted whenever we found each other in the lab, but neither of us tried to initiate contact outside of those sparse interactions. Did I look forward to seeing him? Not really. Our conversations intrigued me—that I had to admit. But I was continually unsure what he saw in me to keep coming back. I hadn't been lying to get out of an awkward situation when I mentioned his odd presence here.

The boy was strange. That was for sure. If this was the norm for university students, I was sure I never wanted to become one.

Exiting the lab, I made the trek to the train station and caught the 7:00 back to Loyala. Once the train dropped me at the town square and I was confident I was alone in the quiet town streets, I spoke aloud: "Harlow?"

"Yes, Cass."

It had been too long since I'd spoken with her. *Really* spoken with her, and not just performed scattered database searches mild enough to keep Empress in the dark regarding my intentions.

"We never watched that deep sea documentary, did we?"

I imagined Harlow shaking her head. "No, but I'm in no rush. Are you?"

A woman walked by me, and I went silent until she passed. "I've been distracted with everything going on lately. I could use a break. We'll make time for it this weekend, I promise."

"Sounds good to me," said Harlow.

"Can I ask you a question?"

"Ask away."

I gave one more glance around me, just to make sure no one lingered within earshot. I was alone. "Will disconnecting from the cloud affect your programming?"

"You could download all my code onto your device, but it could max out your storage capacity, and you won't be able to access the metaverse. All search engines will remain accessible, however, as long as you have an internet connection. What are you thinking, Cass?"

I pursed my lips. "I can't talk about it. Not yet. I think I need to see John Brown again."

"You have no way to contact him," said Harlow.

"I know. But I have an idea."

The next day after school, I popped into the clinic and found Tahlia folding bedsheets fresh from the laundry. "Cass," she said, surprised. "What's up?"

"Andie and I need strawberries. We wanted to make a treat for Zinnie. We wouldn't need a lot. Would you be all right telling me where that wild patch is?"

"Of course. Are you going now? I could walk with you."

"That's all right. Andie said she would go with me." It was a lie. I felt bad about it, but the situation seemed to warrant the deceit.

"Sounds fun. It's just about two miles south of town. Follow the dirt road until you get to Gorner's Creek. There's a sign. The patch is on the right side of the road, just a ways into the bushes."

I thanked her and headed back outside. I walked south until I reached the edge of town, passing by the street that would have taken me to Zinnie's house to collect Andie if what I'd told Tahlia had been true. But I couldn't risk bringing anyone with me for this endeavor. I just hoped I was right in my guess, or I'd be walking four miles for nothing.

The long road twisted along flat land, curving around sycamores and sparse wildflowers and scrubby foliage. Wild pecans littered the road every few hundred feet or so. It was a pretty walk. I could understand the appeal, but living so far out from town would be no good for me. After a solid half hour or more, I came across a rock cottage-style house tucked into the trees. Behind the house stretched a wide meadow full of shoots of wild grasses and hints of colored flowers. The dirt road, which curved ahead and disappeared, was visible through the trees on the other side of the meadow. It seemed like the kind of shortcut an old man might jealously guard from groups of trespassing teenagers.

I knocked on the cottage door. From inside came the thumps of heavy footsteps, and then the door opened a crack. Brown's bearded face glared through the slit. He recognized me and pulled the crack open wider.

"What are you doing here? How did you find me?"

My guess was right after all. "My friends told me a grouchy old man yelled at them for trespassing on his property. I thought you matched the description. I need your help."

Brown's glare deepened. "Your job was to be careful what you searched up on the internet. What about that was too complicated for you?"

"That's the thing," I said. "I need your help encrypting my searches."

Brown looked wholly unimpressed. "I think you misunderstand. I'm not your personal IT expert."

"I know that." I tried not to get frustrated, since it wouldn't help my case. "Listen. I can't go around walking on eggshells anymore. You made me a part of this, so you—"

"Correction." Brown held up a finger. "You made yourself a part of this when you got involved with Empress."

"Whatever. I'm a part of this now. I need to be able to do my research without worrying about Day breathing down my back. I'm asking for your help."

Brown stood, unspeaking. He seemed to be sizing up my argument. "Fine," he said finally. "I'll help you." He pulled the door wide, revealing a stunning array of high-tech equipment covering everything. Underneath the chaotic spread, I identified a living area with a sofa, table, and reclining chair with a narrow hallway leading to what looked like a kitchen. Brown stopped me on the threshold. "Two rules," he said. "First—don't speak a word of this to anyone. Second—don't touch *anything* or I will kick you out on your scrawny butt before you knows what's happened. Now get inside. You're letting the flies in."

CHAPTER 13

One thing about Sam Fellow: the streets were also the playground.

I saw children running down the middle of roads, riding their bikes in circles around the town square, and playing on the steps of ancient buildings, unsupervised, during all hours of the day. No one seemed to mind. Besides one or two emergency vehicles, no cars traveled the streets to endanger their safety. Citizens of Meridian might call it neglect. I thought as much, initially, until I started reading books under the monument on the weekends. From there, I was surrounded by distant groups and their laughter, their conversations, their games that they played in the grass and on the cobbles of the town square. It was then that I caught glimpses of imagination running wild, and my perspective changed.

"What are you reading?"

I looked up. Rollie walked toward me across the crunchy yellow grass of the town square. I sat beneath the monument, a nonfiction manual open on my lap. It had been two days since John Brown showed me how to encrypt my network searches and separate Harlow from the public sphere. I was now fully off-the-grid, so to speak.

I replied, "It's medicinal herbs and plants. I thought it might be useful. Citrine lets me borrow books from the clinic sometimes."

"I didn't know you liked reading." He sat next to me. I noticed a faint soapy lavender smell on his person. The memory of my conversation with Tahlia came to mind. I wished she hadn't said anything about him. At the same time, I was strangely happy she did. Believing her was out of the question—Rollie didn't like me as anything other than a friend—but it was somehow nice to think about it.

"I like learning new things. It gives me something to do."

Rollie squinted, looking out across the square. "You could always come work at the sheep farm."

"I could use some extra money," I mused. I had enough saved up from my work at the theatre to pay the university lab dues until the fair, but it felt strange not to work during my off evenings.

"Alternatively, I know Fish Fristrup could use some help on his peacock farm."

"Fish *who* needs help on his *what*?"

Rollie chuckled. "Fish. That's just what we call him. He raises peacocks to sell to inner-sector people. Apparently, they're popular. He usually makes a good profit."

"Well. Maybe I'll swing by tomorrow and ask some questions."

"You know . . ." Rollie started, in a voice that made me wary. I sensed a question coming on. "We've been going to school together for two weeks now. But I still don't know much about you."

I shrugged. "Like what?"

"Like, your name. Is Cass short for anything?"

This was acceptable territory. "Cassiopeia," I said. I so rarely said the name out loud that it felt foreign on my tongue.

"Never heard of it."

I laughed, closing my book and holding it on my lap. "It's a constellation. A long time ago, there was a legend about a queen named Cassiopeia. My mom liked how it sounded." My voice trailed off softly. I sat still, waiting for his response.

Rollie gazed up into the blue sky, the expanse dotted with a few wispy white clouds. "Cassiopeia," he repeated. "It's a mouthful, but I think it sounds nice."

"Yeah, maybe for a centuries-old lady."

I liked the sound of his laugh. The clean lavender smell came back to me, and I had the odd urge to lean closer to him. Did he really want to ask me to the dance? Was that why he was sitting next to me now? I clutched my book tighter.

No, I told myself. *Relax. This is all Tahlia's fault.* Before she brought it up, I'd never had these thoughts and feelings about Rollie. I resisted the urge to roll my eyes. Great—now, instead of being my regular awkward self, I'd have to deal with an amplified level of it until I pulled myself together.

"Will you tell me the legend?" Rollie asked. "About Cassiopeia." He looked expectant, genuinely interested. At least, I thought he did. Was I only imagining it? I couldn't tell anymore.

Ugh. Thanks a lot, Tahlia.

The myth of Cassiopeia was not very inspiring in itself. The queen could hardly be called a role model. It was, however, a story I'd memorized due to my namesake. Cassiopeia's legend, though not a bedtime story for children, held a kind of darkly fanciful quality that gave it allure.

"Not right now," I replied. "Meet me here again tonight, after the stars come out."

Rollie raised his eyebrows. A flash of a smile showed his teeth. "You going to try to scare me?"

"Maybe, now that you bring it up."

"Well, don't try too hard. I'm not as tough as I look."

I couldn't help glancing at the brown bangs draped across his forehead and his smirking lips. Did he look tough? Not in the traditional way. His shoulders looked strong, and he wasn't short, but the feeling I got from him was more . . . aloofness. Not like Nash or Dangelo, who seemed to be locked in a constant battle for superiority.

I looked away. Had he seen me looking at his lips? Of course I would be the one to make a fool of myself immediately after warning myself against it.

"I need to get home," I said, standing. I crossed my arms across my abdomen, the book sandwiched against my body. Rollie showed no sign of having guessed my previous thoughts. "I'll see you tonight?"

He nodded. "See you then." He looked utterly comfortable, so completely at ease wherever he went. I wondered if he would still be at ease if the sky rained sheep this very minute.

Probably.

I walked back to Zinnie's house. According to Andie, our elderly roommate used to be a social worker years ago and still received a monthly pension. Zinnie paid the bills, Andie purchased groceries and household materials, and I helped cook the meals—or, as Andie put it, generally freeloaded.

It was lunchtime when I got home. We ate a meal of fried chicken and cornbread. After, I washed the dishes, and we stayed around the house until evening. We snacked on leftovers for dinner while the sun went down. As dusk settled outside the windows, I slipped on my jacket and said goodnight to Zinnie, who would likely be asleep when I got back.

I walked down the streets to the town square. The night air hummed with mosquitoes' subtle buzzing and the muted sounds of people laughing one street over. The town felt different during the night. Unlike Meridian, which remained busy far into the evening hours, this place turned peacefully solemn when the sun bid farewell and the stars made their appearance. I found the square empty when I arrived. So Rollie wasn't here yet. I sat on the cool concrete base of the monument. A dog lumbered along the street to my left, pausing momentarily to look my way. "Go on," I called. I watched the animal disappear around a corner, and it occurred to me how dark it would be by the time I returned home. I hoped Rollie would have the good sense to bring a flashlight.

Just when I was sure he wasn't coming, I heard the faint crunch of pebbles underfoot and saw a figure appear. It didn't take long to confirm it was Rollie. He wore a maroon sweatshirt, his hands tucked into the pockets. He crossed the square and stopped in front of me.

"Hey. I'm looking for someone named Cass. She promised to tell me a story about the old lady she's named after."

"Did she?" I replied. "I haven't seen her. You must have the wrong monument."

"Aw, man. I hate it when this happens." He sat down beside me. "Mind if I join you anyway?"

"Be my guest." I shivered involuntarily against the cold. We sat in silence for a moment. I could hear his quiet breathing, gently audible in the stillness of the night. A warm sensation lingered in my chest, a candlelight of reassurance after thinking he had forgotten about our meeting—or worse, stood me up on purpose. I realized how pleased I was to be with him. From the moment we parted ways this afternoon, I'd eagerly looked forward to seeing him again.

"Sorry I was late," Rollie apologized. "Had some things to finish after dinner."

"How is your family?" I asked, more out of genuine curiosity than politeness.

Rollie shrugged his shoulders. "Well enough. About as good as we could ask for."

His response caught me by surprise, and I couldn't help but want to know more. "Is something wrong?"

"Nothing really. My little brother is sick," he said emotionlessly, his eyes trained downwards. "I mean, he's dealt with it his whole life, so it's nothing new. Today was harder than usual."

This confession caused me to sit back, unsure what to say. Would I be insensitive to pry any more? I finally settled on asking whether his family had sought medical care from the hospital.

"He takes a prescription. Truth is . . . his symptoms have gotten a little unstable lately. Nothing major. We might need to switch his medicine."

"I'm sorry," I managed to say.

He shrugged again, as if physically shaking the subject from his shoulders. "He takes it with his chin up. Besides, like I said, it's nothing major."

I imagined having a younger sibling that I felt such concern for. I had dealt with my own share of undesirable life circumstances, but those burdens were always mine alone to handle. Perhaps life was easier to carry, in a way, when you were the only one affected. What would it be like to watch a family member struggle against something you couldn't control?

"So are you going to tell me this story or not?" he smiled, easing the solemnity that had come over me and bringing back that candlelight of warm things.

I tilted my head back and examined the sky. Then I spotted her—five zigzagging stars directly across from the Big Dipper, with Polaris situated evenly between the two constellations. "There," I said to Rollie, pointing. "Five stars forming a 'W' shape."

He was having trouble, so I scooted closer and directed his hand until he was pointing roughly in the right direction. "Oh. Yeah, I see it."

"That's Cassiopeia."

"Five dots? Doesn't look much like a person to me."

"You have to use your imagination. The stars are just her core. Imagine her whole body drawn around the stars. She's lounging back, admiring herself in a mirror."

Rollie looked doubtful. "Okay. I'm imagining."

"So," I let my eyes roam over the wide expanse. All that endless, endless matter stretching as far as the eye could see. "The story goes that Cassiopeia was queen of a land far away, where there were all sorts of magical creatures. The queen was very beautiful, but she had a habit of bragging about it." I rolled my eyes for effect. Rollie was attentive. "One day, Cassiopeia boasted of greater beauty than the sea nymphs, and that made them angry, as you can imagine. They appealed to the sea god, Poseidon, to punish her. So the god sent a monster to terrorize the coasts of the queen's land. The only way to save her kingdom was to sacrifice her daughter, Andromeda, to the monster."

Rollie waited. ". . . Well? Did she sacrifice the daughter?"

"Yes. At least, she tried. Andromeda was saved by a man named Perseus. They decided to get married, but Andromeda's ex-boyfriend showed up and challenged the marriage. Perseus turned the other guy to stone. Cassiopeia got caught in the crossfire, and she was turned to stone as well."

"I did not see that coming."

I stifled a snort. "After everything calmed down, Poseidon placed Cassiopeia in the sky, doomed to circle the pole forever in punishment for her vanity. She still sits on her throne up there, always admiring herself in the mirror, never coming down."

Rollie followed my gaze to the constellation, his features pulled together in thought. "Forever is a long time," he whispered. "I don't envy her."

A cricket chirped somewhere nearby, and a door slammed in the distance. I marveled how every sound was audible in this place, unlike the city where anything delicate was drowned out by the bustle of heightened living.

"Why do you think Cassiopeia had to sacrifice her daughter and not herself instead?" Rollie asked.

I'd never thought about that question before. For a minute I searched for an answer, eventually coming up short. "I don't know. Maybe Poseidon thought it would teach the queen a better lesson."

"But the daughter hadn't done anything wrong, right?"

"No, I guess not. I've never really thought about it."

We sat under the stars together, neither of us speaking. Cassiopeia's story had never particularly resonated with me. I didn't find any striking similarities between the queen and myself. She got herself into trouble, after all, and that lack of good judgment could hardly garner sympathy. She brought the punishment upon herself because she couldn't resist egging on the sea nymphs.

Yet I always wondered why Poseidon felt justified in dealing out such a harsh consequence for something as trivial as Cassiopeia's crime. What about the sea nymphs, who might be accused of the same level of vanity as the queen? What gave them justification to respond like they did? This is why I never placed much stock in the legend. It didn't make a lot of sense. Besides, Rollie was right. Nothing about the story seemed very fair. Before I could think twice, I found myself starting to speak. "You know, my mom and dad divorced when I was ten. It didn't feel fair at the time. Still doesn't, really. I think things happen in life that we don't understand, things that we never asked for."

Had I actually said it? I felt Rollie looking at me, but I stared straight ahead. I'd never discussed the truth with anyone besides Letty and Harlow. At first, I only brought it up as a means of sympathizing with Rollie over unfair life circumstances, but I found that once I started, I couldn't stop. "They hadn't been getting along," I continued, "and one day my father just disappeared. Mom basically went into a midlife crisis, saying how she never wanted this life anyway and she couldn't be tied down by a couple of kids. My sister was old enough to move out on her own, but Mom left me with my grandmother in Meridian. I didn't understand what was really going on. Grandam told me she wasn't coming back, but I always hoped she would. It was hard to know that nobody wanted you."

Tears sprang to my eyes, and I forced them down, startled. I had not cried about my parents in a long time. Something about saying it out loud wrenched open a hole in my heart that had barely scabbed over, a superficial layer that only obscured the wound instead of curing it.

"You can't tell anyone else, okay?" I hastened to add, clearing my throat. "I don't want the others to know. No sense giving Venetia more ammunition." I attempted a wry laugh.

Rollie's voice was soft but not pitying. "I won't tell anyone," he said. "I promise. Dealing with something like that, it couldn't have been easy."

"It's nothing major." I mimicked his own words from earlier with the hope of making him smile. I was disappointed. It didn't work.

"Does this have something to do with why you really came to visit your sister?"

A slow, rattling breath filled my lungs. I nodded. "Grandam and I had a fight. I left. Anything was better than staying there. I figured I'd come out here for a few months until—" I stopped short.

Rollie waited. ". . . Until you felt better?"

I opened my mouth, then looked away. "Yeah. Until I felt better."

Across the square, Citrine emerged from the front door of the hospital and shook a rug into the air. She didn't notice us. In the dimness, we were likely no more than two shadowy blobs beneath the monument. After a minute she returned inside, shutting the door behind her.

Suddenly, the awful thought occurred to me: what if Rollie thought less of me after this, now that he knew my ugliest secret? How could I be sure he'd ever treat me the same way again? Instantly I regretted saying anything. This lull in our conversation—was Rollie contemplating whether or not I was worth his time anymore?

"I know it can't be much consolation," he said at last, and I hung on his every word. "But I'm sorry. I don't know exactly how you feel, but I do know what it's like to be angry. You don't have to carry it alone anymore. Not if you don't want to."

Not a rejection. Nothing like it, actually. I frowned. My instincts began to fire like rogue atoms, warning me to be cautious. Rollie meant well, but I couldn't handle another let down. This part of me I had shared, this ugliest part, would ruin everything if I wasn't careful. I couldn't let someone else into my heart only for them to break it.

I became aware of his nearness, the close proximity of him as we sat together, untouching, not speaking. The cold concrete seeped into my bones. I tried not to imagine how it might feel for him to pull me close to his chest and wrap his arms around me. To breathe him in. To feel his warmth. The thought was tantalizing. Oh, I yearned for someone to hold me. And not just anyone, but *Rollie*. My heart swelled as I risked a glance at him, his face outlined in moonlight, his presence both excruciating and irresistible.

I needed a change of subject. Fast.

"Have you ever heard how stars generate their energy?"

Rollie looked surprised. "No, I can't say I have. We probably learned in school at some point."

"The process is amazing, honestly." Heat rose to my cheeks. Was I really about to launch into a lecture on stellar nuclear fusion? Apparently so. Anything was better than the silence, the nerves, the complicated emotions. "Stars are so dense that they can initiate and sustain fusion within themselves. Atoms produce energy as a biproduct when they combine with other atoms. But for fusion to even happen in the first place, there needs to be enough heat and pressure for the atoms to overcome the repulsive force that naturally keeps them apart, which is where the density of the star comes into play. After that, the fusion process sustains itself by using the energy from previous atomic reactions to fuel the fusion of even more atoms." I laughed. Why was I laughing? I really shouldn't be laughing. "Scientists took more than a *century* to engineer the right materials and methods to achieve sustained nuclear fusion in laboratories on earth, but stars have been doing it on their own forever. How incredible is that?"

Rollie stared at me for a while. Then he whistled long and low. "Impressive. All that in a little pinprick in the sky?"

"And more," I said. "There's so much we don't even know yet. The universe is infinite."

"Where did you learn this stuff?"

"I like science," was all I said. Rollie seemed amused by that. When he shot me a sidelong look made of equal parts confusion and admiration, a few of my nerves relaxed. Just a few. Perhaps he didn't consider me a waste of time after all. An unexpected shiver went through me, and I wrapped my arms around myself.

Rollie noticed the movement and stood up. "You're cold. Should we get back? It's getting late."

No, I thought. I didn't want to go. Why couldn't we stay here forever and ever, with only the stars to keep us company? But I didn't say any of it. Instead, I swallowed hard and gave a nod. "Sure. You're right. We better get going."

He walked me home. We said goodnight on the front step. I had one foot past the threshold when Rollie stopped me.

"Hey, Cass?"

I turned around.

"Thanks for talking with me tonight. It was nice. I hope we can do it again sometime."

The house was quiet as I latched the door behind me with a *click*. For one suspended moment, I stood there, heart beating, surrounded by stillness and the sound of my own thoughts.

It was good Andie had already gone to bed.

I didn't want her to see me blushing.

CHAPTER 14

When an overcast sky turned the afternoon sun into a gray blob, Andie and I walked to the edge of town and spoke with Fish, the peafowl farmer. Dozens of the colorful birds stalked around his enclosed pasture. Fish looked to be advancing in years, so I understood why he was seeking a farmhand to help him with the birds. We agreed on the schedule and pay, and I found myself employed.

Andie and I returned home. The door gave a creak as we entered. Andie tossed her shoes into a corner with a *thud*. I slipped off my sneakers and placed them on the linoleum.

"Someone brought by a gift for you," Zinnie said in her lilted, croaky speech. She sat in a chair by the window. More often than not, she could be found in that spot. I realized she was speaking to me.

"Huh?"

Zinnie raised herself from the chair with trembling arms. Once standing, she shuffled to a side table at the edge of the room, where I noticed for the first time a small unassuming gray box. I looked back to Zinnie, bewildered.

Zinnie took the box in both hands. I stepped forward, and she placed the 'gift' in my outstretch palms. It felt light.

"Who is this from?"

Zinnie only grinned, the kind of grin that caused her cheeks to bunch up like two pink rosebuds. I lifted the lid. Inside was a delicate necklace with a star-shaped pendant. An inaudible breath of air escaped my lips. A star. A gift for *me*. Only one person could have been behind this.

"Who is this from?" I asked again, wanting to confirm.

"A boy. Brown hair." She gestured a trembling hand across her forehead.

I swallowed. "That's Rollie. He's my friend." I took the pendant in my fingers. In the center was a cluster of crystals, expanding out into eight tiny silver points. My heart began beating quicker inside my chest. Only Rollie, of all the people in town, knew about my love for stars. How much had a gift like this cost him?

Folded along the side of the box was a note. I slid the paper from the crease and opened it up. Inside was a question, only one line long.

Will you go to the dance with me?

I read the sentence again. And again.

The dance. I had never been to a dance before.

Rollie wanted to go to the dance . . . with me?

"Go on," said Zinnie. "What does it say?"

"He's asking me to go to the school dance with him."

She swelled with a tender smile. "Sweet boy. Will you tell him yes?"

Oh. I closed the note a little too rapidly and eased the necklace back into its box. *Was* I going to say yes? For crying out loud—the dance was just over a week from now, and I didn't have a dress. And even worse, I had no idea what it was like to go to a dance. I would make a fool of myself for sure.

"I don't know," I confessed.

Just then, Andie appeared from the hallway. "I need to get dinner started. Will someone clean these dishes in the sink?" Her eyes dropped to the box. "What's that?"

A compulsive urge to hide the necklace overwhelmed me. "Nothing. I'll help you with the dishes." I slapped the box down on the table in my haste.

"Wait. Seriously. What's in the box?" Andie reached for it.

Panic coursed through me. I stepped into her path, between her and the necklace and the *note*. The note with Rollie's invitation scrawled across it. Andie would make fun of me. I was certain of it.

My sister looked irritated. "What do you have that's so secretive?"

"It's my business. Stay out of it."

Now she looked incensed. She shot a glance at Zinnie. "Fine. Be that way." She disappeared again down the hall, and I followed her with a huff. In the kitchen, I filled the sink with searing hot water and plunged my hands into suds up to my elbows. The heat didn't bother me. I was thinking about the dance—how I absolutely could not go.

Suddenly, Andie dashed from the room. I ripped my hands from the water, droplets flying. "*Andie!*"

By the time I'd found a towel and swiped the moisture off my arms, she'd gone quiet in the other room. I skid down the hall to find her standing in the parlor with Rollie's open box in her hands. The necklace glinted in the sunbeams coming through the window. Andie looked at me, surprised. "Who's this from?"

"I told you to stay out of my business!"

Andie ignored me. She spotted the note tucked into the box's crease and gave me a knowing look.

"Don't—"

But she unfolded the paper even as I lunged for it. She read its contents while holding it far out of my reach.

"Give it back," I demanded, grappling with the barricade of her free arm. I knew I was too late. Her stance relaxed, letting me snatch the paper from her fingers and refold its words protectively, though it was no use. I already felt violated.

Andie's lips formed a perfect 'O' of glee. "You're going to the dance?" Her voice was shrill with delight.

"No, I'm not."

Confusion muddled the joy in her face. "What? Why not?"

"Again, it's none of your business." I tucked the note back in place, closed the box, and marched from the room. Of course, Andie followed me. I didn't look back. Embarrassment had turned my ears warm and my face hot. "Leave me alone," I said aloud without facing her. "I didn't ask you to read it."

"Cass, wait." She touched my arm from behind. I jerked away, but I

141

did stop walking. Andie stepped in front of me. "What's wrong?"

"For starters, my sister invaded my privacy."

She ignored the comment just like she ignored my privacy. Figured. "Why don't you want to go to the dance?"

I ran one thumb over the top of the box, cradling the thing like I might a vulnerable piece of my heart. "Maybe I just don't feel like it," I tried, but it was a pathetic attempt, and Andie saw right through it. I huffed. "Fine. I've never been to a dance before. I don't even know how they work. You happy?"

Andie's eyebrows shot up innocently. "That's no problem. I'll help you. I can take you dress shopping if you want."

Dress shopping. The thought filled me with both excitement and immense trepidation. Dress shopping. Silks, sparkles, heels. Dressing rooms and pedestals and all eyes on me. *Oof.* "Don't you have a dress I can just borrow?"

"Nothing for a dance," said Andie, like the notion was laughable.

I threw my hands in the air. "I can't think right now. I'm going to see Tahlia."

"There's a storm coming. Are you sure you want to go out?"

"I'm pretty sure," I responded, stashing the necklace upstairs before heading out the door, calling out a hasty goodbye over my shoulder.

As soon as I was certain no one could see me, I allowed myself a small pleased smile. Rollie had asked me to the dance. Everything else aside, that fact alone filled my stomach with butterflies and made me feel lighter than ever before.

***

With the window open, cool air drifted through the hospital's upper level and enveloped us in the delicious smells of coming rain. Tahlia lay on the rug, flipping through a book without reading it. The overcast sky cast the room in a dim light. I sat huddled in one of the armchairs, watching storm clouds drift in from the east like bruised sea foam rolling in with the tide.

"You know," said Tahlia, musing over a page of her book. "I've never really liked reading. Can you imagine the libraries they must have had back in the day? So many books. Did people actually get around to reading them all?"

Old rafters creaked as the wind picked up outside. It was a difficult question Tahlia asked. One I couldn't answer. Virtual reality, after all, was so advanced now. If people wanted escape in a fictional world, all they had to do was log onto the right database. Then, instead of reading stories, they could experience them firsthand. The thing was surely faster than reading pages and pages of text. More sustainable too. Trees became a valuable commodity around the time of the climate crisis, and as of now, we had just barely started rebuilding the forests felled by previous generations.

The simple fact was that nobody needed books anymore. Not when such superior technology existed. In a way, the thought struck me with regret.

"I think it's sad," I responded. "My dad liked to read. I bet libraries used to be incredible. Just shelves and shelves of books." I let my gaze drift to the corner of the room, where the empty bookcases sat crammed together collecting dust on their wooden planks.

"Sounds almost wasteful," said Tahlia.

"Maybe. There seems something natural about them though. Something simpler than living inside the metaverse all the time."

Tahlia shrugged, closing the book with a *snap*. I'd debated whether to tell her about Rollie's necklace, but in the end I didn't dare. The nerves stopped me. As long as Andie, Zinnie, and I were the only ones who knew, I could still process the thing in relative privacy. There was some comfort in that. While I wasn't afraid of Tahlia's reaction or what she might say, I was nonetheless inclined to keep the information to myself for as long as possible.

Humidity hung thick in the air. The first droplets had already begun to fall, fat and heavy through the open window. A gust of wind, powerful enough to whip at my ponytail, rushed into the room. It whistled in my ears. Standing, I crossed to the window, reached up, and slid the pane down into place. Outside, the storm continued to rage.

Then I saw him. Down in the square below. I pressed a palm against the glass.

It couldn't be.

"Oh, no."

"What?" Tahlia asked, sitting back on her knees. "Is something wrong?"

I raced down the stairs, out the front door, and braced against the wall of wind that smashed against me. There he was. Shuffling at a snail's pace, stopping, then starting again. Going nowhere. The wind snatching at his clothes.

"Jeremy!" I yelled. There was no indication that he heard me. The fat infrequent droplets were a downpour now, quickly drenching everything they touched. I stepped forward, trying to see through the water rushing into my eyes. "Jeremy! Come into the hospital! You'll freeze to death!"

How had he escaped the jail cell? Where was the police officer who was supposed to be guarding him? Jeremy lifted his face to the rain, either oblivious to my presence or not concerned enough to show it. His arms hung limp at his sides, rivulets running from his fingers to the muddy earth.

"Jeremy!" I tried again.

At last, Polluck looked my way. His eyes were two dull stones set within a sunken face. I stumbled back a step. He looked so . . . so *inhuman*. Bestial.

In a flash, he rushed at me.

My heart stopped.

The following seconds were a blur.

I tried to scramble away, but I wasn't nearly fast enough, and I slammed to the ground when his body crashed into mine. My shoulder hit first. Pain rocketed down my arm. I rolled onto my back, kicking and forcing clawed fingers towards his eyes. Anything to keep him away from my face, my throat. Polluck had one of my legs pinned beneath his weight. I couldn't run. He grabbed my shirt collar and shook me till my vision turned starry. "*You don't care! Nobody cares! I'm dying and nobody cares!*"

Someone screamed from far away. "Get off of her!"

I scratched at his face, but he grabbed my arms at the wrists with unnatural strength. His face was nightmarish, crazed. He gnashed his teeth until saliva flew from his lips. "*Water on the brain,*" he cried, his voice a scraping falsetto. Terror flooded my chest. "*Shark teeth. Shark teeth. Water on the brain!*"

Screaming, I brought my free knee up with everything I had. It connected with Polluck's side. He wavered but didn't release his grip. He shook me harder. I was choking on rain, sputtering and coughing as sheets of it assaulted my vision. My other leg protested under his full body weight. The joints felt like they would tear any second.

"*Shark teeth. Shark teeth. Water on the brain!*"

There was a loud cracking sound, and Polluck lurched to the side, releasing my wrists. I shoved him away. My sole thought was getting as far from the man as possible. I felt the biting grain of gravel under my palms as I pushed off the ground and broke into a run. Citrine caught me at the clinic doors. I was writhing and gasping for air in her grip. "It's all right, Cass. It's all right." She grasped my upper arms, forcing me to stare into her face. "Look at me, Cass. Breathe. Breathe."

Remembering the *crack* which rescued me from my assailant, I spun around. Tahlia stood with her back to me, wielding a crowbar in two hands. Polluck lay groaning at her feet.

"Tahlia, get away from there," Citrine ordered.

Tahlia backed away from Polluck's inert figure, then raced over to me. She was trembling. "Are you okay, Cass? Did he hurt you?" The girl's dark curls, drenched with rain, stuck to her cheeks as she searched my body for injuries. But I didn't get to reply. Light from the clinic doorway flooded past us into the storm, half-illuminating Polluck as he began shifting on the ground. He rose like a shadow, drawing himself up to his full height among the rain and wind. From the corner of my eye, I saw Tahlia tighten her grip on the crowbar. Citrine stepped in front of me.

"*Water on the brain,*" Polluck repeated in a gasp. He stumbled towards the clinic.

"Give me that crowbar," said Citrine. "Tahlia, call the police." And then, in a louder voice directed to Polluck: "Stop right there. Don't come any closer."

Polluck did stop. Tahlia disappeared in response to Citrine's command. I watched the man raise a hand to his eyes, squinting at the light. "Shark . . . shark . . . Do you want to know who did this to me?"

"Stay back," Citrine called loudly.

I placed a hand on her arm. "Wait."

"Cass, don't—"

"I'm not leaving the doorway." I stepped out from around her, just enough to put the man in my direct sights. "Who did this to you, Jeremy?"

Polluck placed his hands on his skull, as if contemplating that question himself. His body seemed to retract, his shoulders stooping, and he closed his eyes tightly. "A droid."

"A droid?" I exchanged a look with Citrine.

"Yes . . . No. I saw people." Polluck opened his eyes and met my gaze. "I saw people. They were . . . they were . . ." his chin jerked to the side. "Swimming in glass. Like sharks. *Shark teeth. Shark teeth. Water on the brain.*"

Whatever brief clarity he seemed to have experienced was fading as quickly as it arrived. "Jeremy," Citrine soothed, "the police are coming. We can help you, but you have to stay right there until the police arrive. Let us help you."

The mention of police startled Polluck. He looked wild again, like an animal ready to bolt. "No."

"Jeremy. Please."

"No. The people in the glass . . ." He shot a look over his shoulder, searching for something in the darkness. ". . . shark teeth . . . shark teeth. I-I have to go." He broke into a jog, heading in a direction away from the clinic—and farther into the storm.

I shouted after him. "Jeremy!"

But the wind was roaring. My voice dissolved only a short distance from my lips. He ran in the direction of the train station. I wanted to go after him, but Citrine corralled me to a hospital bed and refused to let me leave. "We will tell the police which way he went," she insisted. "You are not going back out there."

I let my body sink into pillows which she hastily stacked behind me. I didn't protest as she examined my body from head to foot, lifting my legs one at a time and bending the joints. I responded each time she asked, "Does this hurt?" or "Can you move this?" or "Where do you feel pain?" Once Tahlia joined Citrine at my bedside, I even let her dry my wet hair and apply an ice pack to my swollen knee and shoulder. Already a bruise was budding where Polluck tackled me to the ground. Thankfully, my shoulder had taken most of the hit. My head was unfazed. I was lucky in that respect. There would be no second concussion to deal with.

Even as Tahlia wept over me, recounting the fear and shock of it all bit by bit, only one thing dominated my thinking: Jeremy Polluck was gone. He went into the storm. Would the police be able to find him? Somehow I doubted it. Anger replaced my shock. Anger at Sommer Day. Polluck was gone because of her. It was all her fault.

Everything was her fault.

CHAPTER 15

Once the police arrived, I received an escort back home.

Andie opened the door to see me standing on the step, soaked to the bone and flanked by two officers, and instantly looked like she might strangle someone. "What's going on? What is this, Cass?"

Rain fell all around us. I just wanted to go to my room and close the door. But the officers had something different in mind. They asked to come in, and Andie obliged. We stood in the hallway while they explained what happened. Andie was furious to hear that Polluck had escaped. I shivered in my wet clothes until Andie told me to go upstairs and wait for her. From above, I could still hear the three speaking in the entryway below. I wrapped myself in towels and curled into a ball on my bed.

Eventually, there was the sound of a door opening and closing. Andie's footsteps climbed the stairs. She entered and sat on the edge of my bed. "Cass . . ." she whispered, touching my shoulder. "Did he hurt you?"

I shook my head vaguely. No words would come. A few questions later, all of which I left unanswered, and my sister seemed to decide the interrogation wasn't worth it. I sensed her uncertainty as she sat, silent, most likely contemplating what to say.

"The police said he's gone, that he ran away out of town. He's far away now. You don't have to worry."

"I'm not afraid of him," I said, my words muffled by the bedspread.

"It's okay, Cass. You don't have to be brave."

"No, you don't understand." I sat up on one elbow, wiping tears and rain and who knows what else from my swollen face. "I don't think he was trying to hurt me. He was trying to give me a message. He wanted someone to know what happened to him, but his brain kept short-circuiting, fighting back."

Andie looked skeptical. She picked at her fingernails. "You've just been through something scary," she started. Seeing me bristle, she hastened to add, "I believe you. I swear I do. Let's just talk about all that later, okay? For now, you need to rest."

Citrine had given me pain meds at the hospital, and they just now seemed to be kicking in. The stinging scrapes on my elbows no longer throbbed, and my joints felt numb enough to get some sleep. I settled back into the towels and pulled my pillow closer.

"Do you want me to stay with you tonight?" Andie asked.

"It's okay. I think I want to be alone."

My sister shifted her weight on the bed, looking both guilty and uncomfortable. "Well . . . Well, okay. I'll come check on you in a bit. Promise me you're going to be all right?"

I dipped my chin up and down. Andie left me to my thoughts, which were chiefly comprised of plans for revenge against Sommer Day. I knew I wasn't thinking clearly. Lightning cracked outside my window and lit the room with flashes of white. The storm, the fight with Polluck, it all left me rattled like thunder crashing inside my own body.

I didn't realize how exhausted I was from the whole encounter. My eyelids got heavier the longer I laid in the dimness. Wrapped in the warmth of the towels, my body's temperature returned to normal.

It didn't take long for sleep to overtake me.

***

"Are you sure you want to go to school today?" asked my sister.

It was morning, and I didn't feel like staying cooped up in the house just because of what happened with Polluck. According to a call from the police around dawn, almost all traces of the man's route had been dissolved by the rain, but some people in the next town over reported a stranger trekking through the storm in the middle of the night. By all accounts, he seemed to be headed north.

Was Polluck's exodus the senseless result of a ravaged mind, or did he know something the rest of us didn't? Who were the people in the glass, if they were anybody at all? Everything seemed to line up with John Brown's theory. Could I trust him? I needed answers. The more I thought about it, the surer I was that I'd only find truth by going to the source.

"I'm going," I insisted, stuffing food into a sack for my lunch and crunching into an apple for breakfast. My shoulder ached, but more pain meds kept the swelling down. Remembering my jacket, I ascended the stairs quiet enough not to wake Zinnie since her bedroom sat directly below mine. I held the apple in my mouth as I slipped my arms through the jacket sleeves. From the corner of my vision, I glimpsed the small gray box with Rollie's necklace atop my dresser.

What would he think of me if I didn't wear it? What would he think of me if I did? I opened the box and removed the necklace. The pendant wasn't larger than my thumbnail. I clasped the necklace around my neck and stepped in front of my bedroom mirror. The gleaming silver star lay between my collarbones, winking at me with each movement. For a beat, I stood motionless, admiring how the necklace scattered the light in a dozen brilliant streams.

Wearing it was as good as saying yes. I couldn't keep the necklace in good conscience if I intended to turn Rollie down for the dance. I chewed at my lip.

Then Harlow sent a generic notification reminding me not to be late to school, and I was out the front door before Andie could worry over me any further. The street outside was riddled with puddles leftover from the storm. I munched on my apple as I walked. When I reached the gravel road heading to the school, I saw six figures walking with their backs to me, and I started jogging to catch up with them. "Tahlia," I called. She turned her head.

"Cass? I thought you would stay home from school today."

The others caught wind of my approach and stopped to wait for me. "Tahlia told us everything," said Evie. "That would have been so scary. I can't imagine. Are you sure you want to come to school today?"

"Everybody keeps asking me that," I said. "It's almost like you don't want me here."

"No, no, no!" Tahlia waved her hands emphatically. "Of course we want you here. We're just worried about you." She pulled me into a tight hug that made me squirm, and I wriggled out as soon as she would let me.

Everyone else looked uncomfortable. Everyone except Rollie. He fixed me with a look so intense it took me aback to meet his gaze.

"So, uh." Nash scratched at his head. "If you want to talk about anything . . ."

"That's all right," I hastened to say. "Why don't we talk about something else?"

Nash began telling us how his sister got a job in the inner sectors as a live-in housemaid in some executive's fancy estate. I glanced at Rollie one more time from beneath my eyelids. I couldn't help it. Sure enough, there was that same scrutiny, that hooded expression, even something akin to anger. Why was Rollie angry at me? The star pendant rested against my chest. I knew it was halfway visible from beneath the neckline of my t-shirt. Was I wrong to wear it? Oh, great. I knew I shouldn't have put it on this morning. What was I thinking?

We walked the rest of the way to the school. Rollie held the door for the others as they filed into the building. It was the perfect opportunity to talk with him in private. While everyone else went ahead, I lingered in the entryway. "Do you have a minute?" I asked.

Rollie nodded, and we stepped inside. The door closed with a soft *whoosh* behind him. That same intensity from before, though tempered now, still lingered in the shadows of his face. He stuffed his hands into his pockets. "What's up?"

I felt my cheeks going pink and tried to hide it by looking anywhere except at him. "Zinnie said you came by yesterday . . ." I trailed off, searching for the words. "I just wanted to say thank you. For the necklace."

His face remained neutral for all but a half-hearted smile that didn't reach his eyes. "You're welcome. It looks good on you."

"Also, I would very much like to go to the dance with you."

There was a beat of silence between us. He didn't smile. He didn't even *say* anything. It was not the reaction I'd expected.

Oh, no, I thought, embarrassment curdling my stomach. Bad move. I shouldn't have said it. *Bad, bad move*. It was the wrong thing to say, and now I'd offended him. Or, more than likely, I'd blown this whole dance idea way out of proportion. *Stupid*. Why had I been so quick to say yes?

Then I realized Rollie was shaking his head.

"What?" I asked automatically. "What's wrong?"

"You have bruises on your arms."

The statement took me by surprise. I looked down. "You're right. I hadn't noticed."

"It feels strange, doesn't it? To talk about something as meaningless as a dance when—" He stopped short, a crease digging a canyon between his eyebrows. Rollie's brown irises found mine, stayed there for a beat, then shifted away. "Come on," he said. "We shouldn't be late for class." Rollie started walking, and I followed out of obligation. I wanted to press. I wanted to know what he really thought about me. He paused again outside the classroom door, scratching his head and looking anywhere but at me. "Listen. I know you said yes, but I would understand if you needed some time. I don't want to pressure you."

Clearly my neurotransmitters were only functioning at half capacity today. "That's okay. I meant it," I assured him.

"Maybe let me know how you feel on Monday." He entered the room with a finality that left me standing, confused, in the hallway. I would have lingered there longer if the teacher hadn't approached from the opposite end of the hall, attempted jovial small talk, and herded me into the classroom ahead of him. I claimed my seat along with the others.

Mr. Parsons—or just Parsons to most students—was a man of average height and build with a penchant for the word *precisely*. He was one of three other teachers in the school. Two covered the young children, those aged five to ten. One had charge of the early adolescents. And Parsons instructed those of us aged fourteen and above. The setup contrasted strongly with that of the high school in Meridian, where the sheer number of students could have filled this classroom a hundred times over.

Parsons scribbled today's schedule on the whiteboard. "Welcome, everybody. Nash, any updates on your sister's job search?"

"A family in the Capital hired her to clean for them. She'll be a live-in too. I told her, 'Sabrina, you better remember us poor beaters once you hit the big time. Living that Splurger lifestyle, you'll never want to come home.'" His laughter caught on around the rest of the room.

I wondered whether Nash actually believed that. If his sister was to be a live-in, I could pretty well guess her daily work schedule. Sabrina wouldn't have time for any portion of the 'Splurger' lifestyle, let alone opportunities to visit home. I'd give her a greater chance if she were a nanny or personal assistant. That way she could accompany the family on outings throughout the city. As a housekeeper, on the other hand, she might get lucky enough to enjoy the scraps from her employer's luncheons on occasion.

"That's great news," said Parsons. "See what can happen when you put your mind to something?" He looked pointedly among the students. "Sabrina is making a name for herself. Give it a few years, and her salary will exceed mine. Steps in the right direction yield big results down the road."

"C'mon, Parsons," said Dangelo, sinking into his seat. "Do we have to get the 'follow your dreams' lecture? We've all got jobs. There ain't much more to it than that."

"*Isn't*, Dangelo," Evie chided. "There *isn't* much more to it than that."

Parsons nodded her way. "Evie is right. Speak correctly in class, please."

Dangelo stretched his shoulders, arms extended overhead. "Fine. But why should we talk like life has big plans for us when we already know where we'll end up anyway? Twenty years from now, Rollie and I will still be shearing sheep. Venetia will have landed some service position for the Splurges. And Tahlia will be working at the clinic for the rest of her life."

"Hey!" Tahlia protested from across the aisle. "That's not true. I could be a nurse one day. Or a doctor. You don't know."

"Oh yeah? How do you plan to pay for medical school?" Dangelo countered. Tahlia bristled, and Evie scowled at her brother.

"Just a heads up, buddy," Rollie said. "You're starting to sound like a real jerk."

Nash guffawed, everyone looked uncomfortable, and Parsons decided to take control again. "Dangelo, you better apologize to Tahlia."

I expected resistance, but Dangelo actually looked chagrined. "I'm sorry," he said. "I swear I didn't mean it that way. It's just that none of us really have much to dream about. How will our lives be any different from now when we're forty, fifty, *sixty* years old? Work won't have changed. We'll be doing the same jobs as always, living in the same place, just trying to get by."

A heavy silence blanketed the room as we all considered this. Was Dangelo right? I knew from experience how hard it was trying to make something of yourself. Yet I hadn't grown up in Sam Fellow. Schools in Meridian—even the elementary I'd attended as a child in Exulta—had more funding than this place. Was that the difference between me and my new friends? Someone cared enough about my education to set me up right from the start? For crying out loud, Parsons was teaching from a textbook. An *actual* textbook, with pages and all. The thing had to be fifty years old.

"All I'm asking is that we acknowledge our situation for what it is." Dangelo looked around, shrugging.

"What *is* our situation, exactly?" asked Tahlia.

"We're Outmodes. If 'hitting the bigtime' means cleaning some Splurge's house for a living, then who are we trying to kid? Our biggest achievement is serving the *actual* big-timers." He shrugged again. "Why should I pretend like that's a big deal when it's not?"

"You don't need a fancy degree and bigwig job to be successful," Venetia remarked.

"I know that. Still, we shouldn't get excited over such a backwards system. I hope your sister does well, Nash. I really do. And I don't doubt she will. But none of us are going any farther than her. Sabrina is the cap, guys. Don't you see that?" He shot a glance at Evie, as if embarrassed to break bad news to her. "Celebrate it all you want, but in the end, you'll just be celebrating the fact that one of us hit the limit. Anything beyond that—well, it just isn't accessible."

"That's a pretty defeatist view of things," said Rollie.

"Not defeatist, just realistic."

"All right, all right," said Parsons, attempting to get us back on track. "Dangelo has a point. It is difficult to break out of pre-established patterns. Now, if we could all open our—"

Tahlia's hand shot into the air. "Mr. Parsons? Can I say something? I think we have more opportunities than we give ourselves credit for. Say I did want to go to medical school. I could save money for tuition. It might take me a while, but I could do it. Maybe I'd get a scholarship. If we put up these boundaries for ourselves based on where we live or who we think we are, we'll never know what we're truly capable of."

I smiled. It's why I liked Tahlia. Count on her to inject optimism into a conversation.

Venetia rotated in her seat to address Tahlia. "So what? Parsons said it himself—Sabrina's going to make more money than him in a few years. And that's *without* any degree. Why go through all the extra trouble for nothing?"

"Besides," said Dangelo. "How am I supposed to go to college? Some of us aren't in a place to save that much money. I don't have the grades for a scholarship either."

"Oh c'mon, Dangelo, what expenses could you possibly be paying right now? You got a secret house loan you're not telling us about?" Tahlia rolled her eyes.

As if succumbing to the fact that his lesson was derailed for good, Parsons closed the textbook and crossed his arms. "On average, those with a college education do make more money than those without. Over a lifetime, the difference pays off. That being said, Dangelo raises a valid concern regarding the financial demands. Student loans are always a possibility."

"So I can spend the rest of my life in debt to people who think they're better than me? No thanks."

Rollie and I met each other's eyes, unspoken messages carried in the silence. I decided to summarize what everyone was thinking. "You believe the professional sphere would never accept someone from the outer sectors. Even if you could get the money together for a degree, no one would let you be truly successful in your field." I checked Dangelo's face for confirmation.

"See? Cass gets it."

"I get it. But I think it's a dangerous way to think."

"Dangerous to acknowledge reality?"

"No. Dangerous to play into it."

Dangelo looked skeptical, so I forged ahead. "I lived in the Capital for the last six years, but I wasn't born there. Most of my childhood I spent in the outer sectors. Yeah, they called me Outmode, and no, I didn't have a lot of friends, but I didn't let it scare me away from my dreams."

"Oh? You've achieved these dreams already?" Venetia asked wryly.

I heard the deliberate taunt in her voice and thought about the World's Fair this summer. Only two months away now. "No, not yet," I admitted. "But I'm on the right track."

"No offense, but how do you know you'll make it? I'm sure you have what it takes—" she drew out the last word as if highly doubtful I actually did "—but it sounds to me like people on the inside don't want us around. Say they don't accept you into their circles after all. Say no one offers you a job because no one wants an Outmode as a coworker. What then?"

I considered the possibility. I'd always imagined my pariah status would go away once someone bought the CosmiLock. I'd assumed the biggest tech companies would care more about my scientific capabilities than my family's history. Now, I wondered whether Venetia might have a point. My only chance at *real* happiness taken away.

I sensed everyone's attention as I drew a long breath. "That's a chance I'll have to take, I guess."

"Speaking of the Capital," said Parsons, looking like he'd just had a marvelous idea, "this might be a special opportunity to see some real-life government principles in action. As I'm sure Cass knows, there is a special replacement election happening in Meridian today after the previous senator stepped down unexpectedly two weeks ago."

Confused by his statement, I raised my hand. "Stepped down?" I repeated.

"Yes. Just after being elected senator, Sagittarius Seymour stepped down from the office. These things happen sometimes, though I couldn't tell you why. Maybe he wanted to prove he could get elected but didn't want to do the work!" Parsons chuckled at his own joke. "Why don't we watch the broadcast as a class this afternoon? Hm? We'll then discuss the forces of our government at work."

"That's not how it happened," I said. I heard Venetia murmur something to Nash.

"Pardon? Not how what happened?" asked Parsons.

"Seymour didn't step down from the office. He was killed. He and his wife both. They were blown up on the night of the election. I was there."

Silence. The room oozed with it. Within the silence, I felt my classmates waiting, watching to see how Parsons would react. I'd never been one to question a teacher. But this time was different. I couldn't let such a crucial fact go uncorrected.

Parsons lips twitched soundlessly, as if he couldn't pick how to respond. Finally, he decided. "None of the news reports I saw said anything about killing." The teacher laughed awkwardly. "Senator Seymour stepped down from office, and now the Capital is holding a replacement election."

I was starting to get irritated. "I'm telling you—I was there. I worked at the theatre where it happened. Their car went up in flames. The explosion put me in the hospital.

Now the man looked concerned. I realized he genuinely believed his side of the story. Whatever his news outlets, I wouldn't trust them to report on magpie migrations if this was the information they were giving out to people. Tahlia leaned towards me. "Do you mean it? You really saw this guy die?"

"I did. The police found bomb residue in the wreckage. It was an assassination."

"If this really happened," scoffed Venetia, "why haven't any of us heard about it?"

"I don't know," I confessed. "You must not be watching the right networks."

"Yeah, the loony networks," Venetia whispered.

Tahlia glowered at her.

"Here, I'll prove it," I said. I spoke to my watch. "Harlow? Can you connect to the TV in this room?" I noticed strange glances from everyone but Tahlia as I waited for Harlow's response. Tahlia, of course, knew now about Harlow and inner-sector technology. She grinned at the others.

"Watch this," she said.

Right on cue, Harlow's voice emanated from my watch's speaker. "According to my scans, it looks like an older model. Casting capabilities might not be enabled but let me give it a shot." With a click, the classroom TV powered on. Parsons took a step away as if startled. "I'm connected. What would you like me to play?" Harlow asked.

"Show footage of the Grand Theatre on election night."

Immediately, images of the blazing vehicle lit up the screen. Fire fighters in bright coats were visible with their chemical-filled hoses, showering the fire with powder as smoke rolled into the sky. Parsons looked astonished. Venetia too, I was pleased to note, stared at the screen in disbelief.

"Well, you weren't lying," Dangelo muttered.

"Harlow, switch to a news broadcast from that night." Obediently, the TV traded the smoldering car for video of a reporter sitting inside a studio. Text rolled across the recording, displaying the date and time and names of Sagittarius and Amalthea Seymour. I let the reporter talk for a while about the bombing, long enough for my classmates to get the gist. "None of this sounds familiar to you?" I asked.

"No," said Nash and Rollie simultaneously. Evie, Dangelo, Tahlia, and Venetia shook their heads.

"Don't you receive this network here?" I asked Parsons, indicating the still-rolling broadcast.

"Yes, and I watch it quite faithfully, but I never heard of this incident until now. They all said he stepped down from office. That's very strange."

Strange was one way to say it. Harlow shut off the TV, and we continued with class like usual. I couldn't stop thinking about the implications of it—if people in Sam Fellow weren't receiving accurate news from the Capital, were the rest of the outer sectors lacking as well? How about the inner sectors surrounding Meridian? I could understand some minor miscommunication of details, maybe, but covering up a domestic terrorist attack and assassination? Someone had done it on purpose. Someone who didn't want the news leaking to the rest of the country. I wondered if Meridian officials requested the cover-up as a means of reducing unnecessary national panic. Still, I couldn't justify it. People had a right to information, positive and negative. It made me wonder what else the media had neglected to report to the outer sectors. And why.

After a morning filled with math lessons and writing responses, we broke for lunch. Tahlia and Evie had questions about the bombing. I related the story to them, but the whole time I kept an eye on Rollie. He was hovering somewhere near Nash, Venetia, and Dangelo. I caught him looking at me more than once. Finally, I confronted him. "Look," I said, pulling him aside under an oak tree. The others were distracted by a soccer ball someone brought with them. "You have to stop treating me like a wounded animal. I'm *fine*. Won't you try acting normal?"

He ignored that, which annoyed me, but I didn't get a chance to say it. "What do you think it means," he asked, "that we couldn't get that news story in the outer sectors? Why would they lie to cover it up?"

"Maybe they didn't want it panicking the public."

Rollie hummed doubtfully. "Yeah, I don't believe it. I've seen national news stories worse than that."

"Worse than an assassination?"

He crossed his arms. "Okay. Not worse. But pretty close."

I looked across the grass to where Dangelo was dribbling the ball towards a rusted metal goal missing a net. When Tahlia, acting as goalkeeper, missed the ball by inches as it sailed between the posts, Dangelo threw his arms in the air victoriously and ran in circles.

"Maybe someone thought the story could damage their reputation if it got out to the whole country. Someone powerful." I paused. ". . . Like Sommer Day."

"Who?"

"Sommer Day. She's the president of Empress Industries. And she's the one Sagittarius Seymour was running against in the election."

Rollie put two and two together. "You don't think she was responsible for the bombing?"

"I don't know. I didn't at first. But now I'm not so sure." First there was John Brown and his conspiracy theories, claiming Day was experimenting on people and killing her way into the Senate seat. And after last night's encounter with Polluck, I was more inclined to believe it. Then there was this issue with the media. If I were Day, intent on preserving my good name, I might not want any more of the nation than necessary knowing about the murder of my political rival. Too many suspicions. Too much underground gossip. No. If I were her, I'd do whatever was in my power to cover it up. "She's going to win the replacement election, you know," I said, squinting as the sun shone threw a gap in the leaves overhead.

"How do you know that?"

"No one can compete with her now that the only person able to hold a torch to her is dead. She'll be the new senator. Wait and see."

We finished the lunch break with the rest of the group. Grass stained and breathing hard from a soccer match in which Rollie, Evie, and Venetia emerged victorious, we made our way back inside the building. The results of the election were set to air at 1:00. The procedure for these things must be different than the regular elections because I'd never heard of results being announced in the middle of the day.

Parsons switched on the TV as soon as we were all gathered. It opened on an aerial view of a large crowd. I recognized the Capitol building in the background, with its grand wings on opposite ends, one each for the Senate and House of Representatives. The camera zoomed in close on someone speaking at a podium before the crowd. Surprised, I identified the speaker as none other than the Republic's president himself, Epsilon Montesquieu. They were making this election a bigger deal than I thought. President Montesquieu wore a pale blue suit, a mandarin collared shirt, and diamond cuff links that glinted with each movement. His hair was almost nonexistent, but what little still remained always seemed to stick straight up on his head. He shared some pleasant sentiments with the crowd about the strength of our nation, the "trials" we've overcome together, etc., but not once did he mention the deaths of the Seymours. I wondered if he'd been instructed against it since this broadcast was airing to all the Republic, outer sectors included.

The Method To Infinite Things

There was voracious applause at the conclusion of his speech. "Did you see his suit?" Tahlia asked no one in particular. Laughter spread around the room. Parsons, even, cracked a smile before hushing the class.

"Remember your assignment. Three observations from the broadcast that demonstrate an important piece of our government. Tahlia, maybe you can write a sentence or two about the president's role in addressing the union."

"Hopefully not *dressing* the union," she whispered, "because that suit was hideous."

Another speaker, someone I didn't recognize, took the podium and explained the procedure for the replacement election. This part I didn't much pay attention to. I scribbled down something about fair representation in a democracy. It wasn't until another nameless face stood to announce the results that I began listening carefully.

"After counting all the votes in accordance with established regulations and procedures, the people of Meridian have spoken. It is my pleasure to announce our sector's newest senator . . . Sommer Day."

I twisted in my seat to look at Rollie. "Told you so."

CHAPTER 16

I neared the end of my chores on Fish's farm for the day. The sun was getting low in the sky. The last of the eggs were hatching, bringing delicate new peachicks into the world of the living. Their mothers guided them around the open pasture, teaching them to hop over logs and roost in the safety of the wired enclosure at night. Most chicks would need a week or more before they could fly, so the proud hens led their families over the rocky earth in tightly knit groups.

I had already finished cleaning the roosts and sweeping the floor inside the enclosure. All that was left was to refresh the birds' water and feed. They received a variety of feed throughout the week to keep their diet balanced. Today I poured a grain-protein mixture into the dispensers. The cascade sent plumes of dust into the air which I blew in vain away from my face. At least it wasn't mealworms. I disliked that food rotation most. The smell from the dried bag of grubs always made me gag.

Peacocks fought their way to the newly poured grain, while the hens, with their fragile chicks, clucked and warbled along the edges until the others had cleared out. I counted the hens and chicks before locking up their enclosure for the night. While the older birds could roam free in the pasture and roost in the trees, the newly hatched young were still too vulnerable to fend off predators that might slip through the pasture fence. Picking the water hose off the ground, I towed it to a hook on the outside wall of the enclosure, wrapping it round and round and round. The humidity hit me especially hard today. I wiped at beads of sweat that had gathered on my forehead.

Everything was quiet. Peaceful, even.

It felt wrong. Somewhere out there, a man descended into madness because Sommer Day valued his existence at less than her own. Jeremy's contorted face hovered in my memory, mixing with images of a burning car and lives stolen in a rigged election. Since last night, my certainty had only grown: I hated Day. I wanted to destroy everything she stood for. She harmed for her own benefit. She used and discarded people like the scraps on her dinner table.

My new world was peaceful when theirs weren't. It made me an impostor in this place, enjoying a life I didn't deserve. Could I hide in a dream when I knew the truth? Brown's warning echoed in my mind: *You must swear* . . .

Day couldn't find out that I knew about the neurochips. She would come after me worse than ever. Would I end up like Polluck? Would she implant one of her chips inside my own brain, turning me into a walking experiment? A tingle ran down the base of my skull, and I rubbed my neck. Briefly, I saw myself in the same deranged state as Polluck, growing more unstable by the day, losing my closest friends to the insanity inside my head . . . I shuddered. No. She couldn't find out.

I had one advantage no one else did. Day wanted to see me. She knew I wasn't one of the countless inner-sector acolytes under her perfect illusion, and no doubt the fact drove her nuts. My existence was a splinter in her side.

Maybe I could make use of that.

"Harlow?"

"Yes?"

"What's the contact information for Ashcroft March?"

"I-I can look that up for you. What are you saying? You're not thinking about contacting him, are you?"

"Please, Harlow. Just get me the information."

She paused, and in the meantime, I stepped into the sun-drenched pasture. I closed my eyes to the warmth on my face. When Harlow's voice returned, confirming that she had located contact information for the office of Ashcroft March, Director of Public Relations, I swallowed all inhibition and acted on pure justice-driven adrenaline. "Send him a message. Tell him I would like to speak with Senator Day at the earliest convenience."

"Are you sure about this?" Harlow's anxious tone returned.

"Yes. Send it." I stood in silence, and sure enough, Harlow's confirmation of the delivery came through. I'd done it. Now, all I had to do was wait for his answer. I felt surprisingly sure of myself, the pasture's long grasses pricking at my ankles and the blue sky stretching endlessly above me. For once in the last week, I felt a sense of control.

Exactly five minutes after Harlow confirmed the message's deliverance, she announced the reception of a reply. I tapped the screen to life to read the message myself. The text confused me at first. It was an official aircraft travel report.

DESTINATION: LOYALA SOUTH, SAM FELLOW
ETA: 0743
STOPOVER: NEGATIVE
PASSENGER: AFFIRMATIVE

That time, 0743. I checked my watch's clock. That was half an hour from now. March was sending me a hovercraft. Landing . . . landing where? In a light bulb moment, I registered the wide-open pasture in front of me. The Empress manager couldn't be planning to land an aircraft *here*, in plain view of Fish and everyone else this side of town? Actually, I realized, that sounded exactly like something Ashcroft March would do. Still, I'd expected something a little less conspicuous.

I'd have to hope that Fish stayed inside his home until the craft had come and I'd disappeared along with it. I checked my watch once more: 7:15 now. From the enclosure, the adult birds watched me carefully, their heads always tilting this way or that, their babies poking around their feet in the trampled bits of feed and wood shavings. I settled down on an old railroad tie next to the enclosure that served as a good enough bench for me now. The hens pecked at my hairs through the wire, and I shooed them away.

So peaceful an evening. It seemed impossible that an airship could disrupt the cloudless sky at any moment and descend into the grasses that swayed, uninterrupted, in a gentle breeze.

7:40. I wondered if I ought to hear the ship approaching overhead. I'd seen high-tech aircrafts before on the news. They were sleek machines, known for their speed. A good craft could travel from one edge of the continent to the other in less than two hours. But I didn't know what they sounded like. I listened closely, expecting to hear the beating of propellers or the roar of engines any minute now. Could it be late? I found that unlikely. What was Empress's technology known for if not efficiency? I waited.

Then, somewhere between blinks, a charcoal gray ship appeared. One second, I'd been gazing at an empty field—next, the craft popped into existence right before my eyes. I gasped involuntarily. I knew some advanced technologies could make the ships invisible through light refraction, but I didn't know they could be so silent. The craft settled into the field with hardly a sound. Its loading ramp unfolded from its body, welcoming or perhaps taunting.

Ashcroft March emerged from the lion's den. He stood on the ramp, unmoving. I could only assume he was waiting for my approach. I picked my way across the pasture. March watched me through dark sunglasses. He wore an olive green suit with a puce-colored tie—so far, my least favorite of his designer looks. The man smiled as I got near.

"Miss Atwater. What a pleasant surprise this is. Please." He extended one arm to gesture inside the aircraft. I stepped onto the ramp, feeling its inflexible surface beneath each footstep, and ascended. Inside, a row of seats lined the walls of either side of the ship. March directed me to one and claimed the other directly across. The ramp folded back into place, sealing us inside the beast.

"Couldn't stand being away from home, I see." March smirked.

I stared out the window as the craft lifted silently into the air.

CHAPTER 17

Countryside rolled by at a breakneck pace until our elevation reached a point that the ground was only creeping instead of speeding. March picked up on my social cues and stopped trying to make conversation. I had never traveled by airship before, but I wasn't afraid of heights. I locked my gaze somewhere beyond the window and tried to plan what I'd say to Senator Day.

Gradually, urban cityscapes replaced the outer sectors' rolling greenery. Buildings stretched taller and taller, creeping ever closer to grazing the bottom of the craft. Soon I recognized the telltale landmarks of Meridian. But instead of descending towards the Capital offices, as I expected, the craft continued its flight over the city entirely.

"Where are we going?"

March lifted his gaze from some unknown work occupying his attention. "Ostentia." He said it like it should have been obvious. "Headquarters."

So Sommer Day wasn't fulfilling Senatorial duties today. She would be acting in a business-professional capacity for our meeting. This fact didn't much affect me. I was driven by determination, and nothing could deter me at this point.

Ostentia was a sea of sprawling deciduous forests and lavish mansions nestled into mountain slopes. I saw a clearing in the forest up ahead. As we neared, the tops of buildings came into view, spread out in an amorphous strip like a sandbar in the midst of a green ocean. An enormous compound drew the eye first. Even from this elevation, I could read the large name displayed on the side of its largest building: Empress Industries. Away from the compound, accessible through a few sparse wooded areas by a series of curving roads, stood another set of buildings. Rather than connecting all together in an industrial style like the compound, the layout of these lent greater opportunity for leisure and landscape. This, I suspected, was the campus of Empress Industrial College.

Our aircraft began a measured descent toward the monstrous compound. So this was Day's meeting place of choice. Was it an intimidation factor? I rehearsed my lines again a few more times in my mind. I had requested this meeting. I was in charge, not Day.

The compound roof rushed toward us as the craft swooped down. Before crashing into certain death, we pulled up, slowed, and touched down with not so much as a jostle. If Empress didn't have such a monopoly on drone and aerospace tech, I might admire the craft's impressive engineering. As it were, I felt grimy sitting inside Day's accomplishments.

We exited the craft, me first, with Ashcroft March a step behind at my elbow. I didn't like the feeling. "This way, Miss Atwater." He extended one arm to a rooftop door, and mentally, I thanked him for his obviousness. How else would we get off the roof, sir? Catapult over the side?

An elevator transported us down two floors, opening onto a polished interior hallway. Dark, glossy wood with decorative trim lined the bottom half of the walls. The hallway led us past a room with large glass windows looking in, though the lights were off, and I couldn't tell what lay inside. Finally, we emerged in a spacious reception area with a view overlooking the forest. A secretary perched behind a tall desk. She smiled pleasantly upon seeing us. "Good evening, Mr. March. Is there something I can do for you?"

March leaned onto the marbled desktop. "Skylah. President Day is expecting us. Please inform her that Miss Atwater has arrived."

"Right away, sir." Skylah flashed her long lashes at March a second longer than necessary before pressing a button somewhere behind the counter. She spoke into a microphone I couldn't see. "President Day, Director March and Miss Atwater."

While no voice responded aloud over the intercom, Skylah looked up as if satisfied. "She will see you now."

Straightening, March once again extended the arm of guidance. He gestured to a set of double doors with elongated crystal windows. I grasped one of the doorknobs. It was solid, like brass. "Please," March encouraged when I hesitated for half a second. This irritated me, so I turned the knob sharply and didn't bother to hold the door for him in my wake.

Inside, I was met by the most breathtaking view of all. The entire back half of the room, it seemed, was made of glass. I could see miles and miles of stretching tree-covered mountains, all enveloped in the dazzling colors of a world on the verge of nightfall. It was beautiful. I couldn't imagine a more lovely image. I had to tear my eyes away to take in the rest of the room. The space was one long rectangle. In the very middle, close against the panoramic window, sat a modest desk with two empty guest chairs. At one end, the area to my left, four armchairs arranged themselves around a patterned rug, and an abstract painting loomed from the wall like the eye of a blue and green sea monster. On the other side of the room stood a stone fireplace and table.

And there she was. Sommer Day. Every detail of her appearance matched the images I'd seen on TV, down to her perfect blonde hair and inexplicably sharp waist. She smiled her customary smile, the one meant to dazzle and win over her opponents.

"Cassiopeia! What a pleasure. Come in, come in. I don't believe we have officially met."

I swallowed. "No, we haven't. Thank you for agreeing to meet with me." Courtesy, I thought, might make my arguments go further with this woman.

"Certainly. Please, have a seat." She gestured to the desk near the window as her heels clipped across the floor. I claimed one of the chairs while March wandered over to the painting. Day settled across the desk from me. "Well." She interlocked her fingers, exuding nothing but innocence and cordiality, and it made me want to kick something. "What can I do for you today?"

I cleared my throat. "I'd like to discuss your offer regarding the work-study program."

Day raised an eyebrow. "You've changed your mind?"

"Not exactly. I'm unsure as of yet."

Day's face was an imperceptible mask. "Director March should have explained the finer details to you already. Do you have remaining questions?"

"Yes." I forced myself to sit still, to copy Day's confidence. Playing my cards right was essential. I must give her no reason not to trust me. If I succeeded, I could finally get the answers I needed and possibly expose Empress Industries for its scientific corruption once and for all. "Yes, I have questions. As I'm sure Director March has informed you—" I glanced in the man's direction, meeting his eyes briefly, "—I intend to present my personal research at the World's Fair in two months. Doing so should open up many professional pathways for me. So I want to know, what can Empress Industries offer me that other companies can't?"

A small smile crossed Day's lips. "Wonderful question. You have the business instinct for discretion, Miss Atwater. That will serve you well in life. Here is my answer: No reputable company that *I* know of provides the kind of immersive work-study experience you will find with Empress and our affiliates. No school in the country could match your education. Now, the joint nature of our students' schooling and professional career is a remarkably streamlined process, as you certainly already know. Many of our students enter full-time positions with Empress after graduation. But not all. Contractually, you would be under no obligation to remain with the company, should you decide to pursue an alternate path."

An immersive joint program. The best education in the country. And no obligation to work for Empress after graduation. Was it too good to be true? The thought, while tantalizing, still turned my veins icy cold. Except, I didn't let my trepidation show. I relaxed my posture and kept my face a mirror of the woman across from me. "My personal research takes up a lot of my time. I doubt I'd be able to commit fully to a program that rigorous."

Day didn't even miss a beat. "Why, you surely know better than anyone the value of a rigorous education in a scientist's career. What would the world's greatest minds be without an arsenal of knowledge, principle, variety of thought? Something tells me you would not be satisfied fulfilling only a fraction of your academic potential."

Perhaps she was right. This conversation, this room, even, frustrated me beyond words. I hated the taunt of such a perfect possibility, knowing what I did about the true nature of Day and her corporation. I remembered the faces of people Empress had harmed, and my anger flared. How dare she speak about things like potential and principle when her hands bore the blood of broken lives?

More than likely, Day knew I did not trust her. Pretending I did would only make a mockery of us both, and I might get farther by putting forth a certain degree of honesty.

"I was there at the theatre the night the Seymours died." I waited for her response. Sommer Day regarded me, and for a moment time hung in the air, frozen. I didn't so much as blink. "How can I believe anything you tell me?"

The same itching smile curved her lips, and she stood, pacing to the panoramic window where she looked out on the forested mountains below. She tapped two delicate fingernails against one elbow, serene as the season for which she was named. The silence unnerved me. My remark hadn't phased her. Nothing phased her, nor did anything catch her by surprise. That's how it seemed. Somehow, I felt control slipping from my grasp, even as I sat saying nothing, waiting. Waiting.

"I understand your skepticism, and I admire it," the woman said at last. She fully turned her back to me. I analyzed the reflection her face cast in the glass against the fading light of day, blurred and distorted. "Sadly, the public eye is a cannibalistic place," she said matter-of-factly. "Rumors will eat one alive, if not handled carefully, if not treated with respect as much as they are discredited. I did not kill Senator Seymour and his wife." At this, she turned halfway, and her ice-blue eyes bore into mine. "You do not trust me. Well—that's all right for now. I do not require your trust. I simply desire your cooperation."

Once again, I sensed the very room stifling me. A slow, twisting contraction that inched ever closer. Why had I come here? I'd wanted answers. I'd been angry, impulsive. Now I faced this woman, and I felt my insignificance profoundly. "What do you want with me?"

"Must I point out the obvious?" When I did not reply, she continued. The tone of her voice took on a different quality, something like fascination. "You are brilliant, Miss Atwater. Your mind possesses a degree of genius I have rarely seen in one your age. In all my years tutoring the young to greatness—" She stared so intently that I felt like a bird stripped of its feathers and laid upon a table for examination. "You are the most intriguing of them all."

I swallowed, failing to concoct any response. Day returned to her desk. The last rays of sunlight streaked the floor through the massive windowpane. It was as if the sun were giving one last hurrah before retreating below the horizon. The light stung my eyes. Day pressed a button on a remote atop her desk, and the glassed rippled, transforming to a darker hue that relieved the painful glare.

". . . I have a confession to make, Miss Atwater," she said. "I know the nature of your prized invention. You've managed to create an inhibiting device that protects against rogue electrical signals. Is that accurate?"

My breath caught. "How do you know that? All the fair entries are supposed to remain confidential until the event."

"No matter. This has become a negotiation between you and me. My methods are none of your concern."

I sat back, feeling violated somehow. I'd kept the Lock a secret from everyone. Its research never left the safety of the university labs.

"Whatever you did, it was illegal," I said.

"You cannot prove anything of the sort."

How did she do it? I imagined hidden cameras, digital phishers, and countless other underhand schemes. Panic began to set in. If she knew about the Lock, she might know its construction. She could steal the technology right out from under me, passing it off as her own. And where would that leave me? My future . . . ripped out of my hands.

No, I realized. I'd already secured the copyright. A rush of relief swept over me. The Lock was safe. *I* was safe. What, then, did she mean by bringing it up? If she meant to offer me a contract under the table, before other companies had their chance to weigh in, I'd refuse. No sum of money could convince me. "You said you wanted my cooperation," I prompted.

"Yes. Yes, I do. You are an ambitious person, are you not? No need to answer; of course, you are. Ambition fuels you." Day glanced in March's direction. He must have grown tired of the painting because now he sat in an armchair, lazily tapping away at his Loom screen. I thought he looked spectacularly bored. "Director March," said Day, grabbing his attention. "Excuse us, for a moment, if you would."

The man closed the panel with a nimble flick of his watch. "Of course. I'll be outside." He exited, the crystal doors hushing closed in his wake.

"Director March is not fully aware of all the particulars I'm about to discuss with you," said Day. The statement only increased my uneasiness. She launched her own panel, turning the screen so both of us had a view of the content. I happened to glance at her hands resting neatly on the desktop. Neither of them wore a watch. How, then, had she opened the screen? Upon a moment's further inspection, I caught sight of a little blue dot glowing from beneath the skin of one of her wrists. At first, I thought my eyes were playing tricks. But no, the blue glow was real enough. It was then that I realized. She'd bypassed the need for a watch completely and embedded a control apparatus directly beneath her flesh.

Day spoke to what I could only assume was her AI companion: "Alphonse, fetch video coverage of Cell B19, please."

Sure enough, the feed on her screen shifted in response to the request. I found myself staring into a pure-white room from a vantage point high in the corner. Medical equipment dotted the space. Near the center, stretched prostrate on a white gurney, lay Jeremy Polluck.

I scrambled to my feet. "What is this? What are you doing to him? Let him go!"

Sommer Day remained collected in the face of my outburst. "Please, Miss Atwater. Have a seat."

I shook my head, my heart pounding hard against my chest. Tears burned my eyes. "No. Not until you let him go. He doesn't deserve what you've done to him."

"What exactly *have* I done to him?" Day tilted her head curiously, feigning confusion, and I knew I'd been caught. The realization that I'd given myself away stung like a slap across the face. Now she knew. Perhaps she had known before. Why else would she show me this footage? Either way, it didn't matter. I'd given Day definitive evidence that I knew about the neurochips.

I watched the screen helplessly. From behind a windowed wall in the white room, scientists in long lab coats pointed at Polluck's prone figure, their mouths moving in silent conversation amongst themselves. A male technician with broad shoulders and a long braid entered the room as I watched. He approached Polluck's gurney with a syringe in hand, and immediately, Polluck began jerking against the restraints which fastened his wrists and ankles in place. My mouth opened in protest, but no words came out. I remembered the rainstorm. Just like yesterday, Polluck's body now seemed controlled by some chaotic force beyond himself. The horrible thought occurred to me: It was almost like Jeremy was gone. Absent. Evicted from his own brain. I was going to be sick.

As I covered my mouth with my hands, the technician finally managed to insert the needle in the crook of Polluck's elbow despite all this thrashing. *No.* What were they giving him? I wanted to scream for it to stop, but no one would hear me. I was useless here.

My only relief, and minimal at that, came when I saw a red liquid filling the tube of the syringe. Blood. A blood sample. They weren't injecting Polluck with anything then—at least not for now. I still tasted acid in my throat. Tearing my gaze away from the screen, I realized Sommer Day was studying me intently. Never had I felt so vulnerable in all my life. Glaring, I lowered my hands back to my sides and imagined how I would make her pay for this.

"I understand you and Mr. Polluck have already made each other's acquaintance," said Day. "We found him wandering the countryside late last night and brought him here for his own protection. You see, Mr. Polluck is a volunteer in an experiment of ours testing out a new neuro-technology. Sound familiar?"

The question seemed more rhetorical than not. Day was building up to something. I just had to sit back and wait.

"Traditionally, Empress Industries builds drones and droids," she continued. "But sometime ago, we realized these machines can only progress so far. They lack human capability and thus remain forever limited. So then came the idea of a neurochip, implantable in the brain, able to increase a person's five senses to droid status and connect a human being to the metaverse with a single thought." Day raised a finger to her temple. "We wanted to create the ultimate mesh of two great powers: technology and organic life."

Now it was coming together. The purpose of the neurochips. Day meant to give droid capabilities to people. If she succeeded, I couldn't deny the lucrative potential for such an industry. I watched Polluck laying there, scientists leering at him through the window, engaged in their silent conversations about another human being, as if he were nothing more than a strange bacterium in a petri dish. Leering . . . *like sharks*, I thought. And it took me a moment to recall where I'd heard that exact phrase.

Sharks . . . sharks in the water . . . people in the glass. Could that be what Polluck meant by all that gibberish? Was he remembering a room like this one, when Day's cronies implanted his brain with the chip and scientists watched him from behind a wall of glass?

"I know you've been aware of our neurochips for some time, Miss Atwater. Once we apprehended Mr. Polluck, we tapped into the video footage stored on his chip. We saw everything, including your unfortunate altercation yesterday . . . Interestingly enough, that is one way the prototype has functioned just as it should. Once the chip connected to Mr. Polluck's senses, his every waking moment became digitized and cataloged." A satisfied smile crossed her face, like this piece of information should bring me just as much pleasure as it did her. "I also know you've been approached by that fanatical recluse in the outer sectors. The veteran. If I may be frank—" Day released a single laugh. "I thought you were smarter than to place stock in the words of a lunatic like that."

"I didn't," I countered, defensive. "I found the chip on my own. And I'm sorry, but testing your technology on people is wrong. Jeremy didn't want this."

"No? Mr. Polluck volunteered to serve his country. Do you realize what a technological breakthrough of this caliber will do for the world? Billions of lives will change for the better. Is that not what Jeremy wanted when he enlisted?"

I was still standing. The longer I stayed there, listening to Day's lies, the more restless I became. With a jerk, I paced away, chewing one of my fingernails to shreds. *Just like Andie*, I thought.

Andie.

Suddenly, my precarious situation became crystal clear. I looked all around me, at this room, at the forest beyond now shrouded in shadow. Reality settled upon me. Here I was, speaking to one of the most powerful individuals in the Republic, one who clearly would stop at nothing to get what she wanted. Had I really spent the last five minutes insulting the woman to her face?

"I apologize for my rudeness, Senator Day," I said, turning back. "Forgive me. I-I'm just confused. What is it exactly you want me to do?"

"Do not apologize, Miss Atwater. I understand your reaction. Allow me to explain. Your invention—what do you call it?"

"CosmiLock," I murmured just above my breath.

"Right." Day gestured me over and instructed Alphonse to pull up another file. A diagram of a human brain replaced the live footage of Polluck in the white room. "Our problem with the chips thus far revolves around an issue of the brain's structural integrity. The chips contain a powerful pseudo-artificial intelligence . . ." Day enlarged the diagram and zoomed in on the brain stem, revealing a shadowy rectangle that I thought must be the implant. "We've tested several prototypes. Every time, we see the same result. The chip overwhelms the brain. More specifically, the pseudo-AI overwhelms the brain." Day swiped the screen to a different diagram, one showing a spiderweb of unnatural lesions covering the organ's entire surface. "Without an inhibitor to prevent corruption, every patient eventually succumbs to the same degeneration."

"You mean . . . you want to use the Lock in people's brains? That's impossible. I didn't create it to be biocompatible."

"Actually, Miss Atwater." Day leaned forward. Her eyes pierced me to the floor. "I believe you did."

My fingernails dug crevasses into the soft flesh of my palms as I sat helpless, exposed, before a woman who professed to know more about my invention than I did. "You stole it," I said, more as a statement than a question. How else could she make these kinds of claims?

"No." Day acted like the notion was ridiculous, casting out her response with a roll of the eyes. "What a juvenile thought. No, I simply make myself aware. For example, I know you created a synthetic material derived from carbon to serve as the basis for your invention, and I am inclined to believe that with a tweak or two it could be modified to function in an organic capacity."

Now I understood. Day didn't want me for my general IQ. She didn't even want *me*. She wanted the Lock, and my copyright—that puny, inconspicuous, *blessed* copyright—was the only thing standing in her way. I hoped the law would remain true in this instance. Everything relied on it.

"I won't sell you the Lock. I'm sorry, but it's not going to happen."

"No, no, no. You misunderstand. I want your partnership."

"Right." I resisted rolling my eyes. Hadn't we already gone over this? "You want me to work for Empress, to attend your school. With all due respect, Senator Day, you've made what you want very clear."

"You do not believe I value your skillset?"

"Only as far as it can get you your neurochips." I shook my head. "Besides, I can't partner with a company whose practices contradict my values."

Day's lips compressed in a line, and I got the sense she was finally losing her patience. "You still don't understand negotiations, do you? You are still very, very young. I want your help perfecting the neurochip; that much is true. But rest assured, I will give you tremendous opportunities in exchange. You must consider this offer at face value. In business, we rarely get everything we want. We navigate a network of individuals who are just as passionate as ourselves. Put simply—my work will go on whether it fits your values or not." Her shallow smile was unapologetic.

She indicated the white room footage with a nod. "You could help these patients. Forgive me for saying so, but the violation of morality remains if you choose to withhold the technology that can save them."

"Your decisions aren't my fault."

"No, but would you be so selfish? These chips will change the world for the better. People currently limited by their own physical frames will find themselves enhanced, stronger, healthier, and capable of solving all the mysteries of the universe. Whether you choose to expedite the process by lending over your CosmiLock or not, this work will go on. I promise you that. Granted, my teams would have to find another way to keep the chips from overwhelming all our patients. Many more minds would surely perish in the interim. But no, don't concern yourself on that front. Far be it from me to compromise your values."

In a flash, I saw a glimpse of this woman's true nature. I heard the venom which underlaid her cool, collected demeanor. I sensed the satisfaction behind every precise word, knowing she was gaining the upper hand. And I felt trapped. Confused.

I hated the feeling.

"Cassiopeia—" Day paused. "May I call you Cassiopeia? Of course I want your device for my company. Who wouldn't? But I want *more* than that. I want you to thrive. I want to see you receive the recognition and success you deserve. I can tell you want that for yourself, as well. This is where you can get it. Here. With this company. In the meantime, you'll save lives and contribute to the advancement of countless others."

I sat, silent, unmoving. "If I give you the Lock, will you heal Jeremy?"

Day's lips formed into the perfect surprised 'O' shape. "No, that won't be possible. Mr. Polluck is beyond repair, I'm afraid. His condition at this point is terminal."

My breath evaporated. "*What*? You're killing him?"

Day released a scoff which she disguised as faux amusement. "Of course not. Mr. Polluck understood the risks when he volunteered for the advancement of science. These things happen. They are always tragic. But they happen."

Too many conflicting thoughts battled inside me. If I refused to conform to Day's wishes, then how many more of her victims would I be condemning? If I did as she wanted—if I joined Empress Industries—could I possibly make a positive difference in the world? No doubt I'd find the notoriety she spoke of. Of all the people who could turn my name into something big, it was Sommer Day. Perhaps this project to develop an enhancing neurochip could be a new threshold for a better earth. What advancements might this technology lead to? Admittedly, the prospect excited the deepest parts of my imagination.

Was the cost worth the result? Was *this* my ticket to my future? What if Day's offer was the best I would ever receive?

"It is a lot to take in," the woman said, seeming to read my thoughts. "Asking you to respond right now would be unreasonable. While we are under more of a time crunch than the previous two times I've made this offer to you . . ." Day put emphasis on the words 'previous' and 'two,' as if she meant to tack on just one more layer of guilt. "I still want you to take the next week or two to think about it. Give me your answer, say, by the end of the month." She closed the Loom panel with its footage of the white room and Jeremy Polluck on his gurney. As the image blinked into nonexistence, I still felt its imprint burned onto my memory. "How does that sound to you?"

Finding my tongue was difficult. I swallowed hard and managed a nod.

"Very good." Sommer Day smiled. "I am very impressed with you. There are great things ahead for you; I know it. Director March will meet you just outside and escort you back home."

I finally stood from the seat, clutching my backpack, inundated by moral dilemmas and possibilities. Day was offering the gateway to it all. Everything I ever dreamed—at my fingertips. "Thank you, Senator Day, for your time." I exited through the crystal double doors, feeling like I was wading through a dream.

"And remember, Miss Atwater—" I turned back, dazed. "The end of the month. I expect an answer. For your own sake and the sake of our common future, please choose correctly."

Outside the office, Ashcroft March stood speaking with Skylah at the reception desk. They both looked up at my appearance, and Skylah coaxed a stray hair out of her face. "Looks like your cue," she said from under long lashes. "Safe travels, Mr. March. It's always a pleasure." The exchange gave me a sour taste in my mouth. I didn't try to hide my repulsion.

Back along the hall, onto the roof, where the aircraft waited for us. I climbed the ramp, seated myself, stared out the window, and made a point to remain like that all the way back to Loyala. March deposited me in Fish's field. When I glanced back, I saw only a glimpse of the carbonate undercarriage before the craft vanished. Grass swished from its departure and peacocks exclaimed in wild earnest.

A glance at my watch told me it was now 9:45. My meeting with Senator Day hadn't been long. And yet, I came back with more questions than I took with me.

Unable to sort it out now, I made the trek back home. Andie would be wondering where I was. It was dark, and the streets were empty. Sure enough, as soon as I entered the house, my sister stood from the sofa, her hand dropping to her side in a clear indication that she'd been chewing her nails. "Where have you been? I thought you would let me know before you went anywhere late at night. I've been scared to death."

"I'm sorry. Really. I was finishing up with the birds and lost track of time." I didn't dare tell Andie about my interaction with Day. Accidentally leaking information about the neurochips would only cause more trouble.

"You know, I wish you would take things more seriously. Sometimes I think you live in your own little world."

"Maybe I do. Maybe I like it better than the wacked one I've been dealing with."

She frowned at me. It was a look somewhere between a glare and a grimace. "I want to help you, Cass. I really do. You have got to cut me some slack here. Believe it or not, I have no idea what I'm doing." Andie released a sharp laugh and collapsed back onto the sofa. "Please, just give me some communication."

"Look, I appreciate the effort, but I don't need you to be my mother. Just don't worry about me, all right?" I unlaced my shoes in the entryway. I needed a shower. The smell of the peacock enclosure, now uncomfortably potent inside the house, lingered on my hair and clothes. I'd been too distracted to notice at the time, but I probably smelled this way during my meeting with Day. There was some satisfaction in the thought.

"Don't worry about you? Of course I worry about you. For crying out loud, that nutjob attacked you last night. He could still be out there. You realize why that makes me worry, right?"

I paused, staring at the floor. Knowing the truth didn't bring me any comfort. Jeremy might not be loose anymore, but his situation was no better. Trapped, lonely, and slowly descending toward madness.

I might be safe, yes, but Polluck was condemned. What's more, his death would be merely one of many until Empress created a successful inhibitor of their own. Could I live with the knowledge that I might have prevented additional suffering and I'd refused?

"Cass? Hello? Are you even listening to me?"

Andie startled me from my heavy reverie. I hurried to give the answer I knew would satiate her so I could finally wash the grime off my body and crawl into bed. "I'm sorry I've been distant. Talking about my feelings isn't really my strong suit. I shouldn't have stayed out so late, but it won't happen again."

My sister sighed. "You're only saying that to get me off your back. I just want you to know . . . that I'm here for you. I already screwed up by being gone for half your life. Now I hope you'll let me make it right. I want you to feel comfortable talking to me."

I nodded reluctantly. "Fine. More talking. Duly noted."

"And no more going out at night alone, at least not until the police find Jeremy. Either you take me with you, or you stay around friends."

"Fine." I threw my hands into the air. "Now you are being my mother." I said it as a joke, hoping to ease some of the tension. Andie smirked at least. Maybe I couldn't tell her about the neurochips, and maybe I couldn't trust myself with the kind of vulnerability she asked for. Yet all her worrying did strike some remote chord inside. It felt nice. Not perfect yet. But nice.

"You know," Andie started. "I was thinking we could go dress shopping on Saturday. Assuming you still feel up for the dance. What do you say?"

Oh. The dance. So much had happened today, the event was the farthest thing from my mind. Consequently, I didn't put much thought into my response. "Yeah, that sounds great."

"Really? Well, all right then. It's a date!"

"It's a date," I murmured through my best toothy grin and trekked up the stairs to scrub the scent of mealworms and poultry off my skin.

CHAPTER 18

"I thought I'd find you here," said a familiar voice behind me. Startled, I flung the hose in a wild half-circle as I spun around, dousing both the wall of the enclosure and Rollie with a stream of water. He cried out and jumped back. The whole front half of his clothes were soaked. His shirt dripped water steadily into the dirt.

"Geez, Cass. Jumpy, much?"

"Oh, no! Rollie, I'm sorry. Ah . . . let me find something to dry you off . . ." The enclosure was so painfully bare that I quickly came up short. I started to take off my jacket.

"No, I don't want your jacket." He lifted one foot, then the other, his shoes making a wet squishing sound each time. I groaned. Rollie flicked a droplet off his eyebrow. "Funny enough, I was just thinking the temperature tonight was a little too perfect, you know? Being comfortable is the worst. Better to be wet and cold."

I tried to offer him the jacket again, but he laughed and held up his hand. "I'm kidding. It's not that bad. Is this what your job looks like then? Watering the peacocks and spraying anyone who gets in your way?"

I turned the knob on the wall that shut off the water. "You think you're funny. Yes, I do the feeding and watering. I also clean and lock the enclosure at night. And you know what else? They're called peafowl not peacocks. Try to get it right."

Rollie hummed skeptically, and I hid my smile from him as I bent to sweep the floor.

"So the reason I came by was . . . I thought I would check in with things . . . you know, see if your thoughts are the same as they were the other day."

I sensed hesitation in his voice and looked up to see him rubbing the back of his neck. Was he talking about the dance? After two days giving me the cold shoulder, acting like he wished he'd never asked me in the first place, *now* he came to talk about the dance? "Look," I said, "If you've changed your mind about going with me, I understand."

"What? Not at all. I mean—that's not what I'm saying. Of course I still want to go with you."

"You realize you haven't been exactly thrilled to see me these past couple days."

Rollie looked at me blankly. "That—I—that was me trying to give you some space, I guess. After—you know, after what happened." He trailed off, looking mildly in pain.

I fixed him with a sidelong look, my eyebrows pulled together. "You mean with Jeremy? Rollie, I was fine. You don't have to worry about me."

"I don't have to worry about you? I'm not sure what things you worry about, but here, we worry about stuff like this."

"I said I'm fine. He didn't hurt me. See?" I held my arms out to my sides to show him. "Nothing wrong." I started winding the hose onto its hook in the wall, internally shaking my head because his concern was so ridiculous.

Rollie was quiet behind me, the faint *drip drip* of water into the dirt being the only sound. Then I heard him approach. Reaching down, he lifted the bulk of the hose while I twisted it up and secured it together. Pieces of wet hair fell into his eyes. They stuck to his forehead. Without thinking, I reached out a hand and combed back a spot of erratic hair near his temple. He blinked. It was then that I realized what I was doing, and I withdrew my fingers with a bit of a start.

"Sorry," I said, and ducked my head as my cheeks burned hot.

He didn't move. In fact, his silence was starting to unnerve me. Had I said something wrong again? Honestly, if he still thought he'd go on about that Jeremy Polluck business, I'd walk out right here, right now. I hated pity. It was like the patronizing pat on the back given by teachers to their grade school students.

And maybe Rollie saw that in my eyes—the stiffness, the set of my jaw as I clenched my teeth, hoping he'd decide to move on. He must have seen it, because his demeanor shifted just slightly, and I watched his chest expand with a deep, time-to-change-the-subject breath. "Are you hungry?" he asked.

"Actually," I said, grateful for the transition, "I'm starving. I should get home."

"Would you like to have dinner at my place?"

The question caught me off guard, much like the rest of this conversation, and I reacted too quick at first. "No. No, that's okay."

He raised his eyebrows. "You sure?"

"Yeah. I mean—I don't want to impose on your family."

"Trust me, they'd love to have you."

"Meh, I don't know about that."

"Meh?"

"Not 'meh' about your family; 'meh' about me. About, uh, them . . . uh," I scratched my head, feeling this all spiraling like a train derailed and spinning off its tracks.

And then Rollie was laughing. I fixed him with a confounded stare. "I'm sorry," he said. "I shouldn't be laughing. That's my bad." But still, he was laughing. "Look. If you want to come, I promise you can leave whenever you want. No obligations. Just food."

This time, I gave it some thought. Admittedly, I was curious to see Rollie's home. More than that, I was curious to meet his family. I wondered how much they knew about me—if he had told them about the dance, if he'd told them my background . . . Even as I thought it, I doubted that last part. Rollie wasn't the kind to go around airing other people's dirty laundry. It was one thing I liked about him. It made our time together feel secure, like no one else would ever partake of those minutes but us.

Dinner was a harmless thing then. Right? Just food, a little conversation maybe, and no more. It was manageable. "Well," I said. "If you really don't think they'd mind, I guess I can come to dinner."

Rollie smiled. It was wider than his usual smirk, enough to show the whiteness of his teeth. "Great. It's good timing too. I don't think I can stand here any longer." He rubbed at one of his arms, where gooseflesh prickled his skin.

I cringed. "Sorry," I said again, leading the way out of the enclosure and locking the door behind us.

"That's all right. Let's just not stay outside longer than we have to. How do you feel about running?"

"Running," I echoed, not sure I heard him correctly.

Rollie took off at a sprint then. His shoes pounded hard on the gravel and left me in the dust. I called out, but he didn't look back, so I gave in and broke into a run after him. He had a fifteen-yard head start, but he must have slowed his pace because I caught up to him quickly. I was laughing hard enough that I had to stop, and we walked the rest of the way to his house. My heart pumped hard in my chest. A good feeling. His clothes mostly dried while we walked. I was grinning over some joke by the time we reached his front step, so I forgot what exactly I was walking into until Rollie turned the knob and led the way inside.

A woman whom I could only assume was Rollie's mother appeared from around a corner. She was my height, with a wide hourglass figure and short brown hair pulled up halfway. Freckles sprayed across her cheeks and forehead. "Well, well," she said. "Look who finally came home. Dinner's almost ready. Who's this?"

"This is Cass," said Rollie. "Do you mind if she stays for dinner?"

"Cass!" The woman's face lit up. "Rollie's told us so many good things about you. I'm Delaney. Please, come in. Come in."

I followed Rollie down the hall and into a living room. The house wasn't much larger than Zinnie's. Lamplight cast a warm glow over the space. On a sofa nearby lay a little boy. His legs were swung up lengthwise on the couch, and pillows propped him up from behind so he could sit upright. He gave me a wave. This must be Yael, Rollie's little brother who was sick.

A man, tall and lanky, stepped out from the adjacent kitchen. "Rollie. You didn't say you were having a friend over."

"She's here for dinner, Dad."

My ears turned hot instantly. "I'm sorry for intruding, Mr. . . ." I realized, with another wash of embarrassment, that I didn't know Rollie's last name.

"Waverly," the man supplied.

"Don't be ridiculous!" Delaney emerged from the kitchen carrying a heaping plate of cookies. "It's such a treat to have you here. Would you like a cookie? Yael and I made them this afternoon. Paul will tell me eating dessert before dinner spoils a person's appetite, but I don't believe it." She extended the plate toward me. "Hopefully you're not allergic to walnuts."

"No, um, I'm not allergic to walnuts." I took a cookie tentatively. "Thank you."

"Mom, can I have another one?" Yael asked from the sofa. His floppy brown hair fell in just the same way as Rollie's.

Delaney smirked at the boy, but she allowed him to take a cookie from the plate. I bit into mine. The taste of brown sugar filled my mouth.

"I'm just so happy to finally meet you, Cass. Rollie says you're as smart as they come." Delaney shot a glance at her son. "Sorry—am I not supposed to bring that up? Never mind, I don't care. He's used to me embarrassing him."

I saw Rollie screw his lips up and fix his mom with a wary sidelong look. His body language, with his hands resting on the back of the sofa so casually, conveyed everything *but* embarrassment.

"Yael is just finishing up his reading time. Aren't you, bud? I hope you don't mind if we read this last page."

"Care to sit?" Rollie's father asked stiffly, motioning to the living room seats. "Food's not ready yet."

"We can help," Rollie offered. "Follow me. Do you know how to make biscuits?"

I trailed behind him into the kitchen, where checkered countertops and linoleum floors gave off the warmth of modest living. A potted plant grew in the windowsill. "The dough is ready to roll out," Rollie's father said. "Don't make them too thin this time."

The Method To Infinite Things

Rollie showed me how to roll out the biscuit dough and use a glass jar to cut out the circles. Yael remained in the living room, where Delaney was helping him read a book about pirates or something to that effect.

"Am I doing it right?" I peeled two stretchy dough circles off the counter, examining them.

"Don't quit your day job, because you don't have a future in baking," said Rollie.

"Rude." I tossed a puff of flour into his face. He sputtered as white specks showered from his bangs.

"I'm just kidding!" He exclaimed, rubbing at his nose. "You're ruthless, you know that?" A floury streak remained on one of his cheeks. "Forget I ever doubted you."

I placed raw biscuits onto a baking sheet and folded the excess dough over itself to cut again. From the other room, Yael's voice drifted into the kitchen, carrying his storybook to our ears: ". . . they called him the—that word, Mom?—a natural, for never had a man joined the Ma-Mar . . . Marauders who fought so well and so f . . . fearlessly. When C-Captain Boots died, the crew chose Old Nat . . . the bravest of them all . . . to be the new captain of their crew." I smiled. Yael, I thought, would make a good pirate captain.

The biscuits all cut and ready for baking, Rollie slid the tray into the oven. I noticed how smooth the work came to him, how quickly he stepped into the helping role, and I wondered if he cooked dinner regularly. "All done. Those should be ready in about fifteen."

"I had no idea you could bake," I said, leaning back against the counter. "You're quite the homemaker."

"Don't speak too soon. You haven't tasted them yet."

"Rollie?" Yael called from the other room. "Can she meet Dragonfly?"

The question was strange enough that I looked to Rollie for an answer. "Who's Dragonfly?"

"That's Yael's goat. Here, follow me." Rollie led me back into the hallway, where I caught Yael's grinning eye from the sofa.

"Wait for me," the boy piped. "I want to come with you."

Delaney, though her brow creased ever so slightly, smiled at her youngest son and nodded. "Off you go, then."

In response, Yael maneuvered his legs gingerly off the couch, paused a minute in a sitting position, then rose to his full four-foot frame. "Come on," he beckoned, plodding past me. "You'll love Dragonfly. She's a hoot."

I exchanged a glance with Rollie, who nodded in affirmation. "She's the favorite child."

Following Yael out a back door into a grassy backyard, I spotted the goat tethered to a post beside the house. She was all white across her body except for some brown spots on her side and cream-colored splotches along her nose and ears. Her immediate area looked picked clean of all vegetation, only a circle of packed earth where grass probably once grew. Seeing Yael, the goat released a long curious bleat.

"Hey, Dragonfly," greeted the boy to the goat. "Lookin' good today. Have you lost weight? This is Rollie's friend, Cass. Don't be scared. She's really nice."

Stepping forward, I crouched by the goat and extended one hand for her to sniff. Her lips tickled my palm. "Hi there, Dragonfly. How are you doing today?"

For my answer, the animal side-stepped a bit and let out a few more bleats. I turned to look over my shoulder at Rollie. "She's cute. I've never seen a real goat before."

"Don't they have goats in the city?" he asked with a smirk.

"They're not exactly plentiful," I said. With my eyes off the goat, I began to feel a tugging on the bottom of my shirt. "Hey, what—"

"Uh oh, watch out," Yael exclaimed. Dragonfly had come close and was nibbling on my clothes. I jumped in surprise. The movement made me lose my balance. I lurched backwards and landed on my backside in the dirt. Yael scared the goat off with a wild motion, to which she bleated out a number of complaints but released my shirt before any damage was done. I regarded the crumpled, saliva-stained patch of fabric with a laugh growing in my belly.

Yael planted hands on his hips and shook his head. "She'll do that if you're not careful. I bet she's hungry. I'll go inside and get her some food." He paced back inside the house, closing the door behind him, and Rollie sauntered to my side, clucking his tongue.

"Rookie mistake. Goats are crazy about clothes."

"Well—" I dropped the soiled hem. "I know that now."

Rollie offered me a hand to help me up. Instinctively, I took it. His palm was rough and calloused. I hardly had time to register the fact before he hauled me to my feet with one strong pull. I landed close to him. We stood nearly at eye level, a realization I hadn't much noticed before but now registered along with a burst of fluttering in my stomach.

Oh no, not that again.

Vertigo. That had to be it. Yes. From jumping up too fast.

Rollie released my hand quickly, and I took a step back. *There*, I thought, brushing dirt off my jeans. If he didn't want to hold my hand longer than necessary, I couldn't care less. Tahlia didn't know what she was talking about.

Still, my fingers enjoyed the memory of his grasp.

Rollie cleared his throat. "Yael got her about a year ago," he said, and I had to remember we hadn't left the subject of the goat. "She came from the Murphy farm on the other side of town. Do you know them yet?"

"The Murphys. No. Can't say I do."

"She's been a godsend for Yael," he continued, his eyes fixed on the animal. "Gives him something to take care of. Something to distract him." Rollie chuckled. "Maybe the goat is more a godsend for the rest of us, actually."

Yael had not yet returned from the house. I took advantage of the opportunity to ask, "If you don't mind . . . what is his sickness, anyway?" I kept my voice low so as not to be overheard.

"Hemolytic anemia." Rollie squinted at me, his pupils dilated by the light of the setting sun so the hazel irises stood out more than ever. "It's autoimmune. Citrine thinks he developed it as a baby."

I knew about anemia, of course. The disease worked by confusing the body's immune system. Then the body would start attacking a person's own red blood cells as if they were a foreign substance. The reaction could cause fatigue, weakness, even discoloration of the skin and heart murmurs. "I'm so sorry. He doesn't seem sick, really," I said, hoping I hadn't upset him. "I've never seen a more confident kid."

"He carries it well," Rollie replied. The muffled sound of Yael's voice just beyond the door alerted us both, and Rollie dropped his volume so that his next words were only between us. "I keep wishing it were me instead. That I could take it from him, you know? He's braver than I would be."

I wanted to tell him it was pointless to think like that. Wishing for something so out of his control would only bring more grief. But that seemed callous. Besides, Rollie couldn't actually believe he was capable of taking his brother's sickness upon himself. No—he was not so illogical. Yet those impossible notions, I knew, were the stuff of late nights alone in bed, staring at the ceiling, wondering whether life might have dealt a different hand if somehow you had been better. I was all too familiar with the back-alley grunge of speculation—those ashen doubts which collected in layers upon the soul until morning when they were brushed off and traded for responsibilities. Logic didn't penetrate there.

And so I didn't say any of that. Lots of good it was sure to do anyway. The story Yael read to his mother came to mind. I found myself thinking out loud. "He's like Old Nat," I said.

"Who?"

"From the story. The pirates. Only the bravest of them all was fit to be captain. That's like Yael, huh?"

At that exact moment, the boy pushed through the wire screen door with a thick handful of carrots at his side. He held up the treat with pride. "Look what I got, girl!"

Rollie gave me a simple smile, the kind that spoke loads beyond what could be conveyed in a single look. He accepted a portion of the carrots from his brother, handed me several, and crouched to pat Dragonfly's head while she nibbled the vegetables from his palm. The screen door creaked again. It was Delaney. She called us in to dinner and stood over Yael's shoulder at the sink to ensure he used soap to wash the goat smell off his hands. We ate the hot biscuits with white gravy and sausage.

After dinner, Rollie walked me home again. I carried cookies from Delaney on a plate with plastic wrap. We said goodnight to the sound of crickets chirping, their sounds amplified by sheer numbers.

The woods creaked out a slow cadence on the edge of town. Far into the trees, John Brown would be working his conspiracy theories, all in an effort to undermine Sommer Day. Maybe he was only a crazy recluse after all. Maybe Day had a point. Maybe enough people suffered in the world that I ought to prevent whatever amount of pain I could. Sure, the circumstances weren't perfect—Day was manipulative, and her reasoning was flawed—but was her ultimatum much worse than what the rest of the world had to offer? Don't we all live our lives trying to make the best of the imperfect situations which surround us?

I looked up. Far above, Cassiopeia glinted in her inky expanse. Silent, distant, and entirely unhelpful. If I were looking for answers, none appeared immediately forthcoming.

"Why am I even asking you? It's not like you made all that many great decisions."

I went inside and locked the door.

CHAPTER 19

"This one's too tight." I smoothed blush pink satin along my abdomen, hating the way it hugged my hips and flared at my knees into a tail-like cascade reaching the floor. Walking—not to mention *dancing*—would be a nightmare.

"That's how it's supposed to be," Andie reassured. She stood behind me, both of us staring at my figure in the full-length mirror of the dress shop. Andie convinced me to spend the afternoon searching for a gown to wear to the school dance. The event was a week from now. According to Andie, we were barely skating the edge of having enough time. I didn't argue. We had decided on a small boutique in Honora, one of the outer sectors geographically close enough to the nation's interior to stock a wider range of dresses than those offered in the countryside.

"Well, it's too fancy, then. I can't wear this to the dance."

"Dress shopping isn't about looking for the right dress," my sister insisted. "It's about the experience. When Mom and I shopped for my school dances, I think I tried on two dozen dresses or more. You should have fun."

"But I don't want to try on two dozen dresses."

Andie huffed and helped me out of the pink sausage casing. She left me in the dressing room while I peeled the rest of the dress off and replaced its hanger.

"Here me out on this one," Andie called from beyond the curtain. She stuck her hand through just enough for me to hand her the pink gown, which she then exchanged for something emerald green and strappy.

"Seriously?" I complained. "Who do you think I am?"

"It's *cute*, Cass! At least try it on."

The green fabric fit looser than the pink, but I still frowned at the sleek, tantalizing style. I turned every which way, trying to find an angle from which I didn't look like a string of seaweed. "Can't you find me something . . . less slippery?"

"Less slippery," Andie repeated in a dead tone.

I groaned. "Think less black-tie and more high school dance."

"How are you supposed to know what people wear to school dances? You've never been."

"Well, I have seen what rich old ladies wear to the theater to make themselves feel better, and I'm not leaving the house looking like one of *them*."

My sister threw one hand in the air in the melodramatic way I'd grown used to. While she disappeared once more behind the racks of dresses, I shifted inside the green gown and imagined myself meeting Rollie like this. The thought scared me so bad I called out to Andie to please hurry up.

"Okay, okay, I'm coming. How about this one?"

The dress was midnight blue. A tingle ran through my toes when I first saw it. This dress was shorter than the others. Knee-length. A full ruffled skirt met a wide waistband and starry speckled bodice. The whole piece appeared to have rivulets of light running through the fabric. *Like comets*, I thought. *Like stars and comets.*

The logical side of my brain told me it was just a dress. Fabric and thread and beads. Nothing to get worked up about.

The other side of my brain wanted to kick logic to the curb, because this was the most beautiful dress I'd ever seen in my entire life. I took the gown into the dressing room to try on. Andie was waiting for me beside the mirrors when I came out. She looked me up and down, something unidentifiable in her expression. "What?" I asked, worried. "Does it look bad?"

She ushered me forward without saying a word. I positioned myself in front of the mirrors. A flutter went through me. "*Oh*," I breathed.

It was not like the ladies' theatre dresses. I looked ready to either run a mile or attend an event at the Kennecott Art Center in Meridian. The skirt hit barely above my knees, and it sprayed out from my waist in puffed multi-hued pleats. The top was a little loose on my small chest. I'd have to get it taken in. I smoothed my hands along the fabric. Stars came to mind once again. If the night sky had an earthly embodiment, this dress would be it.

"Beautiful, Cass," Andie said from behind. I caught her eye in the mirror. She looked impressed as much as I felt enchanted. "Is that the one?"

"I like it. It needs to be altered." I fingered the excess fabric along the top.

Andie turned me around, pulling the neckline tighter at various places. "You're right. But not by much. It's almost perfect as it is." She stepped back, and a misty sheen entered her eyes.

"What are you doing? Don't cry. Stop it. Don't be weird."

"Oh, relax." Andie pulled herself together. "I just never thought today would happen. I can't believe it."

I stood in my dress, arms limp by my sides. What she meant was clear enough; I didn't need any more explanation. She meant Mom and Dad. She meant my move to Meridian. Frankly, there had been days when I wondered whether I would ever see her again either. Those shared experiences sisters should look forward to, frivolous things like school dances, disappeared from my radar at a young age. But I'd never considered how Andie felt. Had she regretted our lost time? Did she miss the memories we never made together?

I hugged her. At first, she seemed surprised. Then she squeezed me back.

"Thank you," I mumbled, my chin against her shoulder.

"For what?"

"Everything."

"All right, all right, that's enough." Andie held me by the shoulders and pushed me back to look at the dress once more. "I like it." She signaled an attendant, who walked over to us.

"Do you offer in-house alterations?"

"We do," said the employee. He took my measurements and stuck a few pins in the fabric along my neckline and shoulders. I went off to change back into my jeans and t-shirt. I couldn't stop running my fingers through the full skirt, twirling this way and that in the privacy of the dressing room. I regretted finally having to take it off.

With the blue gown draped over one arm, I found Andie speaking with the same attendant from earlier at the checkout counter. The man stated a number somewhere in the low hundreds, and Andie paid the amount before I could protest.

"What did you do that for? I have plenty of money. I don't need you to pay for my things."

"C'mon, Cass. Let me do this *one* thing for you, okay?" Andie took the dress from me and handed it to the attendant over the counter. "We'll come pick it up on Wednesday. That should give us a few days before the dance in case there are any problems with the alterations."

I wanted to be mad at her, but that was difficult when I was already so excited. The most beautiful dress in the world belonged to me. I could hardly contain myself. Nothing else in the world mattered in that moment, not even Sommer Day and all her schemes. Everything was perfect. Absolutely perfect.

I should have known it wouldn't last.

***

John Brown cornered me in the bakery again on Monday. Why did he always choose the bakery?

"Psst, Genius. Over here."

There I was, bread in hand, trying to decide between a loaf of cranberry orange and honey wheat. I looked towards the source of the voice. Brown wore a baseball cap and sunglasses—the stereotypical undercover image. I placed both loaves back on the shelf and hissed back at him, "What are you doing here? And what's with the sunglasses? For crying out loud, it's raining outside."

Per usual, the man ignored me. "You went to see Day, didn't you?"

I held my ground. "So what if I did? Someone needed to act. Turns out, I might be able to stop Day from hurting more people just like Jeremy, and to me, that sounds a whole lot better than sitting in a hut in the woods spying on people. Now, if you'd excuse me. I'm a bit busy."

Brown snatched off his sunglasses, his eyebrows morphing angrily into one furry entity. "Don't you realize what you've done? You've damned us all!"

"Calm *down*," I spat, pressing a finger to my lips and glancing around us. "From the sound of things, you were already damned to begin with. Day knows who you are. You're not fooling anybody. At least I'm being realistic."

"What did she tell you?"

"Yeah, right." I turned away from him. I'd just get the cranberry loaf. Andie might complain, but we had honey wheat last week.

"Hey, genius. Have you considered that she might be lying to you? Who says she'll even make true on her side of the agreement?"

"My chances with you aren't any better. You approached me out of nowhere, followed me around, violated my privacy, and now you expect me to believe whatever you say? You won't even tell me who you are!"

Brown worked his jaw back and forth as if seriously contemplating this. He flicked dust off the packaging of a dozen English muffins. "If I tell you, you will reconsider aligning with Day?"

I folded my arms. "No promises. But it would make me a lot more inclined to listen to you."

The man sighed deeply, gruffly. He claimed a chair near the window, motioning for me to do the same, and glared at the floor for a full sixty seconds before speaking. "It was my fifth deployment. My third in Africa. The Heritage Wars had just started, and my unit was stationed near a village in the northeast. We kept a number of drones on standby for patrols and the like, all Empress Industries models." He inhaled long and slow before continuing. "One day, my men found a group of village children playing at the edge of camp. A drone had been left unattended, not properly secured, and the kids got hold of it. My men came on the scene just as the drone powered on, initiated attack procedure, and started firing."

Cold seeped into my veins. "The kids . . . ?"

"None were hit. Thank heaven. The little squirts know how to run. One of my soldiers took fire, but he recovered. My problem with Empress was not over the drone itself. Accidents happen. Mindless, yes—but still an accident. When Empress gave their report, their solution was to blame the enemy, to paint the villagers as guerilla insurgents. Day preserved her good name, feds pumped our division with funding, and by the time the smoke of battle cleared, Empress staked claim to one of the richest resource deposits on this planet or otherwise."

I didn't know what to say. What words could possibly fit such a gaping need? If Day really was the one who covered up the deaths of Sagittarius and Amalthea in the media, then an account from Brown along these same lines was not unbelievable.

"Is that when you left?" I asked.

"That was when I realized there was a greater evil to fight. I learned more over the next couple years—heard the rumors, read between the lines. Sensed what was coming. Finally, I decided I couldn't do what I needed to do while still a service member, so yes, I left."

I remembered what Letty had said about foreign dignitaries at Day's vacation home. While getting information out of Jeremey proved to be impossible, maybe I would learn something useful from Brown.

"You say you heard rumors. What kind of rumors? Anything about Day conspiring with foreign leaders?" I asked.

The man sniffed. "It's all part of her plan. She never intended to stop with this Senate seat, you know. Getting the world's most powerful rulers on her side—that was just the start. She's been buying them off for years. You can't do what she wants to do without neutralizing all the Republic's allies first."

"What do you mean, part of her plan? I thought the neurochips were her plan. All these unsanctioned human trials—I thought they were just her way of making money without all the steps in between."

"Oh, no. The neurochips are only a step. Day wants control more than anything. Control, control, control. That's all. And what's the best way to be in control? Set up your own country."

I sat back in my seat with a *thump*. "You can't be serious."

"Do I look like I'm joking to you?" He raised a tufted brow. "I've lived a long time trying to piece these things together. Trust me when I say it's been going on much longer than you think. Day wants her own Republic, and she's got enough people on her side now to just maybe make it possible."

I thought this through. To arrive at this conclusion from such ambiguous beginnings was definitely a stretch. Just because Day met with foreign leaders didn't mean she was plotting the nation's overthrow. I couldn't believe it without further proof.

"All right. You left the service because you had to do something about it. What exactly was it you needed to do?"

"I doubt your new buddy Sommer would approve."

The nerve. I threw my best imitation of Grandam's dagger eyes his way.

Brown half-smirked in response, and it only incensed me further. "In a way, my purpose is still the same today as it was all those years ago. To put down tyranny wherever it arises. I knew Day would never settle as long as there was more power to be had. She'd already won over the media. No journalist could touch her. It was only a matter of time before we passed the point of no return. So, I began subverting Day wherever and whenever I can. Maybe I'll slow her down. Maybe not. All that matters is someone will have stood up to her."

"I don't get it," I protested. "If Empress is so inevitable, why not make the best of it? The more you fight, the more people she hurts to get what she wants. Isn't it better to make it stop?"

"No," said Brown emphatically. "No, you don't understand. It's never going to stop. Not ever. Because life under tyranny guarantees nothing. There *will* be pain—death, even—at the hands of those in power. You have to understand. Life under coercion can never compare to death in liberty. *That* is why fighting is the only choice. It's always been the only choice."

I sat still in my seat, at a loss, overwhelmed.

Brown's chair made a shrill scraping across the bakery floor as he rose to his feet. "Sommer Day is no philanthropist, kid. She's not even your average cutthroat CEO. Do you know why she needed the Senate seat so badly? It's because she intends to take it all. Everything. Every last city, sector, house, home, and human in this nation. Don't let her fool you. Those neurochips aren't for any good. She has plans. And if you play into her game, mark my words. You're going to lose."

CHAPTER 20

He arrived in a quadruple-rotary hovercraft ten minutes before their scheduled meeting. The turbines had yet to power completely down when he exited the craft; the resultant hurricane whipped at his tie and snatched his hair in a dozen directions until he took shelter in the rooftop elevator. While the elevator descended, he tended to his disheveled appearance. His checkered button-down—red today—had acquired a number of wrinkles from the flight. It wasn't ideal for a meeting with the company president, but it would have to do. He ran fingers through his golden brown hair to tame the spots beaten chaotic by the propellors.

The elevator opened with a chime. He navigated the maze of hallways easily. At eighteen now, he'd traveled these same corridors for enough years to know them by heart. It took him only a few minutes to reach the conference room. A scan of his watch provided clearance for entry.

"Ah, Leo. Welcome. As usual, you are right on time. Please have a seat."

"President Day." Leo nodded a greeting before claiming a chair around the elliptical conference table. Half a dozen others filled the room. Over the next few minutes, more trickled in and occupied the remaining seats. Only two of the attendees were over the age of twenty: President Day and Dr. Kyzer Berberich, Head of the Aerospace Division. All the rest were Leo's age or younger, the youngest being a fifteen-year-old girl whose hairstyle mimicked the president's almost to exactness.

Unnerving. He didn't care for it.

President Day began the meeting with a review of last month's minutes, presented by one of the younger teenage boys in the room. She then asked each attendee to share an update on their work within the division. Each had more or less identical reports: Deep space travel. Was it viable? Countless failed prototypes would suggest not. Incineration. Disintegration. Implosion. Explosion. Vaporization. Plain old systems failure. On the other hand, what about this new theory . . . ?'

When it came Leo's turn to report, he shared minimal details about his project in quantum aeromechanics. These accounting sessions always bored him to tears. The shorter he could make them, the better.

But President Day had something else in mind. "One more thing, Leo. How goes your special assignment at the university?"

He refused to make eye contact with anyone around the table but the president. He knew all his peers were jealous. A special assignment was enviable; it meant trust and favor on a higher plane than most could hope to achieve. Leo maintained his composure, though mention of the assignment roused a nagging frustration. "My position remains uncompromised. However, relations with the subject are . . ." he searched for the word, ". . . poor, at best. I have no new information to report." He might have added that the girl hadn't shown up at the university lab for some time. For a while, he'd begun to suspect she was on to him. But he doubted it. More than likely, the girl had become too preoccupied for the frequent trips. With what, he couldn't imagine. Wasn't she living in the outer sectors now? He nearly shuddered at the thought. Imagine living among such primitive people.

The president steepled her fingers on the tabletop, seeming deep in thought. "I see. How many times have you made contact with the subject?"

"Only three times."

"Ah. Perhaps your efforts would best be utilized elsewhere. The initial report you provided fulfilled our primary objective well enough. Consider yourself released."

As the next attendee began their generic review, Leo thought about the girl with long, dark hair. How obstinate she had seemed, barely speaking a word to him, behaving like he was nothing more than gum on the bottom of her shoe. Just the recollection infuriated him. No one had ever treated him with such indifference.

One thing was for certain: he would be glad never to see her again.

At the conclusion of the meeting, President Day requested Leo's presence in her office in fifteen minutes. Of course, he agreed. It would be a prime opportunity to pitch the Aerospace Division's newest prototype proposal. He entered the office at her command and stood with his back to the crystalline double doors while she finished a video call with the Director of Public Relations, Ashcroft March, who was away overseas meeting with foreign dignitaries. Leo was surprised she didn't keep him waiting outside until the end of the call, but he took it as a good sign. Every positive action with the president counted as a win for himself. True, he'd garnered more favor with the president than any student-employee in the program and enjoyed the notoriety of being within her closest circle of associates, but a bit of extra merit never hurt.

President Day ended her call with Director March and breathed a long sigh. "Thank you for your patience. Do you have something for me to sign?"

Leo presented the proposal. She flipped briefly through the folder, and Leo noticed her eyes barely skimmed the pages. "Very good. Your team has my permission to proceed." She signed her name across the front of the proposal in hurried script.

"Thank you, President. If I may ask, are you feeling well?"

She nodded. "Perceptive of you to ask. Yes, I am quite well. I believe I have a favor to ask of you. It's why I've called you here. It concerns the girl in Meridian—Cassiopeia."

Just the thought of her made his blood pressure rise. "Yes?"

"I'm afraid she has taken advantage of my leniency for too long. She exhausts me. My sources tell me she is sympathizing with that pathetic agitator again, and I'll have no more of it. Please arrange a meeting with Dr. Porter from the chemistry department. Say, 4:00 this afternoon."

Leo bristled somewhat at being treated like her personal secretary, but of course he remained compliant. It wouldn't be long before he left Empress behind for good. Not long before he could function out from under the president's thumb. "Certainly, President. And what should I tell Dr. Porter this meeting is about?"

Day was already moving on to the next item on her agenda. She waved one hand in dismissal. "Tell him we're conducting a field test for his division."

CHAPTER 21

The day of the dance arrived.

I almost laughed at the flawless blue sky, the mild breeze which drew warm air through the house's open windows and turned the curtains to flowing angel's wings with every breath.

"This is ridiculous. I'm not going. Tell Rollie I ran away to be a hand model in Galanta."

"Fat chance. I bought that dress for you. You're going."

The morning came and went, followed by an afternoon too fast for my liking. Andie made me start getting ready two hours before Rollie was supposed to arrive. She insisted on curling my hair too.

"I haven't curled my hair in years," I complained as I sat in front of the bathroom mirror, Andie looming above me with hot iron in hand. "Swear you won't go crazy with it. I don't want to look like a poodle."

She screwed her face up in the mirror. "Who do you think I am? Honestly," she added under her breath and ran a brush over my head. I sat compliantly while each long straight strand was wound around the curler and released as a delicate wave. I refused any product besides a spritz of spray to keep the curls in place. Thankfully, Andie didn't wear much makeup. I got away with only a layer of lip gloss and some slight color on my cheeks.

Fifteen minutes before Rollie arrived, I put on my dress. The gown had the same effect as it did in the store. The girl staring back from my reflection wasn't the awkward science nerd I'd come to expect when I looked in the glass. This time, she was beautiful.

I paced to the dresser. Pursed my lips. Then I picked up Rollie's necklace and fastened it around my neck. My dark strands framed the crystal pendant, melted into the fabric of the midnight dress, and settled just above the waistband. The diamond sequins scattered across the skirt matched the necklace perfectly. I thought of Cassiopeia, the queen in the constellations. For the first time in my life, I thought we might have something in common.

I made my way downstairs. As I entered the kitchen, Andie looked me up and down. She smiled. Relief swept over me. I hadn't realized how much I'd been hoping for her approval. "Good," she said. "What shoes are you going to wear?"

The thought hadn't crossed my mind. I only had three pairs of shoes, and none of them seemed appropriate for a formal occasion. "I'll probably just wear my sneakers," I replied eventually.

"Oh, no. You can't wear sneakers with that dress. It'll ruin the whole thing."

My relief from earlier evaporated. "Well, you should have thought about it earlier. It's a little late now to go shopping."

Andie began chewing a nail furiously. "You don't wear the same size as me. You can't borrow any of mine." She said it to herself more than me.

Zinnie rose from her seat the kitchen table, a trembling finger poised in the air. She shuffled from the room one labored step at a time. When she returned, she carried a dusty shoebox in both hands.

"What's that, Zinnie?"

In response, she placed the box on the table, blew at the dust a bit, and set aside the lid. Folded tissue paper obscured the contents. She then removed a pair of low jeweled heels.

I was speechless. "Oh, Zinnie. I couldn't wear these. They're too beautiful."

The woman nodded emphatically, guided me to a chair, and placed the heels in my hands. When she spoke, her voice was stronger than I'd ever heard it before. "I wore these to my brother's wedding fifty years ago. I want you to have them." She patted my arm with a degree of finality.

Sitting, I tried the shoes on for size. Nearly a perfect fit. The kind gesture took my breath away. I was about to thank her when a knock sounded at the door. I jumped, startled. It was him; he was here. My heart was going to explode—I was sure of it. Andie began shoving me in the direction of the staircase. "Get upstairs. Hurry."

I struggled to gain my footing in the unfamiliar shoes. "Wait, I—"

"Move it!"

She shooed me up the steps, and I had no choice but to obey. As soon as I reached the landing, I heard the front door open. My sister's voice traveled up to me. "Well, hello! It's so nice to meet you. Rollie, isn't it? I'm Andie, Cass's sister. I think she's still upstairs getting ready. Why don't you come in?"

There was the sound of footsteps on the hardwood. My breathing was ragged. I pressed my hands to my chest, hoping to still the nervous spasms that racked my body. I was already sweating under my arms. Oh, what if this whole thing was a disaster?

"Cass, Rollie is here," Andie called from below. "Whenever you're ready."

I'd never be ready in a million years. But I couldn't stay up here forever. Not after promising Rollie, and certainly not after Zinnie's tender act of generosity. I inhaled deeply and forced slow, steady breaths out through my mouth. *You can do this. It's only Rollie. You can do this . . .*

Somehow my feet found the courage to move. I grasped the handrail and descended each step with precision. Tripping would do me no good now. As I reached the bottom and came around the corner, I met eyes with Rollie and my sister where they stood talking in the entryway.

". . . Wow," said Rollie. A smile spread across his face. "You look amazing."

He wore a plain blue button-down and slacks. His hair, normally shaggy across his forehead, had been gelled and combed back. I felt myself blushing. "Thanks. You don't look bad yourself."

A beat of awkward silence ensued. Andie leaned against the wall, arms folded, looking like she was enjoying herself far too much. Could she be *any* more obvious? I cleared my throat. "Well, should we get going?" I asked. "Don't want to be late." I stepped towards the door.

"There's no rush. Don't you want to stay and talk a while?" Andie looked innocent, but I could have throttled her.

"I don't think Rollie wants to stay and talk, Andie. Let's go," I urged, my hand on the doorknob.

"Wait! One last thing. Let me get a picture of you two." My sister walked briskly from the room and returned holding a camera. "Get in close. There you go. 1 . . . 2 . . . 3. Perfect!"

"*Andie*," I prompted through gritted teeth.

"Fine, fine. I'm done. Go have fun. Don't stay out too late."

It was a miracle we got out at all. Rollie and I strode down the front walk, then turned towards the school road. Neither of us spoke for a time. I was so busy forcing myself to breathe normally that conversation wasn't high on my priority list.

"I have a confession to make," said Rollie at last.

"Oh really? What kind of confession?"

"An embarrassing one."

"Good. It should be refreshing not to be the only one embarrassing myself tonight."

Rollie smirked beside me. "You have nothing to be embarrassed about. Trust me. Okay then. Here it is . . . I can't remember the last time I wore a shirt with buttons."

Before I could stop myself, I let out a snort. "That's your embarrassing confession? With a buildup like that, I was expecting something juicier."

"What can I say? I'm just a boring guy. I like my days simple and my shirts button-free."

We turned onto the unpaved school road. Zinnie's heels, even low as they were, were no match for the slippery gravel surface. It made our progress painfully slow. Rollie saw my struggle and offered his back. I declined immediately. The idea sounded preposterous.

"C'mon, give it a shot." He stopped, crouched, and held his arms out to the side as if bracing for a tackle. The image was comical enough that I laughed, but I couldn't bring myself to actually agree. No, I insisted we keep walking, though the heels sunk and skid with every uncoordinated step.

The walk took us longer than usual. Big surprise. Light poured from the school windows as we neared. Rollie said we'd meet Tahlia and the others inside—that they were probably already here.

As we approached the entrance, I grabbed Rollie's arm. "Wait."

We stopped just before the steps. I felt his eyes on me, expectant. "What is it?" he asked.

"I-I'm nervous."

He shrugged. "Me too."

"Are you kidding? That's not like you at all."

"No? You must not know me as well as you thought."

Still, I hesitated, but Rollie took my hand and adjusted my grip on his arm, wrapping my fingers just above his elbow. Now he was my escort. A spark of warmth thawed my fear enough to go on.

Double doors opened into the gym, where streamers coated the ceiling like pastel stripes on a cake and balloons scattered across the floor wove themselves among the feet of students in various stages of socialization. Music played over the speakers. It was a song I'd never heard before, fast-paced and loud. As soon as we entered, a wave of embarrassment washed over me, and I clutched Rollie's arm tighter.

"Hey," he said, turning to face me. "Don't worry. Forget everyone else. Let's just have fun tonight."

I took a deep breath and nodded.

Near the north end of the gym, we spotted Nash, Venetia, Dangelo, and Tahlia. Evie danced with a red-haired boy I didn't recognize. Rollie and I walked their way. Tahlia gasped upon seeing me and abandoned Dangelo to embrace me with the force of an avalanche. Holding me by the shoulders, she fawned over my dress. "You look so beautiful, Cass! That color is perfect on you!" Her own dark pink gown glittered under the gym's colored lights. I enjoyed a bit of satisfaction seeing it on her, knowing the part Harlow and I had played in its selection. While Rollie stepped away to greet Nash and Dangelo, Evie introduced me to the red-haired boy. She reminded me of a fairy with her simple green dress and long dark braid cascading down one shoulder.

"C'mon," Tahlia prompted. "Let's see if the city girl can dance."

"I don't know what I'm supposed to do," I confessed. Dancing was heretofore uncharted territory for me.

"It's easy. Like this." Tahlia grabbed my hands and started swinging me in circles. I let out an alarmed shriek that quickly dissolved into unrestrained howls of laughter as the world spun off its axis. Tahlia let go, and I careened into Rollie. He caught me around the waist. His hands were strong and steadying but gentle too. I stepped away. I could already feel my face growing hot.

"Hey, Rollie," said Nash. "Show us those famous dance moves." Nash himself did some odd thing with his knees and swung his arms like windmills. Tahlia bust up laughing. Venetia groaned and hid her face.

"Funny thing," said Rollie. "I can't seem to remember any of them. Must have slipped my mind."

A new song came over the speakers, and Tahlia squealed with excitement. "I love, love, love this song! Dangelo, dance with me."

"How are you supposed to dance to something like this? It's not even a slow song," Dangelo protested. He wore a gray dress shirt with a pink tie he must have bought solely for this occasion.

"Like Nash. See? Just have fun!"

While Tahlia tried enticing her date to dance, Rollie and I exchanged a look.

I shrugged. He shrugged back.

We interpreted the action as a sign of mutual confirmation.

So we copied Tahlia's movements as best we could, and before long, the music had coated everything with a sort of ecstatic numbness. I can't remember when we forgot to keep our walls up. There was just the music. The smiles and the laughs. I thought it was a little like magic. Except . . . that wasn't quite right. Magic wasn't as real as this. It didn't make me feel this way inside, like the center of fireworks exploding in the night or a circuit bursting with electricity.

Then the music morphed into something slower and softer. I realized what it meant as my nerves returned full force. Nash pulled Venetia close to him, and Tahlia took Dangelo's outstretched hand, and Red-Haired Boy stood uncomfortably still until Evie placed his hands around her waist and demonstrated the right way to move his feet.

"Can I show you something?" Rollie asked me.

"Show me what?"

"Just follow me. That's the point of showing you, not telling you, isn't it?"

My nerves were bad enough to send the joke straight over my head, and I only blinked in response. "Okay, fine." We left the gym out a side door that someone had propped open to let a cool breeze inside. I was grateful for the escape. I could breathe easier out here. A crescent moon glowed overhead, the sky around it a creamy inky blue. Shadows lay silently just beyond the illumination cast by the gym's open door. Rollie led me into those shadows. Away from the artificial light. We could still hear the music, but now the darkness engulfed us. And with the darkness came the stars—dazzling and endless and alive.

Rollie stopped us. "Watch this." Moonlight highlighted just half of his face, but it was enough for me to catch the impish look he gave me before tilting his head back and pointing up at the sky. "Ursa Major."

I followed Rollie's gaze to the constellation he indicated. Ursa Major. The famous conglomeration of stars resembling a giant ladle in space. It was perhaps most famous of all the constellations. In fact, most people knew it by its informal moniker, the Big Dipper. That Rollie had learned its real name was mildly impressive. But if this was his big reveal—if the thing he wanted to show me consisted of identifying this one popular constellation—well, I didn't want to embarrass him by underreacting.

"That's great!" I said, a little too forcefully.

Rollie laughed. "I wish you could see your face right now. Don't worry. That's not all." He extended his arm, pointing to one heavenly being after another. "Hercules . . . Draco . . . Cepheus . . . Ursa Minor . . ." Starlight flashed across his features with each quarter turn of his body, light and dark, glinting off his eyes for one moment, then plunging him into shadow the next. "Taurus . . . Perseus . . . Gemini . . . Orion." Some made him pause longer than others. I ticked each off in my head for accuracy, a smile sneaking higher on my face with each constellation he named. Rollie bit his lip and faltered with his finger in the air. Looking uncertain, he turned to me. "I think that one's the moon?"

I hummed in thought. "You would be correct."

"I knew it." His arm dropped back to his side.

The song from the gym reached a crescendo. Soft music swept around us, prodding. I dropped my eyes, grateful for the cool air against my warming cheeks, and swallowed. "You learned the constellations." I felt simultaneously touched and proud of him for the tiny feat that carried so much meaning. "A-plus, Mr. Waverly."

He shrugged. "I'm sure you could name a dozen more."

"Not necessarily. I could tell you about their chemistry, but I'm not an expert on the names." The music swelled again. The feelings it sparked inside me were terrifying and tantalizing all at once. We should dance, right? I could ask him to dance. If only I had the nerve. If only my palms weren't growing moist with each second I stood here debating. I tried rubbing my hands along the polyester tulle of my skirt. The fabric was useless—not absorbent in the least.

"Y-You didn't find Cassiopeia," I stammered.

Rollie didn't look back at the sky. He didn't search for the five-star outline of the ancient queen on her throne. Instead, he met my gaze. "Actually, I already did."

The smell of him drifted close. I took in fresh lavender and aftershave. They were smells I'd come to associate with his presence. They meant safety, warmth, friendship. His eyes, hazel in the daytime, were two exquisite pools now, deep and dark and inviting. I saw heaven's reflection on their surface. And my breath snagged in my throat as I realized that I'd never wanted anything so much as I did in this moment.

Him. I wanted him.

Rollie extended one hand to me, palm up. "May I have this dance?"

My answer hovered on my lips, tingling. I thought I could sense the whole world draw nearer, as if the stars themselves were leaning in to listen. I drew a shaky breath. "You may."

The climactic notes of a song far away washed over us like a caress. Rollie grasped my waist. Stepped towards me. His touch, his closeness, sent warmth through my limbs. I wrapped my arms around his neck.

Slowly, we danced. Everything else faded away.

Rollie raised his eyebrows, a comical look that could only precede a question. "You're quiet. You think I'm a bad dancer?"

"No. You're a wonderful dancer."

"You're just saying that."

"I wouldn't admit it if I was."

He chuckled. "And you told me you'd never danced before. I don't believe it."

"What we're doing is not exactly rocket science, Rollie." My voice sounded casual, which relieved me. I'd be mortified to betray my real feelings by accident. The dizziness that hit me fresh every time his hands shifted on my waist. Did he sense it? Could he read my mind by the look on my face? I didn't want him to know. I *did* want him to know.

Where my hands rested behind his head, I allowed my fingers to slide up just slightly, an inch above the starched shirt collar, to graze the back of his neck. His hair, though tamed with gel, remained its usual shaggy length in the back. I curled it in my fingertips.

"What are you thinking right now?" Rollie asked.

"That I'm happy. I've never been happier than this." It was bold for me to admit, but I didn't regret it. The stars were giving me courage tonight.

The song faded out to an end. It wasn't long enough, but I guess we both knew that when we started the dance late. Rollie suggested we rejoin the others inside, but I found myself not wanting to leave this moment. "Can we stay for just a few more minutes?" I asked. He agreed. So we remained outside, and we swayed to a song with a beat far too raucous for slow dancing. Somehow, I didn't care. I soaked in every pulse of our heartbeats between us, reveling in the fact that right now, there was only me, Rollie, and the infinite expanse of universe above us.

CHAPTER 22

Late into the night, Nash and Venetia were the first to suggest we head back. Tahlia had burned out her energy long ago. She'd removed her shoes and collapsed along the wall, exhausted. Evie roused her, and we made our way out the front entrance of the school.

"Talk about a party, am I right?" Nash slid down the center railing of the steps and stuck the landing. "What are we gonna do now? Pranks? Food? Skinny dipping?"

"How about going to sleep?" Tahlia rubbed one eye, leaving a smear of mascara on her cheek.

"Really? You guys are no fun," Nash complained.

"Maybe you're just insane," offered Rollie.

"*Ow!*" Dangelo slapped a hand to his neck. All attention turned to him.

"What's wrong?" Evie asked.

"I think something bit me. Ow!" This time he clutched his upper arm and began swatting at the air with his other hand.

Nash laughed. "Killer mosquitoes! Everybody watch out!"

Dangelo grit his teeth as if in pain. He rubbed intensely at the bite on his neck. "Don't be stupid. Feels like wasp stings. *Urrrgh*. It-it *burns*." He spun around, searching the air. I frowned. A tiny gray pinprick appeared at Dangelo's side, flying straight at the exposed flesh above his collarbone. He cursed at the new sting, swinging one hand wildly, but the pinprick vanished into the air. Dangelo began stumbling like a drunkard, and Nash's amused laugh faded abruptly.

"Danny?" Evie took a single step toward her brother.

Dangelo shook his head and held out a hand, swaying. "It's nothing. I'm fine."

"You don't look fine," said Nash.

"I'm—I'm—" His knees buckled, and Dangelo collapsed to the ground.

Evie shrieked. Nash lunged forward. Dangelo, sprawled on his back, was racked by jerks and spasms. His eyes rolled back in his head while the veins in his neck turned a sickly shade of purple. Evie repeated her brother's name, trying to protect Dangelo's thrashing head from the ground. Someone screamed. I didn't know who.

Time slowed. Struck by a flash of clarity, I realized I knew these symptoms. They indicated an extreme reaction to organophosphates, chemicals principally found in pesticides and rat poisons. In cases of chemical warfare, they were used to engineer nerve agents that could incapacitate a person in seconds.

But how? And why?

There was no time for answering questions.

Seconds. Dangelo had only seconds.

"Harlow. Get emergency responders here. Now," I ordered. Harlow responded with what must have been a confirmation, but I was already giving my next command. "Venetia." The girl's wide eyes snapped to mine, stunned and fearful. "Go inside. Get help. *Hurry*." I think I shouted the last word. Venetia was off like a bolt of lightning, her dress clenched in two fists around her knees as she raced up the stairs and back inside the school.

Atropine. Pralidoxime

The two chemicals capable of counteracting the poison. Dangelo needed them now. His convulsions were already beginning to slow. Emergency personnel wouldn't make it in time. No one would make it in time.

Think, think, think! I pummeled my temples with the heels of my hands. My feet followed Venetia's path into the school, moving of their own volition. Where was the main office from here? A musical uproar came from the gym down the hall, where students' biggest concern was not embarrassing themselves in front of their dates, rather than the horror unfolding just outside. They were oblivious to it all. Venetia had probably gone there for help.

I sprinted in the opposite direction of the gym, pounding out a frantic rhythm. The main office appeared down the hall. I reached the door and yanked on the knob. Locked.

I released an audible scream of frustration. There had to be a way in. I tried a kick under the doorknob, which led only to a jammed knee and still no open door. I turned my focus to the office window, then a wooden flagpole in one corner with a heavy metal base. "I'm sorry," I whispered, even as I set aside the staff and flag, hefted the base in both arms, and hurled it through the window like a discus.

Glass smashed into a million pieces. I covered my eyes. What used to be a window was now a gaping hole, large enough for me to fit through. Adrenaline gave me strength beyond my usual levels; I dragged a bench below the window and used it as a step to hoist myself through the gap. Shards of glass tore at my dress and skin. I could hardly feel the pain. Inside the office, a line of chairs served as my step down.

As soon as my feet hit the floor, I began searching for medical supplies. I found a room at the back of the office that looked promising. I dug through cabinets, discarding bottles left and right, searching for anything labeled atropine and pralidoxime. Nothing looked promising. My panic skyrocketed. There had to be something. Anything at all. Remembering that some medicines contained atropine for treating upper respiratory symptoms, I began sifting through an assortment of injection vials at the back of a cabinet. My heart soared when finally I read 'atropine' as one of the active ingredients. I snatched the vial in one fist and a syringe in the other and retreated back the way I'd come. Back through the broken window, down the hall, out the exit and down the steps. *Please, don't let it be too late*, I begged. *Please, please, please, please . . .*

Others had gathered around, students and adults both. They obstructed my view as I approached. From down the road, flashing lights came closer and closer.

"Let me through, let me *through*." I shoved through the human barrier. There on the gravel, someone performed chest compressions on Dangelo's immobile frame. His lips, tinged purple, were frozen an inch apart. His face had gone alarmingly slack. I fell to my knees next to him, ripping the syringe from its packaging and loading it with fluid from the vial. In one fluid motion, I plunged the needle into Dangelo's leg.

"What is that?"

I met Evie's tear-brimmed eyes. The pain in her voice was excruciating. Tahlia had her wrapped in an embrace, both of them kneeling like me, so I was close enough to see every raw emotion that crossed her face.

"It's medicine," I explained, softly, hopefully. Tears caught in my throat and distorted my voice. The words came out in a croak. I gritted my teeth and ducked my head, watching Dangelo's chest give way over and over again with each compression. I kept waiting for a change. As the compressions continued and the ambulance arrived, all with no sign of life, my worst fears sank in. I bit the back of my hand to stifle the growing hysteria. Evie continued to cry her brother's name, and Tahlia gripped her tighter. I shifted backwards until I found my feet. Blood trickled down my legs. I stared, confused, until I remembered the shattered window. Had it been all for nothing? Was I too late after all?

Reality began to settle in all its weight. Emergency responders—people I recognized from around the town—arrived at the scene. Citrine was among them. Some shouted commands to the crowd while others started work on Dangelo. I answered a man who asked me about the syringe. I explained my administration of the atropine, and that seemed sufficient for him because he returned to work with a nod. I retreated, trying not to get in the way.

I wanted to hope. Yet as more time passed, the truth became terrifyingly and undeniably clear. I recognized this gut feeling. I had experienced it in the lab many times. This was the feeling that said something wasn't right, that my calculations were off. It meant that problems were imminent. It meant failure.

My heartbeat raced. How could this happen? It was a nightmare. That's all it was. A terrible, terrible nightmare.

Rollie interrupted my downward spiral with his approach. I hadn't seen him much at all after Dangelo first collapsed. I wondered what he'd been doing. Rollie extended one hand to me, the palm up, holding something small. He said nothing. Uncertain, I looked closer and realized the thing was a tiny insect body with wings, only slightly larger than a mosquito. Except instead of the fleshy body of a mosquito, this thing was composed of miniscule wires and gray metal, with a centimeter-length needle extending from its abdomen. A drone. Albeit an extremely small one.

"There's more of them, dropped dead all around him." Rollie inclined his head in that direction. "Do you think . . . do you think someone . . . ?"

I said nothing. This could be no one else's handiwork but Day's. I stared at the tiny needle. Dread filled my stomach. I was going to be sick. "This is my fault," I whispered.

"What?"

"I-I need to tell you something. It's so hard to explain." My breaths came in shallow, rapid succession. "This is my fault. I did this."

Rollie's face was all confusion. "What are you talking about, Cass?"

I struggled to speak, managing only agonized silence and a shake of my head. Finally, words came, but they weren't coherent. "I-I couldn't . . . I thought . . . freedom . . ." Rollie tried to comfort me. I backed away. My tears burned hot with shame. How I wished I could disappear far away from here. Evie hunched over the body of her brother, crying uncontrollably. Watching her was torture. I couldn't handle it.

What I'd done . . . What I hadn't done . . .

It was unforgiveable.

PART 3

CHAPTER 23

Dull sounds of commotion drifted up from the hospital's bottom floor. I could discern no specific words, but I knew the conversations had to be about Dangelo. After trying unsuccessfully to restart his heart with the defibrillator, responders had transported Dangelo to the clinic via ambulance. I had gathered all the remaining mosquito droids. Not sure whether their needles still contained poison, I got Nash to give me one of his socks and wrapped them in the cotton. Speculation abounded as we had followed the ambulance to the hospital. On foot, there was plenty of time for theories and tears and expressions of disbelief. Rollie tried getting me to explain. "What did you mean it was your fault? Cass, please talk to me. It's *not* your fault." No matter how he pressed, I couldn't get over the horror of the possibility: that Day sent the drones as a message to me. A warning. I could almost hear her voice in my head. *See?* she said. *I warned you about this.*

And so I kept quiet despite Rollie's pleadings. We arrived at the clinic. Citrine was there, surrounded by all the paramedics who had responded to Harlow's emergency ping. They wore jeans and t-shirts for the most part. One even wore pajamas. In a town this size, I guessed that fulltime responders weren't financially possible. These people worked on an on-call basis. They'd come from their houses, maybe awoken from their beds, to respond to the emergency call about a boy who'd been poisoned. For some reason, this made me feel even more guilty.

Citrine let me inside because of my bleeding leg. The others weren't allowed in. Evie, as family, had ridden inside the ambulance with her brother. She was here now at the side of the room, sitting stoically beside her mother and father and slough of younger siblings. Their grief-stricken faces only cemented my remorse further. I followed Citrine to an empty bed, where I obediently did as she commanded and lay prostrate while she cleaned the deep gash left from the broken window. Numbly, I presented the sock and its contents to her and, as expected, was met with confusion. "Rollie found these around Dangelo's body," I explained. "It's where the poison came from." Her look of bewilderment was enough of a response. I lay back on the pillow, staring wordlessly at the ceiling. At some point she injected my leg with a local painkiller and stitched the wound closed before going off to speak with the Arroyo family. Wanting to be alone, I slipped off the bed while everyone was distracted and climbed the stairs to the library's upper floor. I now sat in an armchair, knees pulled up to my chest, lost in some kind of reverie of the despondent.

I received a message notification on my watch. The sender's contact information read 'Unknown,' but when I opened the communication, its source became clear.

We need to talk. – JB

JB? It must be Brown. I knew no one else by those initials. I wasn't even surprised that he had acquired my contact information. Whatever his means, I wasn't in the mood to chat with him right now.

Not a great time.

The voice-recognition turned my words into scrolling text and sent my reply into the ether. I curled up against the backrest, ready to sink once more into my depression, when another ping chimed out. I groaned. "Harlow, can you turn those off?"

"Um, this appears to be important. You might want to take a look," Harlow said. Sighing, I tapped open the message.

I know what happened to your friend.

Dangelo's last minutes were burned into my mind, and his death was all my fault. I was miserable as it was. I couldn't rehearse my guilt to this man.

I said it wasn't a good time. Interrogate somebody else.

She sent the bugs to kill your friend.

I grit my teeth, angry at his brazenness, disgusted at being called out so directly. I must have taken too long to respond because another message pinged through to my screen.

I told you not to trust her. You have to do what she asks. You have no choice anymore. For the good of everyone, you have to do what she says.

I sent an immediate reply this time:

It's over. You saw what she did to Dangelo.

It is not over. Day will not give up. Things will only get worse from here. Give her what she wants, or you are a danger to the rest of this community.

My breath caught in my lungs; Brown's words were a kick in the chest. It was true, of course. Brown had only stated the inevitable. I couldn't hide here in the clinic forever. Eventually, I'd have to confront reality.

Harlow tried to comfort me. "Cass, it's going to be all right, you know. What happened to Dangelo was not your fault. You can't blame yourself."

"It was my fault," I whispered. "I didn't give Day what she wanted. I was selfish."

Harlow paused. "But . . . you had no way to know."

"It happened though, didn't it? And if I don't go work for her now, it will happen again. Day will kill other people I love. Maybe Andie or Rollie will be next. I can't risk that."

"This isn't fair!" Harlow cried. "She can't do this to you!"

"Life isn't fair." I stood. A layer of gauzy disconnect had fallen over the world, and I looked around, unblinking, unseeing. I sent one final message to Brown:

I won't become one of them, will I?

A few seconds passed, and he replied.

You will keep as much of yourself as you refuse to let them take.

It was as good advice as any. I went downstairs, past the throng of people huddled around Dangelo's body, and walked home. The house felt unnaturally tranquil when I arrived, like getting onto an empty metro car after an especially hectic night at the theatre. Slow shuffling steps carried me to the kitchen. To my surprise, Zinnie was sitting at the kitchen table in her nightgown. She looked up at my entrance, troubled lines etched into her face. Somehow, she knew. I had no idea how. But she knew. She reached shaking hands out to me.

The sight of her made my heart ache. I walked the short length of the hallway, knelt in front of her chair, and hugged her. Andie's voice carried from upstairs. "Cass? Is that you? We heard sirens. Is everything okay?" her footsteps trailed down the stairs and stopped when they reached the kitchen. I didn't look up. Zinnie's gentle hands stroked my hair, and though she couldn't possibly understand the weight of the situation, I clung to her like she was the only stable thing in the entire world. My cheek pressed up against her soft dress, and the sobs came.

Andie knelt next to me. I explained what happened, but I couldn't bring myself to tell them why. That it was my fault. That my stupid decisions were the reason a family was mourning their son and brother tonight. We stayed there in the kitchen, with each other for company, until Andie suggested we move to the living room. At that point, Zinnie was practically sleepwalking, so Andie helped her get to bed. I remained on the sofa, curling myself around my legs for comfort, and begged the universe to wake me up from this nightmare.

CHAPTER 24

Empress Industrial College spared no expense in appearance. Every hall, every classroom reeked of money. Even the bushes and trees on the extensive grounds looked manicured to perfection. I had arrived via aircraft this morning. This time, I didn't expect to return to Loyala.

Unable to face Zinnie and my sister, I'd made a video explaining everything. I started from the beginning, when Day bombed the senator's car and put me in the hospital. I told them how March tried recruiting me to work for Day because I'd invented an inhibitor that would keep her neurochips from corrupting her test subjects. I told them I loved them, but I couldn't ask their forgiveness.

For Rollie, I left a note on my dresser. I asked Andie during the video to deliver it.

He must despise me. By now he would have read the note and realized my involvement in Dangelo's death. I had considered keeping the truth from him by making up some fake explanation for my departure or—better yet—not writing any note at all. But in the end, I couldn't do that. Not to him. Now that I was gone, chances were I'd never see Rollie again. The boy who laughed at himself, who watched the stars next to me, who held me close as we danced . . . was gone from my life. A piece of my heart had gone dark. Yes, the thought of leaving without saying goodbye was torture, but if I had gone to him, he might have tried to talk me out of going. I wore his star necklace around my throat, and the pendant reminded me of Loyala, the only place where I'd felt unconditional love.

Everything had changed now.

Ashcroft March did not accompany me on my journey to EIC this morning. He sent a charcoal aircraft, the same model as the last, manned by only one pilot. Perhaps he was tied up in corporate business, but I couldn't help believing his absence was a sign of my defeat. Why supervise a girl who had already been bought? I realized that this was Senator Day's expertise—buying people. That was how she'd made it so far. I didn't have the strength to even be angry anymore. She had won the game. And I now belonged to her.

Now, some girl gave me a tour of the campus. She waited for me on the ground level of Empress's main compound, the building where I'd met with Day. We didn't say much to each other. Something told me she wasn't exactly happy to be stuck showing around the new girl. She led me to a shuttle that carried us from the work facilities to the school campus. The details were a blur. First, my host took me to the admissions office, housed in a monstrous building that reminded me of my high school in Meridian but with a white-washed brick exterior. I filled out sheets of paperwork while the girl fidgeted beside me. The admissions secretary wore a plastered façade of a smile. It looked unnatural on his face, like a clown's overwrought grin. "That's everything. You are now officially an EIC Caribou. Welcome, and enjoy the rest of your tour."

"Thanks." I followed my guide back out of the building. On our way to student housing, she introduced me to the research labs, an assortment of department buildings, the observatory, the indoor amphitheater, and the cafeteria. I had to admit, the layout was impressive. I regretted not being here under different circumstances. Cass from a month ago might have gone berserk over the promise of a campus like this one. But all the grandeur was tainted by the knowledge that my presence here was involuntary, and any scientific progress made in this arena would be used for the advancement of Empress Industries.

"This is where you will stay," the girl said, pointing out a large housing hall. "This is the female dormitories. Someone will show you to your room inside." This seemed to be where her portion of the tour ended. I did as she directed, letting myself through the large double doors into a spacious reception area. Just like my guide had promised, a woman emerged from an office. Her cheekbones looked fake. I told her my name upon her request, and she bid me wait while she returned to the office and checked some files. Soon, the woman reemerged and beckoned me to an elevator that we took to the third floor.

We walked down a window-lit corridor lined with doors. Finally, the woman stopped at a room labeled 311. "May I see your watch?" she asked. At first I hesitated, but she beckoned so vehemently that I extended my wrist. She removed a handheld device from her pocket and hovered it over my watch until the device made a faint beep. "There. I've given you the entry code for your room. Simply swipe your watch at this sensor." She tapped the said sensor with one long fingernail. I did so, resulting in a flashing green light and the unhitching of an internal lock. The knob gave way when I turned it. To my relief, the room inside held only one bed—so no roommates—and was large enough not to feel like a jail cell. Almost.

"You may unpack your belongings." The woman failed to conceal her distaste as she glanced at my meager backpack. "After you're settled in, please report to the auditorium for orientation."

I was relieved to be left alone again. My room, admittedly, was more akin to a hotel suite than a university dormitory. I had my own personal bathroom with a gilded golden mirror and porcelain sink and toilet. There was a small living area with a fine wooden writing desk and cushioned office chair. The whole thing, minus the bathroom, was really one big room. The walls angled expertly to create a geometric feel, directing one from the entryway to the living space to a bed and dresser area in the back. Senator Day seemed to pull out all the stops for her beloved students.

The day drug on, and I remained in a semi-living state, only existing because people told me to, desensitized to everything but the memories of better days that had ended far too soon. I told myself being Day's captive was my penance for Dangelo's death. But that failed to ease my conscious. If I had only been less selfish, less preoccupied with childish things, I would have had the good sense to acquiesce to Day's demands earlier. That way, I'd have become one of her student-employees anyway. Only Dangelo wouldn't be dead. So I remained trapped by my guilt. My fate had been inevitable. His was unnecessary. Pointless. Not even the life of a prisoner was enough to make up for the pain I inflicted on that family.

Reality was cruel that way.

I received my class and work schedule at orientation, a fifteen-minute video presentation probably meant to hype up new students, at which I was the only one in the large echoing chamber. Apparently, the middle of spring semester was not a popular time of year for students to begin their careers at EIC. Most administrative information I had already gotten from the girl on my tour, so the video felt redundant. I wondered whether I would soon look like the smiling students on the screen, lab coats donned, seemingly elated for the opportunity to be working with such high-profile scientific equipment.

After dinner in the cafeteria, I took the shuttle to the facility labs. One other student accompanied me on the shuttle, a girl with short curly hair and glasses who held a brown leather satchel in her lap. I tried to make conversation.

"Hi. What's your name?"

The girl blinked at me through bubbled lenses. "Nicolette."

"How long have you been going here?"

The girl looked utterly confounded, like talking to her was the biggest of social infractions. "I'm sorry. Are you new?" she asked.

Taken aback, I cleared my throat. "It's my first day." When Nicolette took too long to respond, I thought that was the end of our interaction. I looked at the rushing scenery outside the window and pretended I couldn't feel her eyes boring into me.

"Welcome," the girl said unexpectedly. "I hope you like it here."

". . . Thanks."

"What's your name?"

"Cass."

"That's an interesting name."

"Oh." I forced a too-harsh chuckle. "You're sweet."

"What's your specialty, Cass?"

This conversation had gotten weirder despite my doubts that such a thing was possible. "No specialty yet. I'm still in high school. I like chemistry."

"Everyone has a specialty here. That's what makes us different from other schools. Mine is metatranscriptomics."

"What?"

"I analyze metagenomic data as it pertains to group populations." The girl acquired a self-satisfied look on her face, as if this should be impressive information.

"Genetics," I echoed. "Do you work with the neurochips?"

Nicolette's smirk vanished and her eyes bugged out of her head. "That is classified. You can't talk about that anywhere you want."

"Whoops."

She narrowed her eyes. "Who told you about that, anyway?"

"The CEO," I said casually, and Nicolette's eyes got even bigger. She hunched back in her seat, looking at me warily.

"Well. As a matter of fact, I don't work with the brain chips at all. My department is currently focused on some top-secret genetic research. It's all very classified, so don't ask me any more questions."

That was fine by me. The shuttle, propelled upon high-speed maglev rails like a miniature version of the national train system, took only a few minutes to zigzag through the forest and deposit us at our destination. Nicolette walked beside me to the sensor-activated door, where she flashed her watch and led us inside. "I take this elevator to the gen labs upstairs. Which way are you headed?"

I briefly launched my Loom panel for the digital schedule someone had sent me during orientation. "I have to go to the production floor. Where is that?"

"That's just here on ground level. You'll want to follow this hallway until you reach the big double doors on your right. That'll be it."

Nicolette's elevator arrived, and she stepped inside. "Thanks," I mumbled. The girl pushed her thick lenses higher onto her nose and adjusted the satchel hanging from her shoulder. Turning, I followed her instructions until I came to the large double doors she'd mentioned. From inside, I heard sounds of whirring and the distant screech of welding. Was this where Empress produced all of their models? If that were true, I was headed into the heart of operations for the company that manufactured the drones that poisoned Dangelo. My hands started shaking, so I clenched them into fists.

I pushed through the doors into the enormous hangar and felt my jaw nearly drop to the floor.

CHAPTER 25

Machines everywhere. That was my first impression upon entering Empress Industries central manufacturing zone. The floor extended farther back than my eyes could see around the numerous conveyor belts, clicking ceiling tracks carrying dangling pieces of metal, and autonomous robot arms performing every function from cutting to assembly to welding to engraving. The sheer amount of movement overwhelmed me. I saw a few people walking around the floor wearing hard hats and carrying clipboards under their arms. It was then that I realized no one had told me what to do once I arrived at the production floor. Instead of wandering like the employees who clearly had their own purpose to be there, I stood absently, taking in the sight and sound of mass manufacturing and hoping somebody would catch my eye to direct me to where I was supposed to be.

Then a familiar click-click-click of heels reached my ears. I turned in their direction. Toward me walked Senator Day herself, clad in a gossamer business suit, not a hair on her blonde head out of place. "Miss Atwater." She smiled her signature half-smile. "It's good to see you again. I'm so pleased you decided to enroll in our program."

I had no words for this woman. Too many emotions, ranging from anger to hate, hit me full force, and I didn't dare speak lest they all come tumbling out in a ferocious storm. Finally, jaw clenched, I managed just one meager sentence. "Thank you for allowing me to be here."

Her lashes fluttered with pleasure, and it perturbed me to know she was reveling in her victory. "Come. Allow me to give you a brief overview of our facility." She led the way up a staircase to the side of the room, which ended at a floating observation box that offered a significant view of the entire floor. Plexiglass separated us from the noises below. Day stood, hands clasped behind her back, surveying her grand empire. "This is our great pursuit, Miss Atwater. Producing the lifeblood of this nation. It is exceptional, don't you think? Each of my machines are designed with a specific purpose in mind. Some give us transportation. Some supply medical care. Some protect us from aggressive forces. Every machine has a purpose, as does each of my students." She looked at me. "You, Cassiopeia, possess valuable intellectual abilities. If you freely lend your talents to this corporation, you will learn more than you ever thought possible, and your contributions will benefit billions around the world."

"I don't understand."

Day's brow creased. "What is there to not understand?"

"You claim Empress Industries is all for good. But then you hurt people. You killed my friend. You killed him in front of his sister. How can you call yourself good for the world when you harm the people in it just to get your way?"

A tense moment passed. Day searched my face, her gaze inquisitive—challenging, almost. I did not look away. "*Good*," she breathed, "is such a relative term." For an instant, her ruby lips and blossom perfume no longer professed warmth and kindness. Her lips turned to the color of blood, and the flowery scent became sickeningly sweet, like the aroma of fruit decaying. "What do you think is more important, the lives of a few individuals, or the welfare of a whole population? Because I would argue that the preservation of society's best institutions justifies whatever means necessary to ensure its success. Wouldn't you agree?"

"I-I don't know. Maybe if you were fighting an oppressive system, one that took away people's liberties. But that's not what you're doing, is it? You're the oppressor."

Day rolled her eyes. "Sometimes I forget I work with teenagers. Your thinking is so black and white. Of course your initial reaction is to condemn anything that interferes with human liberties. You are a moral person, after all. I am too. My morality, however, has simply acquired a higher perspective. I believe in furthering the common good. Sometimes, a sacrifice is required to line up the necessary pieces. For example, I saw a need for your talents in our corporation. Empress Industries needed you, for the greater good. You would not join us on your own, though I gave you multiple chances. Finally, when you still did not accept my offers, I had to play the card that was certain to secure your cooperation. You were standing in your own way, Cassiopeia. I only made the sacrifice that had to be made."

"That's insane."

"It's the moral high road. Sometimes, we are our own worst enemy."

I contemplated this, simultaneously blown away by Day's delusions and wondering if she was right. No institution that killed innocent people in the name of righteousness could be good. I was sure of this. Day had murdered the Seymours; she had murdered Dangelo, and who knew how many others had fallen victim to her "moral" philosophies. On the other hand, what if there was a grain of truth in her words? What of Empress Industries? Was it truly a champion for the greater good?

I clung to this idea, hoping that one small victory might emerge from my now hopeless situation. The neurochips, when released to the public, had the potential for good. At least I could have a part in that. At least I could stop Day from harming anyone else with her vicious human experimentation. "When do I start adapting the CosmiLock for your neurochips?" I asked.

"Hmm? Oh, I forgot about that. Actually, we won't be using your CosmiLock after all. We never intended to, really. It was simply a vehicle for enticing you here once you proved more difficult to recruit."

"*What?*" I breathed.

"Don't blame me. I had to! You weren't willing to join Empress under normal circumstances." Day flipped a piece of blonde hair from her face. "I was forced to introduce something with higher stakes, something to appeal to your moral side. Sadly, that didn't work either. Really, it's your fault that boy is dead. I gave you plenty of chances to make the right choice."

This revelation felt like a hammer to the gut. Day never actually needed the CosmiLock? It was a ruse the whole time? "But what about Jeremy?" I asked, not believing. "The neurochips are faulty without something to control the AI. Are you saying you fixed it without me? No one else is going to suffer?"

"Our scientists determined nearly a month ago that a device like the CosmiLock could never solve our problem. Its design is incompatible with our needs. I'm sorry to have lied to you. I needed a way to get you here." Day shrugged. Then she smiled. *Smiled?* How could she be smiling at a time like this? "There is good news, however. We've solved the rogue AI issue. We finally have a prototype that's performing consistently. Soon, we will release it to the public. Isn't that a good thing? Think of all the people we could heal, all the ailments we could cure. I'd say this is a final result that's been worth a few outer-sector sacrifices."

"You invaded people's brains. You destroyed their lives." I couldn't bear to stand here anymore, to look Sommer Day in the face, knowing what she'd done. And all without blinking an eye. "If you don't need me to fix your neurochips, then what am I here for?"

Day acquired a look like I'd just gifted her the moon and stars. More than ever before, I felt the cold press of fear enter my heart when she smiled like that—a distorted smile, something you might have expected from Jeremy Polluck with the chip overriding his brain but not from anyone sane. "I remember every person who's ever wronged me in life," Day started. The smile remained. "I don't forget. Because to rise above the rest, you must not let anyone think they have an advantage over you." Day ran one hand along the room's steel railing, closing the space between herself and me. I wanted to back up, to put as much distance between myself and the snake as possible. But I stood my ground. "You're here because of your mother," Day hissed. At last, the smile vanished from her face, replaced by a wicked glare filled with triumph.

". . . My mother?"

Day took a step back. "Yes. "Did I know her? I spent every minute of my senior year with your mother. Mercury Magnusson and I were good friends. All until she ripped every one of my dreams out from under me." Day shook her head, her eyes focused far away. She sucked the inside of one cheek as she spoke. Her lips formed a snarl. "I was furious. I thought I'd never recover. Though it took some time, I came to realize that your mother had given me a valuable gift. Ambition. See, now? I refused to be my own worst enemy, and I took control of my life. As you can see—" She gestured all around. "It paid off."

I was still reeling from the revelation that this woman had known my mother as a teenager. They'd been friends. All these years, my greatest desire was always to be worthy of my mother's love. Every day, I yearned for another glimpse of her. Another chance. If I could only see her again, I'd prove that I was better now. And she would want me back.

Day spoke my mother's name with acid in her voice. I didn't understand. How could anybody enjoy such a degree of closeness with Mercury Magnusson and come away harboring such hatred? Impossible. If my body were made of bricks, it would have been crumbling. It couldn't be. Not when I'd been proving myself for all these years. Day had to be lying.

"I don't believe you," I whispered.

"What? About your mother? Oh, dear, trust me. I have no incentive whatsoever to lie to you about *that*. Find the story in any old news report you want. Mercury stole away my slot in the Capital's foremost youth internship. She knew I'd been vying for it my entire high school career. When my father heard the news, he called me a disappointment and cut off my allowance. I was left with nothing. As icing on the cake, how do you think Mercury showed her appreciation for such an honor? She didn't give her entire being to the work, like I would have done. No. She quit halfway through. Ran off with that outer sector boy to prove something to her mother, I suppose."

My mother, a Capital intern? It was not unbelievable. She was sharp enough. I pictured Day as a teenager, not much older than me, and my mother. Friends. I found myself angry and wanted to defend her. How dare she speak of my mother that way? What did *she* know about Mercury Magnusson? What did she know?

I shook with contempt for this woman. "You never knew my mother then. How could you speak of her like that? When she met my father, they were in love."

"Perhaps," Day allowed. "But Mercury was always fickle. Flighty at best. Full of her whimsies and never satisfied after she chased one down. It was always onto the next thing for her. I suppose that's why she left your family, dear. I'm sorry, but it's best to confront the past as it is. The faster you get over the fact that your mother left you, the better."

Venom. She was venom in its purest form. Worse than a snake. At least a snake tempered its poison with the breath of life. A snake was only an animal—it killed for the basest survival, for the perpetuation of a natural life cycle. Whatever Sommer Day was, nothing about her was natural.

I wanted to break all the windows in this insufferable place and then dissolve into tears. "Is that why you brought me here? To make me hate my own mom? Well, I'm glad she won that internship. I bet she deserved it. If you were half as good as her, maybe they'd have picked you instead."

Day smirked. "I've been waiting twenty years to repay your mother for what she did to me. Remember, Cass, that even the past has a grip on the future. Thankfully, with your arrival, there's nothing left in my past over which I don't have full control. It's time to move into the future." Breathing deeply, she turned away from me, effectively signaling this conversation as over. "You may go now. I trust you've been shown around. I expect you'll start classes bright and early tomorrow morning."

How I got to the woods, I couldn't say. Frigid air consumed the surrounding mountains as the late evening sun descended below eternal peaks. Having acclimated to Loyala's humid warmth, the icicle breezes here threatened to freeze me to my core. There had been a shuttle at the platform outside the building, but I didn't take it. All I saw were the trees, the evergreens standing tall like silent soldiers, their company much preferable to that of human beings. I'd come far enough into their pine-needle protection that I could now place the trunks between me and Empress Industries and convince myself the thing wasn't there at all.

My breath fogging before me, I leaned my back against the crisp bark of a towering pine. I thought only of my mother. My mother. My mother. Tears filled my eyes. *What did I do wrong?*

The Method To Infinite Things

Brittle quiet hung in answer. I thought of our life back in Exulta. It hadn't been a bad life. We were a good family. I remembered Christmases and Thanksgivings, when my parents used to wake me and Andie up in our beds. I treasured memories of warm fireplaces with hot cocoa, glistening lights, ham dinners, and piano resonating softly from another room.

The weight of six years suffocated me. I threaded my fingers through my hair. *Why? Why did she do it?* Was our family another internship to be abandoned when she lost interest? I had hoped otherwise. All this time, I'd always hoped I was missing some piece of the picture. Another reason. Another explanation.

But to realize none existed? To learn the truth about my mother and confirm my worst fears?

I couldn't help it. I screamed at the top of my lungs. "*You shouldn't have done it! You shouldn't have left us!*" My whole body trembled. A great void filled my stomach, aching. Agonizing. I sucked stiletto breaths and sensed hyperventilation around the corner. Reason told me I should stop. Calm down. Control myself. It was no use. Great rolling tears dripped down my nose, and I pressed my fists against my temples and sobbed without restraint. "*Why wasn't I enough for you?*" I cried. The pain doubled me over. My body, sick for air, racked with spasms, launched into a sort of survival mode. I stole gasps between the wails. Oxygen. I needed oxygen! But still I cried. There was nothing left to stop it.

"I *tried*," I whispered. A coughing fit took over, and I braced one hand against the tree for support.

When finally the coughs subsided, teardrops wet my crusted lips. They fell to the ground. Where they hit, there formed little star-shaped splatters in the dirt. My voice was nothing more than a croak. "I tried. I swear it. I tried-I tried-I tried-I tried . . ."

My voice dissolved among the trees, falling quiet until my lips moved without sound. Time lost its meaning. I shivered, hoping the forest would swallow me up and take me away from reality. I wanted to go home. Home. *Home . . .*

Images of Loyala drifted into my mind like boats on a slow-rolling sea.

Andie wrapping me in a hug. Strawberry jam for breakfast. Dancing with Rollie under the night sky. A young boy leaving the hospital surrounded by family.

But Loyala was gone, I reminded myself. There was no going back. I'd ruined my chances for a home like that. Empress Industries was my home now.

Alone. I was alone.

Like a distant echo, a sentence drifted forward on my sea of memories. *You don't have to carry it alone.* It was Rollie's voice, from a night sitting under our monument, watching the stars. I caught my breath. The remembrance should have been painful, a shadow of times now beyond my reach, but instead of pain, I felt the familiarity of our shared space in time, and I clung to it. I would have given anything to hear the words from his lips once again.

What neither of us knew then was that we would soon be separated for good. Sommer Day played her cards, and she had won the game. My brief sojourn to Loyala was over. Neither Andie, Rollie, nor anyone else, could change that.

I hesitated at the thought. Change. Change what? The fact that I was stuck here in the north, essentially a prisoner to a corporation bent on controlling the country and everyone in it? It was impossible. Day possessed too much power. Her pawns were everywhere; they infiltrated every square inch of this place, and they could gain access to anywhere else Day saw fit. She would track me down again even if I escaped. Besides, what purpose would an escape serve for me to simply return to Loyala, risking the lives of all I cared about and incurring more wrath from those same people whom I loved?

No, I couldn't look Evie in the eyes again. Not without some kind of retribution for the death of her brother. Returning to Loyala, at least right now, was not an option.

The pit in my stomach returned full force upon remembering Dangelo. Like the burden of my mother's departure, I was sure this weight would remain with me for the rest of my life. Some things were infinite. That much I knew. The past was a stringent creditor, always coming back to collect its dues.

You don't have to carry anything alone anymore. Frustration surged inside me. What did Rollie know of pain like this? His family loved him. Right now, he was probably walking home from the pastures, free of guilt or blame's burden. The past had no claim on him.

I remembered Yael, his small frame on the sofa, and my heart softened a degree. I chided myself. Was pain not pain? What difference did it make, whether our pain was caused by the past or the present? *Only the bravest of us all*, I remembered. Yael persisted in the face of life. Life, in fact, belonged to him. And his future? He owned that too.

It was a novel idea. What of consequences? Aftershocks, fallout, equal and opposite reactions? I thought of my mother. My adolescence—a product of her choices. I'd lived to make up for those choices. To correct a mistake. Whose mistake? My mistake. My mistake. I'd worked my fingers raw, studied till the night turned into day and my body screamed for rest. My body, my soul. Screaming. Screaming. And I couldn't change anything. The burden remained. I was to blame. She left. She left because of me.

At what point do stars collapse? Do they scream long enough into emptiness that they can't scream anymore? Do they watch the people below who stare and stare but never reach up, and do they grow exhausted from giving their light? In the vacuum of space do they burn, burn, burn, UNTIL—

—they change?

Change.

My toes and fingers were numb from the cold, but I was barely conscious of the pins-and-needles sensation. I didn't want to burn anymore. Not anymore.

It was a tentative thing—hope. Yet it persisted unlike the hottest flame. I swallowed it up with every throatful of tears, and it warmed my core as it spread through my bones. Hope didn't burn. It remained. A tentative thing, yes, but once you caught it, too delicious to ever give up. Hope. *Hope.* The infinite thing. The future and its promise.

Maybe it was my turn to take it.

CHAPTER 26

On day two, I started class. I attended advanced courses on every subject from aerospace engineering to biometrics. They had me working in the labs by day three. A man called Dr. Porter assigned me to a project developing new variations of space-travel capable metals, adapted for deep space exploration, which he called the "frontier of existence itself." The work was tedious. I was glad of it. In another division of the chemistry department, I sometimes glimpsed a team developing poisons from a variety of chemical compounds. They tested them on Thursdays under the observation of ranking executives. I thought that if I'd been assigned to such a division, I would never get out of bed in the morning, no matter how Day threatened my friends and family.

I met others. Nicolette, I found, never took the shuttle at the same times as I did. Our first-day meeting seemed a fluke. We rarely saw each other after that. In my department, two teens, roughly my age, introduced themselves as Pegasus and Gabriel. Pegasus—or Peg, as she liked to be called, and little wonder why—was from Gateway, an inner sector adjacent to Meridian and known for horseracing. Empress recruited her for its work-study program as a twelve-year-old in middle school. Gabriel, a recruit from the only inner sector further north than Ostentia, had also joined Empress in young adolescence. Once, I asked them if all students were brought in at such a young age.

"Most, yes," said Peg. "A few, like you, come in when they are older, but it's rare. One day a man came to our school and called three of us to the principal's office. Our parents were there waiting. It was all very exciting. I knew a bit what to expect since my older brother had a best friend who was very smart, and Empress Industries chose him to come here when he was twelve, and my brother had to say goodbye to him. It was very sad in the moment, but it would be silly to pass up such an amazing opportunity. That boy was the only one chosen out of his class. My class must have been very smart because there were three of us selected."

"If Empress recruited you when you were twelve, how did they know you would turn into a good chemist?"

"I had always gotten good grades in chemistry," replied Peg. "I had perfect scores on exams."

"Me too," Gabriel hurried to add. "They only chose the best. At my school, I got the best marks in science of anyone. My parents were planning to send me to a private school anyway because my courses didn't challenge me enough." He looked satisfied with himself. Immediately I didn't like him, but I cut my eye roll short because offending people right out the gate wouldn't do me any good. Who knew how long I'd be working alongside these two? So I forced myself to laugh along, knowing it couldn't hurt to have a couple allies in this place.

Our conversation nagged at me for other reasons though. If Empress selected their recruits in middle school, why hadn't I been chosen? Like Peg and Gabriel, my science marks were nothing but the best. I'd outshone all of my classmates in chemistry from a young age. Why, then, hadn't Empress Industries recruited me like all the others? Wasn't I just as capable? My skills just as desirable?

Perhaps it was my wounded pride, but this question pricked at my consciousness relentlessly. Eventually I decided my outer-sector heritage was to blame. No one in the city liked admitting an Outmode was as smart as them. It was a prejudice which permeated every facet of my social life, so why not this too? It was the only plausible explanation.

The days passed. I kept up my work, kept my head down, and adjusted somewhat to the fast pace of an environment always on the brink of scientific breakthrough. I'd never imagined such a perfect place could feel so lonely.

I missed Rollie. I missed my sister. The Cass from a month ago never would have cared about such pointless sentiments. Nothing had mattered more than my work then.

How could so much change in such a short amount of time?

At the end of my first week, I let slip a comment deriding Sommer Day in front of Peg. I regretted the mistake immediately, but I wasn't prepared for the girl's reaction. She fixed me with a gaping stare—a combination of shock and horror. "Don't talk like that about President Day," she scolded. Anger flooded her tone.

I froze where I stood, hands hovering over the controls of a machine that was combining lithium and deuterium in a contained environment. Peg's response seemed so violent, so unnecessary, that I almost misplaced my hands and caused a cataclysm inside the vacuum unit. "I didn't mean to offend you. I was only saying how I felt."

"Don't say those kinds of things," Peg repeated, less harsh this time, and swung her attention back to her work. But the anger in her eyes remained. "You only just got here. You don't understand the magnitude of our mission. President Day needs our loyalty."

"What's that supposed to mean?"

"*Loyalty*," Peg snapped. The sudden clench to her jaw, the severity in her voice, silenced me for all intents and purposes. "If you don't understand something, don't criticize it. You shouldn't say those kinds of things."

"I'm sorry," I murmured, but Peg had switched machines, and I didn't get another word out of her all day. Twice, I caught her eyeing daggers at me from across the lab. The whole interaction left me with prickles along my skin. From the way she defended Day, you'd think the woman was larger than life itself. And what about that word choice? 'The magnitude of our mission?' As more days passed like strange dreams in the night, I couldn't help testing whatever amorphous theory was forming in the back of my subconscious. I found myself alone with Gabriel one afternoon and tried another comment along the same lines as the first. His angry reaction mirrored Penelope's almost to a tee. I began to wonder what the other students knew that I didn't. And I started to think that Sommer

Day was planning something bigger than I'd suspected.

Then, suddenly, it had been two weeks since March's hovercraft dropped me at EIC. Fifteen days, to be exact. Roiling suspicions plagued my thoughts at all waking hours, and I sensed a turning point on the horizon. For a while, I resisted. Two halves of reason fought a war for supremacy inside me. All the while, I knew what choice I would make. The pursuit of truth is a burning desire that grows when fed *and* neglected. You never forget the taste. It's a compulsion of the mind and the soul, and only fear prevents a person from accepting its inevitability. In a surge of reckless abandon—perhaps all the best decisions in life are made in this way—I returned to my dormitory and sent John Brown a message:

I have an idea. I need help.

His reply came as a clap of thunder rattled the windowpane and signaled the approach of an early summer storm:

Are you being rash?

I wet my dry mouth, then whispered my response through chapped lips as the first raindrops streaked the glass.

No. I'm doing the right thing.

There was a pause, a long tenseness that made me wipe my forehead and gnaw at my cheek. Then came the ping of the notification and the wave of adrenaline that accompanied his response.

What is your idea?

***

It was dinnertime, and I sat alone in the dining hall staring at the half-eaten steak on my plate.

I didn't usually eat steak.

Moving from my seat proved difficult since I knew that as soon as I stood from this table, there was no going back. I had a plan in place. I knew what I had to do. Figuring out logistics was not the problem; it was gathering the courage to execute the steps.

Brown had helped me establish each part of the plan, right down to the steak I ate for dinner on the day we agreed upon, three days after our communication. Oh, how these past three days had dragged on. I picked at the green beans on the side of my plate. My eyes glanced to the steak knife on my left, which had come with the meal, and my lungs filled with several preparatory breaths. It all seemed unreal. The feeling reminded me of those stories claiming out-of-body experiences. How had I gotten here, to this moment? What happened to that invisible girl in chemistry goggles who only wanted to present her work to the world?

My fingers tightened around the plate because I knew it was time. Time to fix all of this. Or at least die trying. I tried not to think about that part, really.

I sent Brown one line of text:

Go phase 1.

Thank goodness I'd had the sense to have him encrypt my communications while in Loyala. None of this would work without Brown's help. He arranged the most crucial parts of the plan. My job was to execute the details without screwing up the whole thing.

Standing, I carried my leftover dinner to the conveyor belt that delivered used dishes back to the kitchen. But I kept the steak knife. I made sure no one was watching as I slipped the blade up the sleeve of my jacket.

That was step one. Admittedly, there was some relief once I made it out the dining hall doors without being confronted. The knife laid cool and sharp against my skin. Its presence made me nervous, even though I knew it was essential for what I was about to do. I walked the all-too-familiar route between the dining hall and the female dorms, then climbed the all-too-familiar stairs to the second floor. Instead of taking the next flight to my room on level three, I paced down the hall until I reached 209, a number I'd checked over and over again almost obsessively. Refusing to back out now, I rapped hard on the door.

Footsteps approached from the other side. I knew she would be home. I'd checked that obsessively too. The door swung open to reveal the girl with glasses from the shuttle, Nicolette. She frowned at me.

"Can I help you?"

"Hello," I said, faking cheerfulness. "Do you remember me? We met a few days ago on my first day here."

"Not really," she replied, still frowning. "What are you doing outside my room?"

Yikes, I thought. Under no circumstances would I ever want to be friends with this girl. I made sure my smile stayed plastered in place even through my discomfort. "I wondered if you could help me on my microbiology assignment. You're probably a lot better at this kind of thing than I am since you work in the genetics department and all."

Nicolette looked to be considering my request. I held my breath.

"Well. I suppose I can help you." She opened the door wider. "Don't think I can help with *all* your assignments, but one shouldn't be a problem. Come in."

I followed her inside. The room was structured similarly to mine, but with lighter drapes and different styles of throw pillows. I closed the door. Nicolette cleared a myriad of equations from a screen built into the wall. With her back to me, I swung my backpack off my shoulders and removed four shoelaces and a scarf.

"All right. What unit are you—" Nicolette turned around. Her expression dropped as her eyes landed on the steak knife dangling from my grip.

Any sign of weakness could destroy the plan now. I channeled severity into every portion of my body, making my face into a hardened mask. "Sit down," I ordered, gesturing with the knife to the far end of the room. "Over there. Don't make a sound."

Nicolette had frozen with horror. She stammered. "W-what do you think you're doing?"

"I said don't make a sound," I repeated, jabbing the knife more forcefully. "And don't scream or you'll regret it."

The girl whimpered and scuttled to the end of the room, plopping herself on the floor with her back to the wall. She was scared. *Good*, I thought. That was part of the plan too.

"What do you want?" Nicolette had started crying. Tears pooled in her eyes, turning them blotchy red.

I knelt in front of her, allowing the knife to hover between us. "I want the access codes to your department's files."

Nicolette wiped away wetness from her cheeks. "What? I can't give you those."

"You can, and you will," I pressed. I moved the knife closer so only six inches remained between the serrated edge and her chin. Her eyes widened, and she burst into sobs. I couldn't understand her through the blubbering. "Stop it," I snapped. "The codes. Tell me the codes."

The girl hiccupped between wails. "I-I caaaan't!"

"Nicolette. You either give me those codes, or I'll take them from you some other way. I don't want to hurt you. Just give me the codes, and this will all be over."

Nicolette had shied away from the knife's tip. She huddled against the wall, hugging her knees to her chest. "I'm not supposed to give that information to anyone."

I rolled my eyes. "Clearly you have no choice."

"I'll get fired," she cried. "They'll kick me out."

I shook the blade, causing her to lurch against the wall and sob even louder. "*Listen* to me, Nicolette. Nicolette? I said listen to me!" That got her attention. Her gaze snapped up to me in fright. I leaned in closer. "They won't kick you out for this. But you know what *will* be a problem? Not telling me those codes. This is your last chance, Nicolette. What are the codes?" I let the knife barely rest against the skin beneath her chin.

The touch of the steel sent her over the edge. "No! No! Please! I'll tell you. I swear I'll tell you. Please . . ." Another wave of sobs reduced her to a trembling mess, and I removed the knife just a bit. After her cries subsided, Nicolette took several shaky breaths and wiped mucus from her lips. "The first code is 0787," she sniffed. "That one's mine. It'll give you p-p-preliminary access. Then it's 'Carbonbasedlifeform' for the rest. All one word, capital C."

"These will give me access to all your department's confidential files?"

"Yes," she gasped, pressing her body farther away from the blade.

I stood and stepped back. The codes repeated in my memory, vivid and unforgettable. Seeing the girl on the floor, recoiled in fear, struck me with regret. But I shook off the feeling quickly. There wasn't time for pity. I used two of the shoelaces to secure her hands behind her back, hoping the doubled-up cords would keep her immobile, and repeated the process around her ankles. Then I used the scarf, purchased in the clearance section of the campus store, as a gag to keep her from yelling for help.

Finished, I retrieved my backpack from the floor and slipped the knife into one of the pockets. I looked back at Nicolette, who glared at me through glasses fogged with tears. "Someone will come looking for you eventually," I said. Then, perhaps out of guilt, I added, "I'm really sorry about this. Feel free to keep the scarf."

I closed the door behind me.

Dusk had fallen. I'd purposely eaten a late dinner to ensure that my movements would be under the cover of darkness. By the time I infiltrated Empress's system and escaped with Brown, night would conceal us completely.

I sent a brief message to Brown as I made for the head facilities:

Go phase 2.

So far, so good. Time was ticking now.

I walked across campus at my regular pace. Anything else, I knew, might cause suspicion. Another student—a boy—approached me from up ahead. Who was he? I forced myself to breathe normally. There's no way he could know about the plan. The boy got closer, and I repeated a mantra in my head to calm the nerves: *I'm going to work a late shift. I have a purpose. I'm supposed to be here. I'm supposed to be here . . .*

The boy passed without looking at me. My body relaxed, if only by a fraction.

I passed by buildings where I'd attended classes for the last three days. Part of me regretted having to leave. It *was* amazing—the classes, the work. We spent our days learning groundbreaking principles and applied it all in the labs. Some of the best minds in the world were my colleagues.

In theory, EIC was every scientist's dream. Nothing could compete. Of course, Day would settle for nothing less than perfection. She was ambitious unlike anyone I'd ever known. Lethal, even. And she raised her precious students to be no different. That was the problem, wasn't it? Sommer Day would never care about anyone other than herself. How could I work for someone so destructive? Poor Jeremy Polluck. He didn't deserve the fate he got.

And Dangelo.

Dangelo.

All regret fled immediately at the thought of his lifeless body on the ground. Evie's cries echoed, agonizing, through my memory. I wouldn't let Day get away with it. "I promise, Evie." I whispered under my breath. I *promise*.

So I reached the shuttle platform and boarded the waiting car. Thankfully, no one else boarded with me. The automated doors closed soundlessly and then I was speeding off through the trees. It was all a blur of evergreen on either side. The few still minutes gave me time to collect myself after the angst of fleeing the dorm rooms. When the shuttle slowed and arrived at Empress's work facilities, I was ready. I checked myself twice before disembarking to make sure I left nothing behind by accident. Satisfied, I swiped my watch at the door. The light flashed green as the lock disengaged. I knew immediately that I wasn't alone in the building. Light spilled out from the windows of doors along the hallway. That was to be expected. Plenty of student-employees worked on projects late at night. In my personal experience anyway, it was one of the best times for work. I took the stairs instead of the elevator. Given the situation, the less I exposed myself to potential run-ins with my peers, the better.

The fifth floor housed the biology labs. I'd confirmed that fact obsessively as well. All the adrenaline pumping through my veins must have boosted my endurance because I wasn't even winded by the time I reached the top of the last flight. The stairwell opened onto an empty commons area, with steel tables and colored chairs spaced atop a carpeted signet depicting a double helix. I kept walking until I found the labs. Entry required another swipe of my watch.

Access denied

Oh, no. I tried again. The light flashed red, only confirming the panic forming inside. For the millionth time tonight, I forced myself to stay calm. *Think. Think.*

There was a pin pad next to the scanner. Could I hope it was that easy? I punched in Nicolette's four-number code, the one she said was supposed to give me preliminary access to the department files. Maybe the code worked on locks for things as simple as doors too.

Relief washed over me when I heard the *click* of the lock disengaging and saw the telltale flash of green. I thanked Nicolette silently in my head.

Brown claimed he could tap into the facility's security system to ensure no one would be alerted by my presence in the lab so long as I stayed low and didn't attract attention. I paused once inside the door. The room was enormous, full of tech I'd never even seen before. My gaze landed on a computer interface nearby. But I couldn't move. My feet refused. There were people on the far side of the lab, talking with each other, tapping at data that I couldn't see on an enlarged Loom screen. If they saw me, would they know I didn't belong here? I didn't recognize any of their faces. Resisting the urge to curse out loud, I tried to reason with myself. There had to be dozens upon dozens of employees in the biology department. What were the odds that they all knew each other? Andie's advice came to mind. Confidence was key.

Great. Confidence. *Thanks a lot, Andie.* Channeling what I hoped was an air of self-assurance, I strolled to the interface and tapped the screen to life. A glance upward told me that no one had even acknowledged my presence. I needed to get moving.

First, the access codes. Just as Nicolette had described, the screen called for a four-digit pin to even get past the initial lock screen. My hand shook slightly as I typed 0787 into the blanks. The screen transformed from a dark slate to a glowing home screen. Icons appeared on a rotating slider in the center. Finding the correct files would be the tricky part. I swiped until I found the icon labeled Files and tapped it open. A slough of folder names appeared. I chewed my lip. Which one of these contained anything useful? I tried two folders, finding nothing but bacterial diagrams and general reports. One folder labeled Project Daylight caught my eye. And I knew from the acid in my throat that this was the information I was looking for.

I tapped the icon. There was a faint bass notification tone, and a box appeared on the screen.

Confidential File
Enter credentials: _____

This had to be the second code from Nicolette. This time, my fingers shook less as I maneuvered the digital keys. My lips silently formed the words. Carbonbasedlifeform.

I wondered. What dark secrets hid inside Project Daylight? From the pocket of my jeans, I fished out a mobile drive no larger than my pinky finger. I jammed the drive into the port on the side of the interface panel and selected download on the screen.

The next few seconds were agonizing as I waited for the file transfer. Once more, I glanced at the group gathered at the other end of the lab. One of the people looked my way. They did a double take, and this time their stare lingered too long.

Time to go. *Hurry up*, I begged inside my head. My teeth clenched hard enough to break. Almost there. Almost there . . . Finally. It was pure relief when a glowing green check mark indicated the download's completion. Making sure not to appear guilty, I casually—at least, I desperately hoped it looked that way—closed the program and pocketed the drive again.

I didn't dare check to see whether the people were still looking my way. *I have a purpose. I'm supposed to be here.* If I could trick myself into believing it, I might get out of this place after all.

I exited the lab the same way I'd come. Down the hall, down the stairs. I checked my watch. There was a fresh message from Brown:

ETA 10 minutes.

He'd sent it at least five minutes ago. For the first time all evening, I started to breathe easy. The hardest part was over. We might actually pull it off after all.

Voices drifted up from the stairs below me. I was only on the third level, two floors away from freedom. Someone was coming up, and there was no telling who it was. Could I risk showing my face? What if they recognized me? What if they asked questions?

I had no choice. If I ran back up the stairs to avoid them, I could draw more attention.

Draining my face of emotion, I continued down the steps. Two students appeared around the corner. They were engaged in deep conversation and ignored me as they passed. Higher in the stairwell, a door slammed. My head snapped up at the sound. I waited for the echo of hurried footsteps, but none came. Was I just paranoid? My nerves were strung tight as wires. I listened intently for a few seconds, frozen.

Nothing.

That's it, I decided. No more hesitation. No more distractions. I took the stairs at double my previous pace. I had to get out. My thoughts filled with nothing but determination. There was another buzz at my wrist— another notification. I didn't stop to read it. Most likely, Brown was in place and notifying me of his arrival. I reached the ground floor and had a clear shot to the exit.

"Stop."

I almost tripped. A shock of alarm ran from my head to my toes, crashing through every inch of my being. I spun towards the source of the voice and was met by the barrel of a gun trained directly on my chest.

CHAPTER 27

My mouth gaped open as I stared, wide-eyed, at the weapon and the person pointing it at me.

It was Leo.

He looked the same as when I'd last seen him, doing homework in the lab at Potomac University. But shadows hooded his eyes now, and hard lines clenched along his jaw. I looked from his face to the gun and back.

"You took something from the bio lab," he said, his voice a deep monotone. He held out his other hand, the one not holding the gun. "Give it to me."

I might as well have been caught in between time and space itself. My fingers twitched at my side, and the drive seemed to burn in my pocket. Leo pinned me with cold, unfeeling eyes. The barrel of his pistol stared me down.

"The files," Leo barked. "Hand them over. You're all out of choices. Give me the files, and I'll let you live. Don't, and I'll shoot you and take it back anyway."

Brown was probably already in position, waiting for my escape from the building. I glanced at the door down the hall. And to think I'd almost done it. This was the end. All of that planning for nothing. Leo would shoot me, and I'd bleed out on the floor of Empress Industries. Another pesky fly crossed off Sommer Day's list. Would it hurt to die?

"I-I thought we were friends," I stammered.

"Hardly. You made it clear enough you didn't want anything to do with me at the university. But I wasn't there to make friends. I got what

I needed."

The pieces clicked together. "You told Day about the Lock?" My voice came out childish, twisted by the devastation that filled my chest. Had I been so ignorant? How had I not seen it before?

"You should have been more careful with the pin to your storage unit."

No. No, this couldn't be happening. Leo, another of Day's pawns? My breath came faster. Angry tears threatened behind my eyes. "Did she recruit you too? Raise you in her lies like all the others?"

Leo's frown deepened into a scowl. It was a vastly different image of him than the one from the university. "You think you're so smart. Just cut it out already. You have no idea how this works."

"How what works? Indoctrination? That's what this is, Leo. She lures you in with promises and fills your head with the things *she* wants you to believe. Can't you see that?"

"This isn't about what I think. I can't let you take those files."

"Please, Leo," I begged. "She's a murderer. She killed my friend."

His lips compressed into a hard line. The gun remained trained directly on me. I heard footsteps up the stairwell, and my heart jumped in alarm. Leo heard it too. He glared in the direction of the sound, looked around us, then gestured me into a room. "In here. Hurry up."

I obeyed. Once inside the room, Leo shut the door behind us. We were surrounded by drawing tables—large rectangular surfaces all with embedded screens. It was dim with the lights off, but windows on the far side of the room let through streams of moonlight. Leo stepped closer, so the gun was only a foot or two away from my abdomen. "Here's something you don't understand," he hissed finally. "Day may think she's got all of us wrapped around her finger, but I'm not one of her sheep. My work is all my own. For now, I'm just biding my time until I see a good chance to split."

"Your work is not your own as long as you work for her. She's a psychopath, but she's a genius. It's all about control for her. You've got to see that."

Leo shook his head, exasperated. "I'm not doing this. Hand over the files." His other hand, the one not holding the gun, gestured open and closed.

"... I can't."

He glowered. "Then you won't walk off this campus alive."

My fingers grazed the fabric of my pocket. I looked down, and in doing so, caught a glimpse of my watch. Just one message glowed up from the screen:

In position now.

"Hurry up," Leo prompted.

How could I give up? With Brown waiting for me, risking his life at this very moment, how could I let him down? This was my chance to redeem myself. If this plan succeeded, it would mean the difference between Day's success or failure. It all counted on *now*.

I needed to get out of Ostentia. Tonight. Leo said I had a choice, and maybe that was true, but my mind had already been made up. Whatever it took, I would get this data to Brown.

I hesitated. I looked from the gun to the face of the boy carrying it. He had been molded and morphed according to Day's philosophies for years. Just like she had all the rest, she had taken him and made him into a cookie-cutter model of unfailing loyalty, raised to worship none but herself. Maybe he wouldn't admit to it. Maybe he believed he would walk away once it was all over. However, I was finally starting to understand Sommer Day. From the beginning, she entangled each one of her loyal students in a complicated web that either forced them to remain her pawns forever after or convinced them they wanted nothing else in the world.

"I can help you get away from her for good."

"Forget it. I don't need your help," Leo scowled.

"You do if you really want to get out of here someday. You know she'll never let you go. Think about it. How many students do you know who haven't become either top executives for Empress or members of her Senate office staff?"

Another eye roll. "Obviously I know where you're headed with this."

"And *obviously* you don't care!"

His eyebrows pulled together in a confused crease. I didn't much mind the impression I gave off in a moment like this. If it came to it, I'd throw the drive out the window and tell Harlow to notify Brown of its location even as I wrestled the gun from Leo's hands. I knew my chances of beating him were slim to none. *If* it came to that, I'd probably be dead before I had any chance to get a message out to Brown. My only chance was to persuade Leo to let me go.

"You don't have to do this. Please. Someone has to stand up to her. You know it better than anyone. She's too powerful, Leo. She's going to keep hurting people if no one does anything to stop her."

"Sorry, but the only person I'm watching out for is myself."

"What she does affects you too. What happens when she launches the neurochips full-scale? You think there won't be implications? She wants control, and your life will be just as unimportant as the rest of ours. Especially if you try to split from her. She won't forgive you, you know. You'll get the same fate as everyone else."

He was rigid, the gun still leveled straight at my chest, but he said nothing to contradict me this time. I took this as a sign of progress.

"Leo. Give me a chance. I just need a chance. Please."

His eyes, locked on mine, were hard as carbonized steel. Shadows passed over his face, diving and twisting with the clouds that moved across the moonlight shining through the window. I held my breath. Standing here in this dark room, I was at his complete mercy. His decision would decide whether I lived or died. Part of me feared the possibility of death. Nevertheless, I forced myself to maintain strict eye contact. I tried to convey my pleas through my gaze, one last-ditch effort to convince Leo not to end my life right here and now.

I saw his jaw working back and forth. A thin layer of scruff covered his jawline, and I thought with unexpected clarity how it was now the middle of the night, and he probably hadn't shaved since this morning. It's funny—the details you notice when you're facing potential death. I doubted I would notice such things if my mind were not so calm. As it was, I felt consigned. What more could I do? Drop to my knees, grovel, plead? This was it. Leo's eyes indicated an internal debate. I prayed that my words would be enough.

His grip tightened around the gun, and my heart sank. Let it be quick, I thought. I hoped I wouldn't feel the pain of the bullet. A piece of me, strangely, was curious: Would it be peaceful? Disorienting? Perhaps the greatest mystery of science was—and always had been—the true nature of humanity's common ending. Now, I would get to experience it for myself. My only regret was that I would not be able to share my findings with others.

Then Leo released a sharp exasperated breath. I had squeezed my eyes shut while waiting for the inevitable shot, but I opened them now. The gun hung at Leo's side. The sight of it there, no longer trained on me, felt like the release of a massive weight around my neck.

"Go," he said. His free hand motioned out the door. "Check that the hallway is clear. Do *not* be seen."

My feet wouldn't move. Impatient, Leo pointed more emphatically to the door. "I said, *go*. Now."

Something restored my ability to function. Not waiting any longer, I made for the door past Leo. Then, only steps away from my escape, the gun fired.

I shrieked, clamping my hands to my ears as the ringing echo of the shot ricocheted against my eardrums, and felt my heart leap from my chest for one agonizing moment before I realized . . . The shot was not for me. My body was intact for all but the ringing in my ears.

Leo, though, was on the floor. The moon as a backlight, I could see nothing more than his curled shadowy outline. Alarm caught in my throat. I feared the unspeakable.

But no. Leo was alive. He was moving. When he turned his head just right, the moonlight reflected off his white teeth clenched in a grimace. One hand grasped his foot, his fingers turning dark and wet, while the other grappled with the fabric of his shirt to rub clean the handle of the gun.

I didn't understand. I was torn between the form of the man in agony and the escape looming so close within my grasp.

Leo ducked his head, and I heard the command once again, guttural against his chest, muffled by his teeth: "Go."

I took one step toward him, then stopped. "I'm sorry," I whispered. "Thank you."

Then I turned. And ran.

CHAPTER 28

Brown waited for me in a beat-up hovercraft at the edge of the forest like we had discussed. He started the engines as I approached, sprinting and clutching the straps of my backpack like they were life itself. The craft's side door slid open, and I jumped inside. Almost immediately, Brown began pulling us into the air. The propellors beat out a heavy concussing rhythm. I didn't relax until we reached maximum elevation and had left the sight of Empress Industries far in the distance, obscured by shadowy mountain peaks.

"Nice run, genius," grumbled Brown. "You ever heard of something called good form?"

I crouch-walked to the cockpit and collapsed into the second pilot's seat with a groan. "Try booking it for your life sometime. See how good your form is."

"Did you get the data?"

I reached in my pocket and pulled out the thumb drive, holding it up between two fingers. Brown made a grunting sound. "Good job. That should give us some head start."

The cockpit fell silent for all except the dull beating of the propellors. I debated whether to ask about Loyala. I settled on a question about my sister instead, a safe middle ground.

"Fine," Brown responded. "She's fine."

I waited. ". . . And?"

He shot me a look. "What else do you want me to say?"

I let out a scoff of disbelief. "Well, it's not like I haven't seen her in weeks or anything. Really, you've got nothing else to say than 'she's fine'?"

Brown growled loudly, a sound somewhere between a shout and a grimace. "All right. Hold it. Cut the condescending tone. Let me remind you that it was *your* butt that *I* just rescued. In my ship! So if I have nothing more to say about your sister than she's fine, then fine is all she is!" The copter gave an untimely groan and shuddered in the air, causing Brown to clutch, alarmed, at the controls. As the difficulties finished, he stared straight ahead, his lips pressed together in a hard line.

I contained a laugh, knowing it would only make the man angrier. For a while I allowed us to fly in silence, but eventually I couldn't help myself any longer. "What about my friends? Rollie and Evie and the others? Are they . . . okay?"

"Okay is a relative term, you know. In light of recent events, they are doing as well as could be expected."

"There was a funeral?" I swallowed. I had to ask. I wanted the solace.

"Yes, there was a funeral." Brown had taken on a gentler tone—at least, as gentle as befit a man of his nature. "There was a large turnout. If one thing can be said about that stinking sheep pit, it's that people look out for each other."

I shook my head, staring at my cuticles, not bothering to stop myself from picking away at the dry skin. "I know they must all hate me."

"Look . . ." Brown sighed. "I was not the most sensitive after the boy's death. I . . . I suppose I want to say I'm sorry. I shouldn't have been so harsh with you."

"Wow. I'm surprised. I didn't know you had a sympathetic side."

"Sure I do. I'm selective about when I turn it on. I could take back everything I said right now if you keep pushing it."

We passed over miles and miles of stretching forest, the peaks of trees tall and mysterious beneath us. And, for the first time, I realized how beautiful they were. The hours passed, and the mountains gave way to rolling hills and flat stretches of farmland. I glanced at the ship's compass built into the dash. West, the instrument proclaimed. I had never been out west before. The region was exclusively outer sectors.

"While you were gone, I found something," said Brown. "Information.

Years ago, a paralyzed girl was healed via a chip implanted in her brain. Right after the operation, she and the scientists who worked on her disappeared. Most of her medical records seem to have been destroyed."

"Was this a case with Empress?" I asked.

"No. A different company. It took some digging, but apparently the girl expressed some unique symptoms before the experiment was terminated."

"What kind of symptoms?"

"Odd things. Interesting things. I think she could be useful in figuring out how to undercut Day."

I thought about this. "I thought you said she went missing."

"True. But we're going to find her. I have a lead."

As we flew, rays of sunlight began peering over the horizon. First, orange illuminated the underside of a few scattered clouds and transformed the night to a tentative in-between indigo color. The stars faded. And slowly, streams of yellow lit up the dimness, and the sky turned to a brilliant blue. Finally, the sun itself broke the horizon, flooding the world with the reminder that there was freedom from yesterday and new hope for today.

I touched the necklace at my throat, thinking of Rollie and Andie and all the rest. I might not see them again for some time, but I would think of them every day. Because I'd be fighting for them. Sommer Day could give these people her best shot. She could manipulate and threaten and do her worst in her attempts to control all the world.

But for all her efforts, I would be there to match them. I wouldn't go away. I wouldn't stop. Not until we were safe from her, and no one else had to seep out their lifeblood to quench her savage thirst.

It didn't matter how long it took.

My mind was always my greatest weapon. And I was only beginning to realize how infinite it could be.

END OF BOOK ONE

ACKNOWLEDGEMENTS

Writing *The Method to Infinite Things* was definitely a journey. So many friends supported me along the way. Many thanks to my family—Davids, Goodsells, Winwards, Boyers, Olsens, and my mom and dad especially—for their tremendous love and a treasure trove of memories for me to draw inspiration from. (Don't worry, guys. All good things, all good things).

I need to thank April and Mike Rich, who sat in my living room one day and told me about a company called Future House Studios that publishes young adult books. More than that, they've been with me every step of this process, and their enthusiasm for *Methods* has helped keep me going. Along the same lines, I'll forever be grateful to the Smithfield 21st ward young women. I love you! Can you believe this book is finally happening?

Now for all my students—I wish I could address every single one of you by name. But since that would take way more pages than I have room for, please know I remember each of you very well. How could I forget your smiles and sassiness and support? I'd like to thank Nate Henrie, who helped me work out the finer scientific points of this book and whose own writing experience was invaluable to me, as well as Wynnde Whittier, who carries with her a ray of sunshine and taught me how to live life well. Wynnde, along with Christie Hansen, Christa Bell, and Darlee Dyer remain some of the best English teachers on the planet. They pushed me, encouraged me, and fostered my love for writing

My editor, Kelly Taylor, dedicated 100% of herself to this book, and I'm so extremely grateful she did. The team at Future House is overflowing with talent. *Methods* have their handiwork all through it. I don't know why they decided to take a chance on this rookie writer, but I'm still ecstatic that they did.

Finally, I'd like to thank my husband, Matt, for always pulling me forward. I'm glad to have you as my partner.

Finally, I'd like to thank my husband, Matt, for always pulling me forward. I'm glad to have you as my partner.

ALSO BY FUTURE HOUSE PUBLISHING

We appreciate your purchase of this book. We hope you enjoyed it, we had a lot of fun making it! To help us keep telling great stories, we'd love it if you could take a few minutes to leave us an honest review. Thank you in advance!

If you love *The Method To Infinite Things,* then stay tuned for the next book in the series! Until then, you might also like other books published by Future House Publishing.

Caretaker by Josi Russell
Horizon Alpha: Predators of Eden by D.W. Vogel
Stuck in the Game by Christopher Keene

And many more! Look for your next read by visiting
www.futurehousepublishing.com

ABOUT THE AUTHOR

Madison grew up daydreaming. Her idea of a perfect Saturday involved waking up at 6 a.m. to write stories on the family desktop computer. (She didn't care how weird that made her look at the time). While a junior at Utah State University, Madison wrote her debut novel. She has since graduated with her bachelor's degree in Social Studies Composite Teaching and balances writing with a full time teaching career.

Madison and her husband live in the beautiful mountains of the Wasatch Back in Utah.

GET IN TOUCH

Interested in having Madison Boyer come visit your school? Have a question about the series or want to talk with the Future House Publishing team?

We'd love to hear from you! Follow us on social media, visit our website, or send us an email.

For more information visit us online at
www.futurehousepublishing.com or contact us:
books@futurehousepublishing.com

Please join our mailing list for new releases, exclusive offers, and our best deals. You can join by visiting www.futurehousepublishing.com!

Made in the USA
Coppell, TX
25 August 2023